THE
FLOATING ZOMBIE

By The Same Author

THE FALL OF COLOSSUS

D. F. Jones
THE FLOATING ZOMBIE

A BERKLEY MEDALLION BOOK
published by
BERKLEY PUBLISHING CORPORATION

BERKLEY MEDALLION BOOKS are published by
Berkley Publishing Corporation
200 Madison Avenue
New York, N.Y. 10016

BERKLEY MEDALLION BOOK ® TM 757,375

Printed in the United States of America

Berkley Medallion Edition, NOVEMBER, 1975

Old-fashioned seamen view their advent with alarm, contempt . . . and fear. Before ATl—rightly, it has no name—ground down the slipway, it had been dubbed "Zombie." That sinister name will stick.

Shipping Gazette-Record
March 1979

I

"I've said it before, and I'll say it again." Tediously, the shipping superintendent kept to his word. "Full automation is mad—dangerous and mad."

"Mr. Chairman," put in the chief accountant smoothly, "no one can claim that our seafaring colleague has been anything but consistent throughout all these planning meetings. Observing this is the last, might he not care—just this once—to be specific?"

The chairman and the managing director exchanged hopeless glances. They were at it again; the only thing those two agreed on was their mutual dislike. The chairman examined the backs of his hands as if he had never seen them before. He'd stop them in due course, but meanwhile he was prepared to listen. Home truths could come out in anger, and he wanted to know anything which might bear on the decision that had to be made, and made now. He looked inquiringly at the red-faced, glowering superintendent.

"You mean to tell me that spending seven million pounds on the world's first crewless ship after a couple—?"

"Four."

"Very well—four—voyages testing equipment isn't mad? To wind up its bloody clockwork and push it off with four or five million quid's worth of cargo on a five-thousand-mile voyage isn't *dangerous*?"

"No, it isn't, and even you have to agree the tests have been perfect." The accountant smiled maddeningly. "Or are you saying it won't work at all?"

1

"Of course the bloody thing will work—on a pond! But we're talking about the *sea*! I bow to your superior knowledge of figures—and Bognor Regis beach—"

The accountant stiffened, but the chairman intervened. "Gentlemen, this is getting us nowhere." Obviously, old Blood-and-Guts had no concrete objections. "Naturally, there are risks in everything, but the trials have been an unqualified success, the seaborne evaluation group's report entirely favorable. We are assured the equipment reliability rating is on a par with the automated blind landing equipment in an aircraft. What more can we ask—or do?"

"That, Mr. Chairman," said the shipping superintendent, "is not a fair comparison. In a plane, there's a pilot sitting watching his box of tricks. This—this thing has no one—except its armed guard. And that's another point. Our guards in manned ships are under the command of the captain; this thing, armed to the teeth, is in the charge of the equivalent of a sergeant!" He shook his head. "Maybe I'm getting old, but I stick to it: mad and dangerous."

"Mr. Chairman," said the accountant. "Only the hopelessly biased can say AT1 is not practicable. Many respected seamen accept it. They too may not like it, but they agree it has to come. Moreover, while we are first in the field, we know others are not far behind." He pointed a bony finger at the superintendent. "Assume you take his advice, automate the engine room only. Fine: we save five percent on capital costs, ten percent on running costs, and we do well—until someone else builds the fully automated ship. They'll save fifteen to twenty percent on capital, up to forty percent on running costs. Where does that leave us?"

"Money, money!"

"Yes indeed," rejoined the accountant. "Money. . . . If we were running a nautical museum, I might incline to your view, but we're not! Finally, the armament question." He pointed unnecessarily once again. "He seems to think this is a novel situation. Not all my weekends at Bognor have been spent staring at the sea. I find that historically, armed merchant ships have been the rule, rather than the exception, up to the end of the Napoleonic Wars. Now the wheel has come full circle. In an oil-hungry world, tankers must be protected."

"Rubbish!" snapped the superintendent, red-faced with anger. "And even if you are right, it would be a damn sight safer to have a crew of forty than a guard of four!"

"I hoped you'd say that," said the accountant candidly. "Piracy last flourished in the China Seas in the 1920's." He fell to polishing his bifocals. "Security-wise, give me the automated ship. Back in the twenties they called it piracy—as indeed it was—but now we'd call it hijacking. The rather enterprising Chinese pirates infiltrated the passengers or crew, or both. No, Mr. Chairman, give me a carefully selected guard any day."

The shipping superintendent muttered something about "slab-sided abortions and pen-pushers," which only made his opponent smile. The old boy knew his stuff about ships—the obsolescent manned variety—but was totally at sea in a board room. A bit of polishing, thought the chief accountant, and I'll make a useful epigram out of that.

"Gentlemen, time presses. Unless someone has something *new*"—he leaned on the word—"to contribute, I will put this to the vote." He looked inquiringly at his committee.

The chief accountant smiled again. With Mammon on his side, how could he lose?

That was in March 1976.

II

The Boeing bumped heavily; hearts contracted, bowels loosened. Runway lights flashed past; more than one passenger's foot pressed urgently on a nonexistent brake pedal; then the thankful relaxation for the best part of any flight, the sedate trundle to the arrival terminal. Stewardesses, unfamiliar in faintly ridiculous hats, assumed their farewell smiles as the doors opened; the alien atmosphere, feeling and smelling like a dirty velvet wrap, wound itself around the emerging passengers.

Al Muharraq Airport, Bahrein, Persian Gulf, June 30, 1979. For romantic innocents, their first taste of the magic of the Orient; for the disenchanted, a good deal less. It is claimed that the Garden of Eden once graced this island, but that was long before airports.

If asked, ex-Para Sergeant William Langley would have unhesitatingly ranged himself in the disenchanted class, although to be fair to Bahrein, enchantment in any context was not a word that sprang readily to his practical mind. Insular by nature, travel and experience had done nothing to broaden his outlook. Two or three times the Army had staged him through Muharraq, and this was his fourth trip as a civvy.

He waited patiently in the aircraft's aisle, in no hurry to renew his acquaintance with Bahrein or the Bahreini, watching with faint contempt the muddle and confusion ahead, the dropped bag, the missing camera.

Bloody civvies! No order, no discipline. . . . "Do as you like, mother's drunk" was the motto these days.

4

He consigned his fellow passengers and the entire Persian Gulf to some private limbo, concentrating yet again on his new job. All the way from London he'd fiddled with it, tossing it aside, only to find it back in the center of his thoughts.

Well, soon the guessing and the speculations would cease, and he'd have to make the best of it, but only one of the many novel aspects of his assignment really worried him: this woman. Four men and one female stuck in a floating steel box for the best part of six weeks—crazy! All right for the daft bastards back in the head office, with their slick phrases about "team comfort," "job satisfaction," and "recruit attraction," plus a lot of other compound words he'd forgotten. He'd like to compound the lot of 'em: bunch of bloody fags who judged other men's sex drive by their own thin-blooded standards—and he was the poor sod who had to make their scheme work. And if it went wrong? Who'd carry the can?

Unconsciously he braced his shoulders back a fraction more. Only a blind man could make any mistake about him; from close-cropped gray-tinged black hair to well-polished shoes, he was Army, and one glance at his cold stare put invisible stripes on his sleeve. Dressed up, he would have made a fine subject for a recruiting poster—except for one slight weakness, his mouth. Behind that outward sign did, in reality, lurk a certain flaw, one that he knew, one that had made him embrace Army discipline with unusual keenness, armoring himself against himself. The Army had been all to him; the best twelve years of his life; like a bloody fool he'd let himself be talked out of it—weakness again—and all the rest led inevitably to this moment. Thirty-eight now, he'd have been a sergeant major; instead, here he was, a despised civvy, a security guard, doing a boring job which had nothing to commend it except the money—and how he needed the money! All because of a woman; weakness. . . .

Now, in the one job which he'd reckoned would keep him clear of females, he found, far too late in the day, he was stuck with another of them. He half-hoped she'd be wall-eyed, fat, and forty. Langley felt confident he could handle the men, but could he handle her? Above all, could he handle himself? Just one pass, and his authority, the discipline of the team, would be right up the spout.

Down the steps, across the short strip of tarmac. Even before he entered the bright-lit terminal, he was sweating. Midnight in Muharraq . . . title for a song.

Like its owner, Langley's kit bag was antisocial, rolling down the shute onto the carrousel, banging civvy-style cases aside. Through customs and immigration, a mere formality, and to his regimental mind all the more annoying for that: nothing but a stupid waste of time.

In reception he dumped his bag and waited; let 'em come to him. He stared uninterestedly around; usual bunch of grubby white-suited vultures pouncing on travel-dazed passengers. Bet none of the bastards approaches me. Somewhere in that untidy rabble were two of his men—and the woman. He hadn't sought them on the plane, and sure as hell he wasn't going to start now.

The public-address system announced hollowly the arrival of the company transport. Langley shouldered his bag, picked up his grip, and marched out into the soft darkness. In the bus he allowed himself a quick look at the dozen or so passengers. Four were women; she had to be one of them. The dim light was no help, but as far as he could make out, she wasn't fair, fat, and forty; neither was she the reincarnation of Marilyn Monroe. He slumped down into a seat, aware of the pvc sticking instantly to his back. He shut his eyes, letting his thoughts drift; a fantasy vision of the unknown woman, naked and desirable, flashed across his mind, a vision banished with such mental violence that his head shook.

Think of money: as senior guard he'd be getting—was getting, ever since he left London—U.S. $350 a week, tax-free, to his Bahrein bank, plus all allowances, overtime, free board, and lodging. Yes, the money was good: bloody well should be, for this job.

Deliberately he let the rest get out first, glancing covertly at the women. He learned little, but reclassified one as fat and forty and at once concluded she had to be his private millstone. In his irritable frame of mind, he couldn't decide if he was glad or sorry.

The hotel clerk worried over a list, ticked each arrival, allocating rooms. Last out of the bus, but not in the queue, Langley noticed his team were grouped together. Even upside-down, "AT1" was not hard to read. Three names were ticked: he knew two were on an earlier flight; that meant one had to be ahead of him. He glanced at the small knot of travelers waiting for their main baggage to be unloaded. Yes, that had to be his.

Around twenty-five, he looked like a Yank—they alone have the knack of appearing uncrumpled, fresh, after a three-thousand-mile flight—and his clean-shaven head could only indicate a military man, or a sea guard facing five weeks out of touch with a barber.

The younger man caught his glance, hesitated fractionally, and sauntered over, hands in pockets, offensively casual. His round, rather featureless face was not so much clean-shaven as hairless, and his expression no better than neutral.

"Should we know each other?"

Langley stared at him frostily; he was a Yank, all right. In the senior man's insular mind, that was one strike against him for a start, but even if he'd been a Brit from his own home town, Langley would still have disliked him. "AT1?"

The Yank nodded, managing a thin-lipped smile which Langley found faintly supercilious. Before he could speak, Langley heard a quick-stifled exclamation behind him; the sound threw him, for the voice was female. He glimpsed a woman's profile, half-hidden by a headscarf and dark glasses. Even as he turned, her head moved, and he was left with a vague impression, no more than a tantalizing glimpse of a beautiful nose, a well-shaped cheek. Reluctantly he let that promising vision go, glowering at the man.

The Yank's amused expression showed he had missed nothing of Langley's thoughts. "Julius Colmar, late of the United States Army—God rot them!—now, you-know-what." He bowed slightly, ironically, his hands still in his pockets.

Langley's dislike for the American was powerfully re-

7

inforced; Colmar's manner was bad enough, and his disloyalty to his old service, in Langley's mental imagery, put the tin lid on it. Colmar was instantly graded as a dropout serviceman, a type he rated even lower than a civvy dropout. A renegade is always more hated by the faithful than a plain enemy. Bleakly, Langley said, "What?"

Colmar repeated his name, but before Langley could go to the second part of his gambit, porters arrived with the baggage, breaking up an awkward scene.

They had adjoining rooms; entering his, Colmar gave his senior a mock salute and that same thin smile, and got a blank stare in return. All the same, both knew who had the points decision.

In his room, Langley's ill-humor was going full bore. That young bastard was too cheeky by a long way. Was he shy? No, Colmar wasn't that; his expression said it all: Colmar reckoned he knew the lot, and had a talent for showing it. Well, he'd learn—and Langley would take great pleasure in teaching him. The fact that the run-in with Colmar had distracted him from that female only added fuel to Langley's fire. But for that bumptious bastard, Langley saw himself chatting her up in the bar. That fleeting glimpse had intrigued him; she was young—certainly under thirty—and what he'd seen of her profile had been good news. A blond? He couldn't be sure.

Langley swore to himself. Christ—what was he thinking of? If he was this way before they even stepped aboard, what would he be like after a couple of weeks at sea? Again he cursed the head office. Annoyed with Colmar, the woman, the world in general, and himself in particular, he missed out on his usual exercises, showered, and went to bed.

If he could have seen Colmar in his room, Langley would have been even madder. The younger man was contained, quite unruffled by the meeting, taking a casual interest in his surroundings. He turned back the bedclothes, examining the sheets for any trace of a previous occupant. Satisfied, he checked the cleanliness of the bathroom. Whistling softly to himself, he wandered around the bedroom, found no fault, and raised the louver blind, staring into the dark night. That too appeared to pass his inspection. He called the desk; how about two cans of Coke, iced—like now?

The drinks arrived; Colmar glanced away from the window, jerked his head at the table. The waiter put the cans down. Colmar flipped a half-dollar not so much to as at the man, who missed it, and had to hunt for it on his hands and knees. The coin recovered, the waiter hovered uncertainly—fifty U.S. cents for two Cokes was a lot of money. With a negligent backhand flourish Colmar dismissed him, picked up a Coke, and returned to the window.

That limey had "Army" written all over him. They were all the same, Yank, Brit, or whatever. A sergeant, most probably; got that stiff-necked air. Bums, the whole lot of 'em.

Colmar stared at the harbor lights, smiling. Jesus! Life could be real funny—if you had the right sense of humor.

In her room, Jane Harris sat on the dressing-table stool, thankful to be alone. For a space she appraised her image in the mirror; slowly she removed the headscarf, the dark glasses, meeting her own gaze unwaveringly. Fumbling in her bag for cleansing cream and tissues, Jane Harris cried, silently.

By accident or design, none of AT1's team met over breakfast, a state of affairs easily achieved in the spacious dining room, relic of the days when the company had virtually owed half the Persian Gulf.

Self-conscious as ever, Langley braced himself for his entry, but if any noted his arrival, they did not show it, nor would he look. Much as he wanted to see the woman, he had no desire to meet Colmar's glance: that young gent could wait.

"All members of AT1's team are requested to report to the shipping office at eight-twenty. Thank you."

Langley went stolidly on with his eggs and bacon without glancing at his watch, apparently reading the ingredients label on a sauce bottle with great interest. How he played the next hour or so would be vital; but for that bloody woman, it would be a piece of cake.

The public-address announcement made Jane Harris' heart thump: thirty minutes to go. Her mouth felt dry; she wished she had the courage to order a stiff Scotch, but that wouldn't do, however much she needed it. She told herself it was ridiculous to be so strung-up, but it did no good. In the sleepless hours of early morning she had decided on her course of action, and that was that. . . .

A fanatical timekeeper, Langley knew from past experience it would take only five minutes to walk to the shipping office; he'd get there at eight-ten, time enough to collect his team list, and watch them arrive. He lingered over a cup of tea, watching people leave—including Colmar—but it was the women he studied. One in particular held his attention, for she was dressed in the standard KD skirt and slacks. He had only a back view, but if that was her . . . Most females over twenty-two, in slacks and shirt, are walking disaster areas, but not this one—and the blond hair didn't come out of a bottle, either.

If that *was* her, they'd got dynamite aboard. . . . His timetable forgotten, Langley left hurriedly.

First in the shipping office, Langley did the usual, very thorough identity check; ID card, fingerprint, and password. Given the inevitable shower of paper, instruction books, a list of his team, and their potted histories, he was allowed to pass into the briefing room. He lit one of his rare cigarettes and concentrated on the list:

Senior Guard William George Langley	SG 10 (ic)
Guard Mark Roger Jacens	SG 153
Guard Julius Colmar	SG 165
Guard Phillip Roscorla	SG 183
Stewardess Jane Harris	SG 228

He flipped through their records. Jacens was an ex-sergeant in the U.S. Rangers, on his third trip. Surprisingly,

Colmar had done four, but Langley noted that only in passing, being more interested in the woman.

Harris, Jane. Miss. English, twenty-six. Qualified state-registered nurse. Ten months' ward and theater experience in London teaching hospital, fifteen months' experience as long-haul airline hostess. AT1 first seagoing appointment.

Airline hostess! That settled it, thought Langley: she has to be the woman—got that smart, bandbox appearance. God—they must be out of their tiny minds, sending a dolly like that! He turned back to the men; only Roscorla had not served as a guard in manned tankers, but he was ex-Royal Navy, well-qualified in light AA weapons. On paper it looked a pretty good, experienced team. Damn well should be; in a quiet way they would be making seafaring history. Naturally, they'd been hand-picked, but that only made the choice of Jane Harris more inexplicable.

Langley glanced up as the door opened. A tall, rangy man, dark-haired and tanned, came in with easy, loose-jointed grace. His strong face was not so much marred as strengthened by a badly set broken nose. Instinctively, Langley liked him.

"Jacens," said the man simply.

As they shook hands, Langley realized he gripped the hand of a very strong man, and Langley was no weakling.

"Langley," he said, not to be outdone.

"Wanna see my ID?"

Langley shook his head. "You wouldn't have got through that door if there'd been any doubt." His expression softened. "And I reckon I know an old Ranger when I see one."

"Yes, sir!" The steady gray eyes smiled. "Somethin' tells me you ain't bin polishing a seat all your life."

For the first time since leaving London, Langley smiled; Jacens was his sort of man; immaculate, reserved, strong. "No. Paratroops." They sat down. "There's another American in the team—bloke called Colmar."

"Colmar!"

"You know him?"

11

"Guess not, but a guy I know did a trip with him. Said he was kinda hard to git along with—no kicks against him work-wise—but somehow ornery, you know?"

"I know." Langley changed the subject. "The other guard's new, but he's ex-Brit Navy."

The new arrival was a bare two minutes early. In his mid-thirties, short, and with a stomach straining his belt, Phillip Roscorla's most notable feature was a mop of thick black curly hair. He seemed to bounce into the room, full of energy, grinning widely.

"Morning, all." His dark brown eyes switched rapidly from Jacens to Langley and back, while he rubbed his hands together, shifting his weight from one leg to the other. "Who'se the gaffer?"

"I am," said Langley shortly. The sailor's KD was clean, but casual. "You'll be Roscorla."

"That's me," agreed the sailor. "Mrs. Roscorla's little boy." He nodded in a friendly fashion to Jacens, eyeing his frame. "Mostly known as Phil."

Jacens gave him a friendly nod and shook hands, his six-foot-plus figure towering over the sailor. "The name's Jacens."

Roscorla grinned up at him. "Don't tell me—you're from Texas!"

"Right in one!"

"Texas. . . . Met a girl in Galveston . . ."

Exactly on time, the door opened. Colmar's enigmatic smile did not flicker as Langley stared pointedly at his watch. Roscorla wrecked the scene: for all his plumpness, he was light on his feet. He swung around. "Hello! The name's Phil." Even as his hand moved in greeting, Colmar forestalled him, raising his right hand in a stilted, mock-Indian salute.

"Julius Colmar." His appraising eye recognized that Phil was distinctly nonmilitary.

"How d'ye do—this is the boss."

"We've met."

"Oh? Well, this is Mr. Jacens, also a citizen of the United

States—perhaps you know each other?'' The feeble joke was ignored; Roscorla felt himself caught in an invisible cross fire; Langley and Jacens just nodded at the new man. To fill the gap, the sailor dug out a packet of cigarettes, offering them to Colmar.

''I don't smoke.''

Roscorla got the unspoken comment, and lost some of his bonhomie. ''Quite right, mate. Nasty, dirty habit—and I'm stuck with it. Every man to his own poison, that's what I always say.''

Then Jane Harris walked in, Langley's dining-room blond. All heads turned.

Langley took the full impact, for she looked straight at him, her eyes in torment. He'd been right; she had a beautiful nose, clear, near-violet eyes, and her right cheek was perfection, but . . .

A jagged scar, alien and livid on her pale skin, ran from the left temple to her chin; the sutures that had cobbled up her wound had imparted a faint, fatal downward twist to the left corner of her mouth. In that battlefield of a face, beauty fought horror, and lost.

''Ah, yes . . .'' Mentally Langley stumbled, inwardly raging at the head office. ''I'm . . . Langley. Pleased to meet you.''

Shaking hands, he tried not to look at the hideous scar, and failed. Ugliness may hold character, dignity; ruined beauty is another thing altogether. Somehow he got through the introductions; to each, Jane Harris nodded quickly, not trying to hide her disfigurement, but unable to trust her voice. To offer herself naked in the marketplace would have been less embarrassing.

Surprisingly, Roscorla found the perilous path between oversolicitude and normality.

''Come on, miss,'' he said briskly, ''you sit here. Smoke?'' He sat on her disfigured side, lit her cigarette, and then ignored her, looking attentively at Langley.

''Yes . . . now we're all here''—Langley looked fixedly at Jacens—''right then . . .'' His carefully rehearsed words had all gone. "We get the full briefing on board from the pilotage officer—he takes the ship to sea—but before we leave here, let me have your expense claims." He distributed the small pile of books. "These are your Bibles—the instruction books. Take good care of 'em—you have to sign for them. They're similar to the books some of you've had in manned ships, but these are written especially for AT1. Read 'em—not now, later. Any questions? Right. Be ready—and I mean ready—outside the hotel main entrance at five to ten. Transport's laid on to take us to a boat and out to the ship. Sooner we're aboard and settled in, the better. That's all." He hadn't said half he meant to.

Jane Harris was first with her expense claim. "Here's mine, Mr. Langley." A nice, clear voice, but hard with tight control. She was clearly impatient to go.

"See you, miss," said Roscorla cheerfully, looking her straight in the face. Somehow he got across to her; before she could stop herself, she smiled. Instantly she turned away, but they had all seen that grotesque leer, parody of a smile. And then she was gone.

Jacens broke the silence. "I've seen a few things in my time"—he shook his head—"but that sure is the saddest, damnedest . . ."

"I've been wondering how the hell they signed a dame for this trip," put in Colmar thoughtfully; he grinned. "Gotta hand it to 'em! She comes, because where better for her to hide; we come, thinking we gotta twenty-five-percent share in a woman!" The grin broadened. "Still, you can always put a sack over—"

With casual ease Jacens grabbed Colmar's shirt. "Steady, son. She's a nurse; don't be her first customer." Gently, he let go.

Colmar was pallid with rage, his voice husky. "Don't you ever touch me—never again—you hear, Jacens!" The voice rose. "Never! I don't let anybody—"

"That's enough!" barked Langley. He glowered at Jacens. "As for you, Colmar . . ."

But Colmar too had gone.

Roscorla took in Jacens' calm, unruffled face and the

14

troubled expression on Langley's. "One way and another," he said, "I'd say this could be an interesting trip."

Langley, tight-lipped, stared at the door, and hardly heard him. Colmar was a brash young loudmouth, but he had hit one truth: with that fearful face, Jane Harris had to be seeking the nearest thing to solitude she could find.

III

All took Langley's broad hint and were ready and waiting before ten; naturally, the transport was late. Outside the hotel's air-conditioning, the heat was intense. To stand still was to be aware of every pore in the body; to move brought faint relief of air movement, immediately paid for by trickling sweat.

Stoically Langley stood in the sun, not impervious, but indifferent. He had served in the Borneo jungle, and after that reckoned himself fireproof.

Jacens sat on his case, idly contemplating his boots, his mind elsewhere. Colmar waited in the shade of the entrance, silent, detached.

Roscorla mopped his face, making no secret of his views. He looked at Jane Harris. "Flaming hot, this. Why not go back inside—I'll give you a shout."

"No." She spoke sharply, then retracted. "No, thank you, Mr. Roscorla." Her eyes smiled.

"Don't call me that—I'm Phil to my friends."

She sensed his sincerity: he would have said no less if she had been a haggard fifty instead of . . .

They piled into the station wagon in silence, grateful for the illusion of breeze, bumping, swaying down to the quay, everything insubstantial in the shimmering heat haze.

Colmar addressed the sailor. Jacens and Langley would not be his buddies; that left Roscorla.

"Hey, Ros-cor-la—is that how you say it?"

"Right in one, mate."

16

"Ros-cor-la—what sort of name is that?"

The sailor looked startled—was this bloke skylarking? "It's my sort of name—why?"

Instantly Colmar toned it down, as if Roscorla had taken the offensive. "Jeeze—I only *asked*!" He shrugged deprecatingly. "Seems a kinda strange name for an Englishman, that's all."

"I'm not English, chum," said Roscorla stoutly, "I'm Cornish."

"You mean there's a difference?" Colmar appeared friendly, interested, yet the sailor sensed a faint derisory note; he glanced sharply at Colmar, but detected nothing in the Yank's inquiring expression. Maybe the guy wasn't having him on; maybe he just had a lousy way of saying things.

"Too right there is!"

"Oh—sorry! Guess I didn't know."

The words were well enough, but the sailor suspected a mocking glint in Colmar's pale eyes. In the boat he moved away from the young American and stood close to Jane Harris.

The boat tok-toked out from the jetty; oil permeated everything—clothes, air, water. The boat rolled gently over the greasy, undulating surface, mud-colored.

"Don't want to fall in that lot," observed Roscorla. She nodded but did not speak, safe behind her large dark glasses and headscarf. The sailor tried again. "Been out this way before, miss?"

"Yes." Her tone would have shut most men up.

"Sorry. We Corns are a nosy lot."

Disarmed by his obvious sincerity and friendliness, she reached out impulsively to touch him, and at once thought better of it. "No. I'm the one who should apologize."

Roscorla tactfully ignored that. "There it is, miss," he said, pointing.

No seaman would ever call AT1 anything but "it": "she" was reserved for ships, not self-propelled oil barrels. It was on the tip of the Cornishman's tongue to say AT1 was no beauty, but he managed to sheer away from that pitfall, just in time.

Even for a tanker, AT1 was certainly strikingly ugly. It had the usual slab-sided hull, blunt bow, and sawn-off stern, but from the ruler-straight upper deck up, AT1 was very different. Manned tankers have towering superstructures, six or seven stories high, edifices which resemble futuristic apartment blocks. Not AT1. Forward of an ugly stovepipe of a funnel, garnished with two whip aerials which looked like the antennae of a giant insect, was a small deckhouse, surmounted by an even smaller structure, the wheelhouse. But the main feature was the large gantry, which, like a gigantic goal, stood as high as the thin funnel, above the deckhouse. Even to Jane Harris' unnautical eye, AT1 looked very odd; bare and unfinished.

Roscorla found the gantry particularly interesting, and with good reason; there had never been anything like it before on a merchant vessel. Supported on lattice masts on either side of the deckhouse, the crossbar, fifty or sixty feet above the deck, was festooned with radar aerials. By naval standards, merchant-ship radars are relatively simple affairs, but not AT1's collection. Roscorla had a fair idea what he was looking at, and identified long-range navigational, close-range high-resolution surface, and air-warning aerials. As the boat drew closer, he digested an even more surprising fact; the whole array was duplicated.

"Just look at it—like a flaming Christmas tree!"

Jane Harris darted a quick glance at the sailor, obviously far too interested in AT1 to notice her. Encouraged, she said, "It's a big ship, isn't it, Mr. Roscorla?"

Behind them, Langley listened. This was the first time the woman had come out of her shell.

"No, not really," said Roscorla. "There's lots twice, three times the size. I don't mean they're twice as long—you know—but twice as big." He saw that was unsatisfactory, and pressed on. "This tub's seven hundred and eighty feet long, a hundred and twenty feet wide, and there's forty-eight feet of her under the water, as she is now, fully loaded." He pointed at another, conventional monster. "There: that bast —er, that one—reckon she holds twice as much as ours, but

18

she's not twice as long. 'Fraid I was never any good at math.''

Langley was surprised at how much the sailor knew about AT1.

Jane Harris had caught his interest, but cared nothing for facts and figures. ''What are all those pipes running along the top—in front of the chimney?''

Roscorla looked at her sharply. Was she pulling his leg? Satisfied of her innocence, he sighed, shook his head, enjoying being the superior male. ''No, miss. That's not a chimney, it's the funnel.''

''If you say so,'' she replied submissively, then spoiled it, ''but it's still a chimney, isn't it?''

Roscorla frowned. ''No. The funnel's only a sort of casing, like. Inside there's flue pipes.'' He sought inspiration, one hand going in a circular motion. ''It's just a casing, there's lots of room inside—you can walk around—there's ladders to get at the . . . the flue pipes. If you like, I'll show you sometime.''

Neither could realize how vital that casual remark would be.

Jane Harris persisted. ''Seems silly to me. Why bother with the funnel, then? Why not stick the flue pipes on that goalpost affair?''

Roscorla took a deep breath. ''It's like this . . .''

Langley grinned.

IV

Alongside, AT1's bulk was gigantic. From the boat, the long black hull seemed to stretch endlessly in both directions, the upper deck as far away as the roof of a two-story building. Roscorla held the bottom of the Jacob's ladder, and soon found his solicitude, for Miss Harris was misplaced; she went up the ladder like a professional, not holding the wooden rungs—Colmar, for one, did—but grasping the rope sides. The sailor took time out from watching her shapely bottom to consider her agility. For sure it wasn't the first time she'd gone up a rope ladder, however ignorant she might be about ships.

Langley went in search of the officer, leaving the rest to get the luggage on deck. As her self-appointed guardian, Roscorla shooed Jane Harris away from any part in the chore. It was a long and exhausting process, and she was glad to be out of it. Sometimes, but not often, it paid to be a woman. She continued her investigation of AT1, self-consciousness lost in genuine interest.

Her overwhelming impression was of sheer size. They had come aboard abreast of the funnel; close to, it looked more impressive, a sixty-foot tube, fifteen or so feet in diameter, and the deckhouse was a lot larger than she had supposed. Walking along the starboard gangway past the deckhouse, she saw the vast expanse of deck, over six hundred feet of it. Down the center line ran a raised catwalk, flanked on either side by massive pipes from which smaller pipes disappeared at regular intervals into the green-painted deck, the whole system dotted with innumerable valves. The rest of the deck, while clear of pipes, had rows of mushroom ventilators and what she later discovered were inspection covers. At the far end rose the bows; she could see capstans, cables. A tiny human figure, busy with a hawser, gave clue to the size of it all.

She walked back slowly, past the funnel. Aft lay a clear expanse of sixty or seventy feet; a large yellow circle marked the center of the helo pad.

"Big enough, miss?" Sweating profusely, Roscorla rested, the baggage aboard.

She nodded. "Makes me feel safe, somehow."

The sailor did not answer; sheer size is no guarantee against the limitless power of the sea. He smiled. On the point of saying, "The bigger they are, the harder they fall," he refrained, sparing her—unconsciously—one platitude.

She pointed forward. "You didn't tell me what those pipes were for."

"Them . . . oh, well, the hull's divided up into tanks, see. Those branch pipes from the two big ones feed the oil into the tanks. When we get to the other end, they just change the process, suck instead of blow, like. Looks complicated, but it's pretty simple, really; only a matter of opening and shutting the right valves."

"They're those wheel things, aren't they?"

"That's right. The mushrooms are ventilators. When the ship's empty, its important not to let gas—oil vapor—build up in the tanks."

"Why?"

"If you get a spark inside, the whole tank could go up in a . . . a big bang." He spoke with commendable restraint. "It's happened; not often, but it's happened. Not that we've got anything to worry about: guards are only going to be carried when these things are full."

"You mean this ship will sail all the way from Europe back here with no one aboard?"

That struck Roscorla as a mighty silly remark. "Unless we're clean out of luck, it's going to sail there on its own." He pointed at another, manned tanker. "Take that hooker.

21

She's got a crew of fifty or sixty. Say the payroll is about four thousand dollars a week; the round trip takes ten weeks, plus a week at each end loading and unloading. That's forty-eight thousand dollars, never mind the cost of leave, pensions, sick funds, training. Guess it'd be every bit of sixty thousand. Against that, this team costs around a thousand bucks a week for six weeks—chuck in another grand for our air fares and oddments, and that gives you a total of seventy thousand dollars." He paused, thinking. "Personally, I reckon the saving's more than that, but at least they're saving fifty thousand dollars each trip—more with food and one thing and another. On top of all that, there's God knows what saving on the cost of building the ship—you know, cabins, bathrooms, and all that, like."

Jane Harris looked at him thoughtfully, for once not frightened to show her face. "You're quite the businessman."

He laughed self-consciously. "Not me! Just interested in the way things work. I'm your genuine jack-of-all-trades. Anyway, the place where this packer gets interesting is up there." He pointed at the gantry. "Just look at it—like a bl . . . a flaming aircraft carrier! Notice the way we've got two of everything?"

She glanced up. "Oh, look—they're turning!" Even as she watched, another aerial began to rotate slowly. "Why do we have two sets—and why are they all going around?"

"They haven't told me, miss, but at a guess, I'd say it was for safety, like. If one aerial got damaged, there'd be another to take over. As for both lots going at the same time, reckon it's just a test. Cor— Makes you giddy to watch, doesn't it?"

"So they're only working when they're turning?"

Roscorla nodded.

"Suppose both lots go wrong?"

"One aerial may fall over, but it's yours truly for the lifeboat if one whole set packs in, never mind both!" He frowned. "That's a thought—where are the lifeboats?"

"You *are* a cheery soul!" She laughed, turning her head away.

"No—don't get me wrong. I'm not worried," he

22

protested, hurt that she should think he was. "It's regulations, see." He glanced quickly around. "Ah, that's it—life rafts." He nodded toward a large white-plastic cylinder lashed to the deck abreast the helo pad, and explained how they contained a raft which inflated on hitting the sea.

Jane Harris half-listened, more interested in his face. Not good-looking, his best feature was his thick wavy black hair. Talking of nautical things, his dark brown eyes were bright, his expression animated. She glanced over his shoulder at Jacens and Colmar, sitting silent on their cases. If men were dogs, Jacens would be a thoroughbred Alsatian, Langley a mastiff—and Roscorla? A retriever—no, a black Labrador. Strangely, by no stretch of her imagination could she think of a dog to fit Colmar.

". . . so you see, that's why they call it a nonreturn valve: once in, the air—gas, in this case—can't escape." He waited expectantly for her to comment.

"Oh . . . yes. Yes, I see." She smiled at him. "Why did you leave the Navy?" Her soft tone robbed the abrupt question of any rudeness.

His face lost its animation; he shrugged. "A better question is why I joined in the first place. No, that's not fair." He shrugged again.

"Sorry," she said. "I didn't mean—"

Instinctively he reached out, touched her hand, shaking his head. "No, I don't mind. It's all such a muddle—and what does it matter?"

She noticed that his West Country accent, strong when he was excited, explaining things to her, had gone.

Langley returned, sweat pouring down his face. "Right, lads, grab your gear." He tucked his kit bag under one arm, took his grip in the other, and was off without waiting, making it plain that there'd be no old-world courtesy to Jane Harris as far as he was concerned, an attitude which suited her.

"Here, let me take yours, miss."

"No, it's quite all right."

Jacens said nothing, just took her heaviest bag, gave her a

friendly nod, and followed Langley, through the deckhouse down a companionway to the main deck. "Right," said Langley. "Leave all your gear here for the moment."

Like everything about AT1, the space was vast, but none of them bothered about that. The first impression was of heat: from the moment they entered the deckhouse, it felt like an oven.

"Wow!" observed Roscorla, wiping the back of his neck.

"Jesus! They can't expect us—"

"Can it," grated Langley, letting the sweat trickle unheeded down his face. "This way."

He led them down a short passage. Passing one door, he nodded. "That's the saloon. I'll show you your cabins; get your baggage in, and report to me in there in ten minutes." He indicated another door as they made a right-angle turn. "In there's the sick bay." He stopped, consulting a list. "Next door to the sick bay is yours, Miss Harris. Mine's the other one aft on the same side. On the inboard side, the first's yours, Colmar. Roscorla's next, and you're last, opposite me, Jacens. Okay?"

The little group dispersed slowly. No one in their right mind would want to exert themselves a fraction more than necessary in the flattening heat.

Jane Harris quickly made her mind up that if any of the men wanted to be gallant and move her bags, she wouldn't fight them; she stepped into her cabin, and was agreeably surprised, momentarily forgetting the fierce heat.

A good ten feet square, there were two large portholes, one at the head of the bunk, the other to one side of the washbasin. A quick check revealed that neither opened. She looked at the mirror over the basin, approving its sensible size, but hastily looked away from her reflection, taking in the rest of the cabin.

A desk with drawers, a hanging cupboard, one straight-backed chair and one armchair, chintz-covered to match the tiny porthole curtains, a wall-mounted telephone by the bunk, and a regular galaxy of lights—desk, bunk, washbasin, and two more recessed into the ceiling. With white-painted walls, blue-vinyl-tiled floor, and a cheap Indian rug, she found it very attractive. If only it wasn't so wickedly hot.

The bunk was made up; spare sheets, towels, and a generous supply of soap were neatly stacked on the blue counterpane. She sighed; a lot of hotels weren't up to this standard, but the heat—

Someone tapped on the door.

"Yes?"

"Your bags, ma'am." Jacens put down her heavy cases, gave her a polite nod, his gaze on her eyes, and had gone before she could thank him.

Idly she opened one of the long drawers beneath her bunk. Inside were a number of discarded shirt wrappings, a dirty handkerchief, relics of the last manned voyage.

Men were a scruffy, untidy lot. If this bunch thought she'd run around clearing up after them, they'd have to think again. No card-carrying member of women's lib, her torn face had taught her much. A romantic at heart, recent experience had given her a hard outer skin, a shell far thinner than she imagined, already slightly dented by Jacens' calm gaze. She had no interest in him or any other man, but she realized she was a lot more conscious of him than the rest.

She was first in the saloon. That too was unbearably hot, but otherwise better than she had expected. A good thirty feet by forty; four equally spaced ports admitted a fair amount of daylight, but that had not stopped the designers' enthusiasm for artificial lighting. She counted a dozen wall-mounted lights, plus four fluorescent strips recessed into the ceiling. Away from the ship's side, close by what she guessed was the serving hatch, lay the dining area—a table and six chairs and a Swedish-style sideboard.

In the other two-thirds were four armchairs, a sofa, all covered with the same chintz, three small tables, another cabinet, which she thought held drinks, a powerful-looking radio on its top, and on another wall, a large, filled bookcase. Near the door was a telephone. Two or three undemanding reproductions, framed and screwed to the white walls, completed the decor. Someone had certainly tried.

Langley entered, his shirt now black with sweat. "Miss Harris, as soon as we're through with this meeting, will you take over in the galley?"

Instinctively she turned her head to conceal her scar, livid in the heat. "Yes." She felt grateful for his brusque, asexual manner.

"Good. Here's the keys, including one to the deep-freeze, which is in the main deck flat—that's this one—just behind the companionway. You'll find the shore services have sent off a packed meal for dinner; after that, it's up to you—okay?"

She nodded, brushing the sweat from her eyes. He paused, giving her the chance, but hoping she wouldn't moan about the heat. She didn't, and he went on, less authoritarian. "Don't worry about the heat, it'll be okay soon."

The pilotage officer came in, a large, beefy figure, mopping his brow. He tossed his cap into an armchair, hardly looked at Jane, and addressed Langley. "They've fixed it." His temper seemed frail.

"Sir!"

The rest of the team trooped in, fanning themselves. Colmar made straight for the officer. "Say, are you the boss? Waddya goin' to do about this goddamn heat?"

The officer surveyed him briefly and without obvious pleasure. "Siddown, and stop generating more heat." He looked at the rest of the team. "All of you." He placed his considerable bulk with care in a chair at the head of the dining table. "First, I want to see your ID cards—pass them along."

He checked each one carefully, impassively, tossing them casually down the table; then he leaned back, a mass of graying hair peeping from his unbuttoned shirt. Slowly he took out a cigarette case, his cold gaze fastened on Colmar. He lit a cigarette with slow deliberation, making them wait.

Langley watched with envy, the old sod hadn't got where he had by marrying the boss's daughter.

Colmar just sat, a nervous tic in one pale cheek the only clue to his state of mind.

The pilotage officer blew a cloud of smoke down the table. "If you watch that"—he kept his gaze fixed on Colmar—

"you'll see it is moving." The smoke was, indeed, thinning, eddying away. "There has been a defect in the air-conditioning, now repaired. Within an hour, the temperature will drop to seventy degrees. This compartment, the galley, and all cabins are air-conditioned. Does anyone want to discuss the matter?" He was heavily sarcastic. "No? Very well, I will pass to less trivial matters. We sail at ten hundred hours tomorrow morning; tugs will be alongside at nine-thirty. There will be no shore leave tonight. Any questions?"

There were none.

"When the tugs have us clear of the moorings, we will go to limited automation; that means the computer assumes control, but pilotage steering remains available to the wheelhouse, where I may override the computer if I see fit." His words conveyed a mental picture of a titanic struggle, man against machine. "Which one of you is the qualified helmsman?"

"Me, sir," said Roscorla. He alone saw the latent resentment in the officer, superseded by a usurping computer.

"Yes, I thought it'd be you." Rightly, Roscorla took that comment as a compliment. "Where did you learn?"

"Navy, sir."

The smile faded fractionally, "You won't find this an ocean greyhound. What's the biggest thing you've handled?"

"Aircraft carrier, sir," said Roscorla expressionlessly.

The officer acknowledged the sailor's hit with a warmer smile, then looked at the rest, his expression hardening.

"When we're clear of local shipping, we go to full automation. I will stay aboard until the ship is in the Strait of Hormuz, then fly ashore with my assistant, and you'll be on your own. Your duties are simple, and will be explained in detail by Senior Guard Langley, but here's some background. First, as near as human skill can make it, this ship is safe—a lot safer than most ships these days, especially tankers. It has many sensors—all duplicated for extra reliability. Depth of water, sea state, wind, and any imaginable navigational hazard are allowed for in the program.

AT1 is programmed for a SOA—speed of advance—of twelve-point-one-five knots, its most economical speed, but do not be surprised at changes: this ship can't do more than thirteen anyway, so you're more likely to find it going slower. Do not be alarmed; the computer will know what it's doing.'' He leaned back, lighting another cigarette. Already it was appreciably cooler.

"Now, your job, security. Alarm bells are fitted in these quarters, on deck, and in the defense citadel. Any surface contact detected by radar which is on an approaching course will set it off at a range of two miles, and the same thing goes for an aircraft below one thousand feet within one mile. You'll have quite a few false alarms, particularly in congested waters—off Bandar Abbas and in the English Channel—but that's what you're paid for.''

"Sir,'' said Roscorla.

"Yes?''

"What about at night?''

"There are very powerful computer-controlled searchlights; one each side of the radar gantry, another aft of the funnel, and a fourth right forward. In addition, you can floodlight the sides, the upper deck, or the helo pad from the defense citadel. It's all in your books.''

Roscorla nodded.

"Remember, you are well-armed, and the citadel is bulletproof. If—and I think it a very big if—anyone wanted to hijack this vessel, the last thing he would want to do is to pump high explosive into it! You, on the other hand, if attacked, are free to hit back with missiles or guns. But, as I have said, hijacking is a remote contingency, very largely because you are here, ready. On top of that, there is the shore alarm.''

"Alarm, sir?''

"Yes. If the senior guard considers a threat exists, his first duty is to press the alarm button. Automatically, and on two different frequencies, a distress call, giving the ship's position, course, and speed, will go out continuously until the alarm is canceled.''

"Supposing," said Roscorla, "they shoot away the whip aerials? I reckon it wouldn't be too hard, sir."

"There are other, less obvious aerials, if slightly less efficient." Clearly he did not want to say more. "In any case, all this is very unlikely—it's only the insurers who insist on a guard, not the company. A final word on communications; in the event of any sort of emergency, you have the radio-telephone in the citadel, but it *is* only for emergency use. That's important; you mustn't give away the ship's position without good cause."

Jacens frowned. "Guess I don't quite get it; how can we blow the ship's location if we don't know where we are anyway?"

"That's true—but you can be fixed by direction finders. The computer will report the ship's position, course, and speed at midday and midnight, GMT, throughout the voyage, but that will be in code and on our own private frequencies. The track of this ship from Bandar Abbas to Ushant is a secret known only to the head office—and the computer."

V

The officer gone, Langley took over. "Okay . . . according to my list, you, Colmar, have done four trips in manned tankers, and Jacens has done three. Roscorla's new, but being a sailor, I don't suppose he'll have much trouble in settling down. You three will work in shifts, starting tomorrow when we've cleared the harbor. If anything happens to me, Jacens takes over. Got it?"

They all nodded, but Colmar was slowest, a fact Langley instantly registered.

"Yes, I know you've got one more trip than Jacens, but he's senior in age, rank, and general experience—including combat."

"I didn't know we were still in the Army," said Colmar softly.

"Son, you're so right—but don't let it worry you. I won't," said Jacens amiably.

"Like it or not," grated Langley, "that's the way it'll be. Read your instruction books! I make the decisions, and if you don't like it, complain afterward, but from here on in, you do as you're told!"

No one argued with that hard voice.

"Now, the domestic situation. Miss Harris here is officially the cook, stewardess, and nurse. Her orders say what she does: I'll tell you what she doesn't do. She doesn't clean out cabins, do personal washing, or clean up the saloon. All of us, including me, will be on a rota for cleaning communal spaces—except Miss Harris. In lieu, she does the laundry;

clean sheets, pillowcases, and towels all around, once a week. A duty cleaner will assist her as she directs—dishes and all that—got it?''

"Yes, Sarge." Roscorla wasn't trying to be funny; Langley let that "Sarge" go.

"Well, that's it. Get unpacked. Dinner okay at twelve-thirty, Miss Harris?"

"I'll let you know as soon as I've seen the galley."

It was more of a luxury kitchen than her idea of a ship's galley. It had everything: large electric cooker with eye-level grill, a separate infrared grill, plastic-topped preparation table, double stainless-steel sink, washing machine, folding ironing board, vast fridge, drying cupboard.

On the table were two big insulated containers, one with three cold roast chickens and two sorts of salad, the other filled with cans of beer and soft drinks. On a sheet of company notepaper someone had typed "Bon voyage!"

"Full marks to the company," she said—women often talk aloud to themselves. She opened a can of lime juice and wandered around, peering into cupboards. Yes, it was all there: floor-polisher, Hoover, dusters, the lot. Suddenly she felt chill, and checked the thermometer: eighty-five degrees. Unbelieving, she tapped it, but it stuck to its opinion.

Langley's interview with the officer was soon over. After observing that that fellow Colmar would bear watching, being a born sea lawyer, the pilotage officer said he would be going ashore, returning at nine A.M., bringing the armory keys.

After his departure, ignoring the fearful heat, Langley remained in the citadel, thinking of a dozen different things: Colmar, the Harris woman. Had he pitched it a bit too strong? Still, better to start off rough; easier to tone down than to harden up. Footsteps on the ladder made him look around.

"Dinner will be at twelve-thirty, Mr. Langley. Cold chicken and salad, bread and cheese—and the company's given us a send-off present of chilled beer." She screwed up her eyes in a smile substitute, turning her head slightly away. Seen like that, she was beautiful.

"That's fine, Miss Harris." He tried not to look at her

breasts. No philosopher, Langley did not try to analyze why that scar made all the difference, only knowing it did—so far; but he wanted to keep the conversation going. "You settling in?"

"I've only just finished checking the galley. Unless you want me to do something, I thought I'd unpack, shower, and check the sick bay."

"No, you go ahead. The shower . . . there's two bathrooms—the two doors opposite the galley. Take the left-hand one; we'll use the other."

"Seems a little unfair; four of you."

"That's not exactly hardship. Anyway, yours is officially the sick-bay shower."

She nodded, relaxing slightly, letting more of her face be seen. "Twelve-thirty, then."

"I thought, first day and all that, we'd have a drink together—specially now we've got some cold beer. I'd be glad if you joined in—say, twelve o'clock?"

Now she was full-face, physically and mentally. "Are you sure, Mr. Langley?"

"Yes, of course!" This was the moment to say something about her scar, but he had no idea how to put it—and knew he lacked the moral courage to say it, anyway. "You come along—with the beer!"

Sharp at ten next morning they sailed; for the traditional seaman, an incredible performance. Up forward, in the eyes of the ship, Guard Jacens stood waiting patiently for orders from the nearby loudspeaker; his charge the two massive hemp hawsers, one to each tug on either side of the tanker's bows. He had only to wait for "Slip Left (or Right)," manhandle the appropriate rope off its bollard, and his work —overtime at seven dollars an hour—was over. Right aft, Colmar did a similar job.

In the wheelhouse, the pilotage officer, microphone in hand, listened to the VHF link with the tugs, watched the swing of the bows, he alone exercising judgment. Behind him, Guard Roscorla manned the wheel. Down below in the computer room, totally enclosed in armor, the officer's assistant waited to engage the computer. Five men to handle over a hundred thousand tons of ship, and only that many because of the attendant tugs.

The officer pressed the engine's starter button, thinking bitterly it was more like driving a bloody car. The "engines running" sign lit on the control panel, and he set them for dead slow. Minutes passed before the giant single screw got appreciable way on the ship. With four tugs pushing and pulling, AT1 edged away from the fueling berth.

Jane Harris watched this historic moment from the citadel. She had no appreciation of the finer points of wind, currents, or the peculiar problems of a single screw ship, but was still impressed by the way it was done, watching the gap between ship and moorings slowly widen. Crossing to the port side, she had a good view of an Arab dhow, in her eyes something straight out of the Bible. Its picturesque sail attracted her; she ran down to her cabin and photographed it through her porthole, happily unaware of the barrage of vituperation directed from tug and tanker at the intruder.

"Stand by fore and aft!"

"Forrard! Slip starboard—right!" The officer swore. "Left" and "right!" Enough to make a man vomit. . . . "Port ten."

"Port ten, sir," repeated Roscorla, spinning the wheel. "Ten of port wheel on, sir."

The officer took time out from mentally cursing the tugs, the dhow, the company, and science to feel a pang of gratitude that at least there was one other seaman on board. "Midships . . . meet her . . . steer zero-six-five." He barked into his microphone, "Forrard: slip left! Aft: slip both, left and right!"

The last line splashed into the pearl-gray water: AT1 was under way, on her own. The pilotage officer had no time for abstract thoughts, watching the bows closely, aware the helmsman couldn't get this bloody great misbegotten barge steady in a few seconds.

Christ, what had we come to? Two seamen and two ex-pongos taking best part of twelve million pounds' worth of ship and cargo to sea.

He sighed and lit a cigarette, thankful for small mercies. On the bigger supertankers, that man up in the bows would come aft on a bloody bicycle.

"Steady on zero-six-five, sir."

"Steer small; keep her steady."

"Aye-aye, sir."

The officer phoned the computer room. "Steady now on base course. Check zero-six-five and engage when ready."

The technician watched the gyro, pressed the input to computer button, saw the digital presentation count out ten seconds; a green light glowed; he pressed another button, which got him a second green light. He rang the wheelhouse. "Computer locked on."

The officer grunted and banged the phone down.

As the phone rang, Roscorla felt the wheel go free in his hands, an unnerving experience for any helmsman. "Steerage lost, sir."

"Very good. Remain closed up until I tell you."

"Aye-aye, sir." At twelve dollars an hour overtime, Roscorla had no objection.

The pilotage officer slumped back in his chair. So that was that: in the not too distant future there'd be magnetic loops laid in harbors, and that really would be the end, even of these lousy pilotage parties. Some bit of a kid, like that wet bastard down in the computer room, would press a button ashore, and away the ship would go; just playing trains. With a transverse mounted bow-thrust propeller, they'd do away with tugs. No crews, no tugs . . . Where the hell was it all going? Automation replacing humans all the time, and all the time more and more humans. It didn't make sense in his mind. Growing old had some compensations.

Langley set a good example down below, helping with the chores. One thing was clear: Jane Harris was a fine cook. Nothing fancy, but well able to produce good, solid grub.

After supper the evening before, a few drinks, and they'd all turned in, highly satisfied; even Colmar had toned down, chatting with Roscorla, and with none of his snide remarks, even exchanging the odd guarded comment with himself and Jacens. They'd all got on first-name terms, but none breached the "Miss Harris" bit. Not that she'd given them much chance. She'd sat on his left hand, which shielded her face from most, and as soon as the meal was over, she'd gone.

Yes; after a shaky start, they weren't doing too badly. Service in the sea guard had something in common with the old-time French Foreign Legion; you didn't ask outright why a bloke joined, accepting him for what he was, not interested in what he had been.

Roscorla had said damn-all on the subject, and Colmar was the same. The big surprise had been Jacens: Mark had confessed—and the way he said it *was* a confession—he was trying to write a book, and reckoned this job gave him the best chance. That had been a right shaker; Mark Jacens a bloody scribe! No great reader, Langley rated writers with office workers; well below soldiers, only fractionally better than lawyers, hairdressers, and pimps. In that order.

After an early dinner, Langley had his men up in the defense citadel, a giant rectangular armored box. The front and back, over ninety feet long, had a dozen windows of armor-plate glass, all easily wound down like car windows. Above each hung a bulletproof steel shutter, pierced with a modern equivalent of a castle's arrow slits, which could be lowered and locked in position. At either end of the rectangle a door led out to a gun position, with waist-high steel protection; only the gun was missing.

Armored doors in the rear wall gave access to the deck on either beam. In the middle of the citadel, to one side of the companionway, was the armory; behind that, the citadel water closet—the man on duty would have no excuse for leaving his post. For his added comfort, a tall stool—which would rest his legs, but nothing else—was bolted to the deck in front of a small red-painted panel. Floodlight switches, the internal phone, and radiotelephone handset were grouped around the external alarm button, its translucent plastic glowing bright red. Below it, the white "cancel" button. A child of ten could master the lot in five minutes, a fact that did not stop Langley explaining the whole setup in detail.

". . . and here we have the radiotelephone, operating on

the distress frequency, 2182 kilohertz, it has a reliable range of five hundred miles, and probably a lot more. It is operated by removing the handset, so, and depressing the switch in the hand grip.''

Colmar and Roscorla, exchanging covert glances, were immediately transfixed by his stare, but their interest grew when, under the brooding gaze of the officer, Langley broke the seal on the armory door. He checked the contents carefully against the inventory, signed it, and handed one copy to the officer, who promptly lost interest, returning to his wheelhouse chair.

They manhandled the two dull black Aden guns out and on to their mountings, one each side. Sealed ammunition boxes holding belts of shells were placed in the ready-use lockers around each gun. The maintenance of these weapons would be Roscorla's charge, and he was quick to shroud them in their plastic covers.

Then came the two Blowpipes. Both launchers and their missiles were racked up in the positions provided on the outside wall of the armory. Finally the four Armalite rifles and Browning automatacs were prepared and placed in their racks.

It was an impressive array.

''Guess there'll be enough to go around,'' observed Mark Jacens in his quiet Texan drawl.

''Better too much than too little, Tex,'' said Langley sententiously. ''Now, pay attention: Roscorla's action station is on whichever Aden is required. Tex—you're an all-rounder, which do you fancy?''

Jacens shrugged. ''That Blowpipe can't be much different from the old bazooka.''

''Okay, you take one, I'll take the other. That puts you, Colmar, on the Adens, either as loader to Roscorla, or if we want both guns, whichever is free. Okay?''

''Okay with me.''

''On top, we've an Armalite carbine and a Browning automatic apiece for close-range work. All guns stay right here in the citadel. The duty man will wear his personal automatic, but leaves it here when his shift is over. Got it?''

36

They nodded.

"I don't have to tell you, each man is responsible for the cleanliness and serviceability of his personal and his action-station weapons. I will inspect them daily, and I won't be kidding!"

"How about the dame?" put in Jacens, more to ease Langley out of his heavy act, which, he felt, was a little overdone. None of them were van recruits.

"Her?" Langley looked surprised. "We'll have to be in a heck of a jam if she needs a gun! Anyway, if we get into a shooting match, I like professionals around me."

Jacens agreed. "Sure . . . sure, but I've got a sneaky feeling—don't know how to put it—but I think she might handle a gun as well as a skillet."

Langley did not reply at once; he too thought there was more to Miss Harris than met the eye. "Maybe I'll let her have a go when we have a practice shoot."

"Yeah—that could be interesting."

"Now we all know where everything is, this is where we start work. Who's got the first shift?" Once again, Langley mentally kicked himself for weakness. He knew damned well it was Mark Jacens, yet did not want to say outright, to a man who was his equal if not his superior in character and experience.

Without answering, Mark moved over, unhooked his gunbelt, and put it on. He drew the Browning 9-mm FN, extracted a full clip from the belt, checked it, and pushed it home. The metallic click, the action, had symbolic significance.

Phil laughed. "Okay, so now we can rest easy—Mark's got the weight!"

Mark grinned, checked the safety catch, and holstered the gun. "Yeah, you might say that."

VI

Apart from Phil becoming Jane Harris' first patient with a prickly-heat rash, the passage from Bahrein to the Strait of Hormuz was uneventful.

Working in the galley, Jane Harris noted that but for a low rumble and the occasional chatter when two dishes touched, AT1 might have still been at the fueling buoy. It seemed amazing to her, a miracle, that those who understood such matters were happy that the unattended engines would churn on for the next five weeks or more. She hoped they were right.

Her confidence was boosted by the pilotage officer. He ate in the wheelhouse, but when she took meals up to him, he appeared to be dozing. In the citadel, the duty guard walked up and down, binoculars slung around his neck, his only excitement the hourly punching of his card in the time clock.

Jane found a difference in the officer when she went up with supper: he was very much awake. Night had come, ahead lay the strait and the consequent increase in density of shipping. She also fed his assistant in the computer room, who appeared more interested in a lurid magazine than his charge.

The only member of the team who really appreciated the situation was Roscorla. Bigger than an old-time battleship, this bastard hammered along at ten to twelve knots, through crowded waters, with one seaman watching, backed up by that spectacled twit gloating over Denmark's latest porn in the middle of a load of electronic guff.

Roscorla went on watch at midnight, and glimpsed, in passing, through the open door, the spectacled twit, snoring on a bench seat, oblivious of the flickering lights and the roar of the exhaust fans. The sailor's surprise reached new heights when Jacens told him the pilotage officer was asleep in his wheelhouse chair and was to be called at four A.M.

Feeling the entire weight of the ship on his shoulders, the Cornishman paced the citadel. Once during his vigil he saw the lights of another ship, inbound for the gulf; he suspected AT1 had altered course, but couldn't be sure without looking at the wheelhouse compass, and he had no desire to disturb the officer—but didn't let him sleep on one minute after the appointed time; it had been a very strange, uncanny four hours.

Dawn came at 5:15, and the quickly rising sun, a huge orange ball, emerged above the black peaks of the mountains of southern Iran. Roscorla greeted the sight with considerable relief, and his spirits rose almost as fast as the sun. Blessed with a happy-go-lucky disposition, he soon forgot his cares and fears of the night.

Clear of the strait, the ship moved gently in the small southerly swell of the Indian Ocean. The officer, after checking with the computer room, radioed Muscat for his helicopter.

The final shutdown of the pilotage party was as impressively simple as the sailing of AT1. The officer stumped up to the wheelhouse, banged down the heavy steel cover to the control panel, and locked it; below, his assistant shut the thick armored computer-room door, shot the banklike bolts, and twirled the combination lock.

As the helicopter approached, the officer unbent to Langley. "It's a strange damned world: here am I, over thirty years at sea, ten of them as captain, stepping ashore as the voyage starts, leaving you—no offense—a soldier in charge of four humans, with a bloody computer in command!" He gave a sharp bark of a laugh. "Ha! I'm too damned old for all this, and frankly I'm glad. The world's moved on; progress—maybe." His washed-out blue eyes openly inspected Langley's face. "I don't envy you; the thing's safe enough, but . . ." The officer looked away, unable to go on, unable to bridge the gap of years, profession, and experience. "Good luck, Langley."

Five minutes, and the helo had been and gone. Jacens, on duty, watched it thoughtfully until it disappeared into the haze that hid the Muscat coast, a buzzing impersonal dot.

Langley had the rest of the team busy rigging the antihelo net on its stanchions, sealing the last gap in the defenses. A pilot would have to be blind or mad to approach that bright-orange plastic-coated steel mesh, firmly secured eight feet clear of the deck.

"Well, that's the bleedin' drawbridge up." Phil Roscorla, tightening the last bottle screw, spoke for them all: AT1 really was on its own. The Cornishman, for one, sensed the change; the world was shut out; they all felt a new sense of unity, including even Colmar. "That's us tucked up."

For five weeks "us" would be the team, "them" the rest of the world.

"Yeah; kinda creepy," said Colmar. "Guess guys in space are about the only ones—"

"No!" Roscorla said indignantly, unwilling to share their situation with anyone. "Astronauts have some control; if they want out, they can do something about it—not us!"

"How about our life rafts—they're our space buggy." The two men went below arguing amiably.

Langley remained on deck, watching the slow movement of the net's shadow on the deck. He had no time for anything he did not regard as practical, yet even he realized the irrevocability of the act of rigging the net. By nightfall they'd be out of helo range and therefore beyond help. All the team had passed stiff medical and dental examinations, and only a man who had had his appendix removed was even considered as a candidate for this job, but suppose there was a really bad accident, something Jane Harris couldn't handle?

Langley shrugged that thought off: she was a qualified nurse, and as the quack had breezily said, they ran less risk than the average city dweller—no roads to cross. Colmar had given no trouble, once he had been told where he got off. God knows, he had little enough to crab about: good grub, moderate booze—he didn't seem much of a drinker—two hundred dollars a week, tax-free, plus overtime, painting upper-deck gear if he wanted it, no responsibilities, except to keep his eyes open eight hours in twenty-four. . . . Phil Roscorla was okay. . . . Jacens; he was the quiet one. . . .

Suddenly aware, Langley glanced sharply toward the wheelhouse. Jacens was leaning out of an open window, looking at him. They half-nodded, and Jacens looked away, panning slowly around the horizon with his binoculars.

Langley went on staring at the Yank, a type he understood. A different army, but like himself, a professional. The world in general views soldiers with unease and faint contempt—until there is some fighting to do. In a jam, Langley would choose Jacens as a partner, and felt quite sure Jacens would pay him the same compliment.

The Englishman considered the proposition: why didn't he pick his own countryman, Phil? A simple if unsatisfying answer: Phil was a sailor; he couldn't feel as sure of him as he would of Jacens. It was all a matter of background, training. Anyway, why was he so sure Jacens would not prefer Colmar? That was another story; Colmar had a spotless record, but he'd been a technician, had no combat experience, lacked that final case-hardening. No: Jacens would not choose Colmar.

And how about Jane Harris? Like Jacens, she seemed to have an inner strength—poor devil, with that face, she needed it—friendly, but detached in an impersonal sort of way, the nurse more in evidence than the cook. And why not? Langley gave it up; in his experience, an unrecognized problem was a nonexistent problem.

Unlike the men, Jane Harris had scarcely stopped since she stepped aboard. Despite the labor-saving galley, three full meals a day for four men—all were realistic eaters—plus the dishes (Langley had helped once, but if the others were like him, they'd be out of plates in a fortnight), cleaning the galley and sick bay, checking stores in both, plus ''shopping'' in the deep-freeze, had kept her going. Langley said the night watchmen would make their own sandwiches; guessing the mess they'd make, she'd taken that on as well. Where they stacked all that food was a mystery—and the gallons of tea and coffee! At their present rate, they'd be bursting out of their clothes in a month, she'd have to tackle the diet question.

Beep-beep-beep!

The sudden, penetrating shriek of the alarm, far worse than a dozen jammed auto horns, made her jump convulsively. She dropped a frozen loaf, nerves tingling, ears still assaulted by the screeching alarm.

Langley flashed past the galley, followed closely by Colmar, stripped to the waist, half-shaven, barefoot. Somewhere overhead there were several heavy thumps. Her blood tingled with alarm and the uncertain novelty of the situation.

"Get a bloody wriggle on!" shouted Langley unnecessarily. Feet pounded on the companionway. At a loss what to do, Jane picked up the loaf. For the real thing—she couldn't believe this was it—her action station was the sick bay. She dumped the loaf and ran.

She stumbled into the sick bay, trembling with excitement. The alarm stopped abruptly. Seconds later, the phone rang.

"It's okay—a false alarm." Langley spoke with curt authority. "Come up and have a look."

Replacing the handset, she decided that had been a crafty way of checking up on her. Still, there must be something to see. She left quickly.

The citadel was much darker, grimmer. In accordance with standing orders, as soon as the alarm sounded, Jacens had released the armored window shields. Unstrapping his gunbelt, Langley, grinning, greeted her, and pointed.

Through a fighting port in one shield she saw a large tanker, high in the water, obviously empty, heading for the gulf. Even as she watched, the ship slid out of her limited field of vision; AT1 was still turning.

"Dim bastards," observed Phil, studying the ship's bridge through binoculars, "waving all over the ocean—bet they still haven't seen us! Expect the officer of the watch has buggered off to the heads or the bar, an' left some solid O.D. to gawp at the radar scan. My dear life! No more idea of the rule of the road than a babe in arms!''

"What happened?" said Jane.

Phil lowered his glasses and looked sharply around. "Oh—sorry! Pardon my French, miss." He looked at the ship again. "Might have known it—one of those PanHonLib packets. Some of 'em are a flamin' menace—including that one!''

"Yes—but what happened?''

"Okay—fall out," said Langley. "Not bad; three minutes. But we'll do better." He nodded approvingly at Colmar as the Yank, lather still on his face, padded silently off to finish his toilet.

Jacens heaved an armored shutter up; dazzling light flooded in. "Waal, I saw this guy sometime back; looks like he's comin' straight for us, but a bit later I see we've altered course, and it all looks pretty okay to me. Then, goddamnit, that guy changes direction—toward us! After that, I lose track, we swing some more, the siren blasts off, the alarm goes, and our searchlights start flashing like crazy.''

"What—like Morse?''

"Could be, Phil. I didn't pay much attention. Yeah; reckon it was Morse, like two dots an' a dash, over and over.''

"That's right!" said Roscorla, impressed. "That's the letter U. In the international code it means 'You are standing into danger.' No doubt about it, you've got to hand it to the blokes that designed this packet; they've thought of everything!''

"I surely hope so," replied Jacens with feeling. "About the time the alarm sounded off, I began to think mebbe we'd need a life belt or two.''

"Come on, lads, let's get the shutters up." Langley raised one that commanded a view of the stern. "We're still turning; suppose we're coming back on track. Flaming uncanny, if you think about it.''

Jane stared after the receding tanker. "Wish I'd had my camera; that would have made a good picture." She remembered the bread and left in a hurry.

The incident put Langley in a good temper for the rest of

the day. Jacens had acted according to the book, and the other two men had moved fast, particularly Colmar; he'd not even stopped to grab a shirt, and he'd cleared the port Aden for action iike greased lightning, and it hadn't been done in a panic. Langley decided he'd have to revise his view of Colmar. Pity he was such an awkward bastard to get on with. Phil had been okay, and the Harris woman had gone promptly to her station. Yes, that tanker had been good news.

At midday, before dinner, he brought Colmar a drink, but felt himself slightly rebuffed; Colmar had an orange juice, nodded his thanks, and said nothing.

Jane Harris felt happy too. In the excitement, she had, for the first time, completely forgotten her face; thinking back, she could not recall even a hint that the others had noticed. Yet, forgetful, she must have smiled. . . . God!

But the experience gave her courage, and secure in headscarf and dark glasses, she went on deck in the afternoon. The weather was beautiful. She wandered along the deck enjoying the hot sun, tempered by the breeze. For a while she leaned on the rail, idly watching the glittering sea, and was suddenly fascinated by small groups of flying fish. Startled, they flashed out of the water, gliding fast and arrow-straight for twenty or thirty yards, swept-wing, aeons-old before Man fell out of the trees. . . .

She marveled at their speed and the way they thumped back into the sea and were gone, such frail creatures, yet able to withstand that impact.

Impact. . . . That was something she did not want to think about. Abruptly she turned away, walking aft, the fragile pleasure gone. Phil, on watch, waved cheerily to her, and she quickened her pace; she could do with company.

Roscorla had transformed the grim cavernous fortress of a few hours earlier. He had cut the air-conditioning, opened all the windows and doors. A warm breeze had banished the smell of gun oil; dappled sunlight, reflected from the sea, danced silently on the white-painted deckhead.

"Bit of all right, isn't it?" Already she realized he dearly loved company.

"Yes," she said, nodding.

"Come and sit on the stool, miss. Do me good to walk about."

She sat down, wanting to tell him to stop calling her "miss," but to do that would inevitably lead to first names, and she was not ready for that yet. Phil was pathetically eager to talk, and explained in detail the simple control panel. Half-listening, she put herself in his place, and realized that being a guard on an unmanned tanker was a fairly lonely job. She had heard that recruiting was not brisk; manning AT1 had not been a problem, but as the automated ships grew in numbers, it had been foreseen there could be problems; she could see why.

It was on the tip of her tongue to ask Phil why he took the job; but to ask for confidences would invite others from her. Instead, she slipped off the stool and wandered around, fingering the cool steel of the Blowpipes, stared at the Armalites clunked slowly from side to side, obedient to the gentle roll, like slightly drunk soldiers. It struck her as seeming so normal, but here they were, a small, well-armed team, yet not soldiers, ready to fight pirates as a private enterprise—and doing it in a giant ship under the control of an electronic box of tricks.

She found the thought vaguely frightening, and sheered away from it. "Is that the door into the funnel?" She pointed toward the back of the citadel.

"That? Oh, yes." Phil remembered. "Like to have a look?" He gave the ocean a careful scrutiny before joining her with a hand lamp. "Mind your step," he said, opening the door. "It's as dark as the inside of a cow."

As he had said, there was a lot more room than she had imagined, very hot and full of reverberating sound from the ventilation fans. He shone the light upward, and she was surprised to see the top totally enclosed. She had always imagined a funnel to be a vast chimney, full of smoke.

He laughed at her illusions and steered her out again, skirting the buckets and mops. " 'Fraid there's not much to see."

"No, but at least I know what it looks like. Thank you."
She chose her words carefully. To have said "Thanks, Phil"
would have implied a closer, more informal relationship than
she wanted, or, she thought bitterly, than he might want.

Given prevision, her reaction would have been very
different.

VII

Forty-eight hours passed without incident. The weather remained good, and the team slipped into a routine which was efficient but would very soon be boring.

At some point Phil remarked they were like flaming lighthouse keepers, but he was wrong in one important detail; keepers do little more than tend their light, a job which may attract men of a solitary turn of mind. AT1's team were different—trained fighters, men of action. Langley saw that boredom could be their biggest danger.

At first there had been great interest in getting news bulletins and sport on the radio, but even twenty-four hours out of Bahrein the interest waned, the outside world fading. Off duty, Jacens spent a lot of time in his cabin or on deck, wrestling with his book. Colmar passed his leisure hours in his bunk, reading or bathing. He was quite the cleanest man aboard.

Phil wandered hopefully around, looking for someone to talk to. Jane Harris discovered the ladder up to the wheelhouse roof and spent an hour or so each afternoon there. What she did was a matter of interest to Phil, and to a lesser extent Langley, but they could not know, for apart from the radar gantry, it was the highest point in the ship. Her polite, slightly distant manner, plus her scar, guaranteed her privacy, reinforced, had she known it, by a comment of Jacens; when asked by Phil what he thought she did, Jacens replied, "Mebbe she sunbathes. I don't know, and don't aim to find out. Could be that scar ain't the only one she's got."

Langley was only too thankful she kept out of the way. Scar or no scar, she was a woman, and increasingly in his thoughts. Sex apart, he stuck to his job, and had little interest in anything else. Any illusions that he would soon slacken off were rapidly dispelled; at all hours he would appear, silent in sneakers, in the citadel. His orders called for four unscheduled visits every twenty-four hours, plus routine checks of the deck log, time cards, and the armament. On top was the daily arms inspection, all living spaces, and the upper deck. Only when Mark Jacens had the watch did he ease off, but even the Texan could bank on seeing him twice in an eight-hour shift.

Colmar, in one of his sudden gusts of rage, confided his vitriolic views of the senior guard to Roscorla, who agreed Langley could safely "take it off his back," but neither expressed their opinions in Langley's—or Jacens'—hearing.

The fragmented nature of the party, their separateness, worried Langley. If it came to action, he reckoned they'd do well enough, and that was the main thing, but they weren't a team, and he set great store by the team spirit. He tried to get a card group going, and that died the first evening. Then he offered overtime, deck painting, to Roscorla and Colmar working together, but Colmar, who clearly detested sunlight, wasn't interested. Phil worked happily enough, glad of the extra money, but that did nothing to foster good relations.

But among Langley's several worries, AT1 was not one. The ship plugged steadily on, the only sign of action the endlessly rotating radar aerials. With the wheelhouse control panel locked, they had no accurate idea of the ship's course or speed, but the sun, and the slowly changing times of sunrise and sunset, showed they headed roughly south.

It was an open secret their route lay well clear of main shipping tracks, partly for security, partly to meet the protests of seafarers who, in the main, regarded the monster as a danger to them all. So high-level policy decreed that until automated ships became acceptable, they should be routed well clear of other vessels. Devotees of automation smiled at the restriction, confident the day would come when the balance tipped the other way and the diminishing number of manned ships would be forced to give up the shorter, more economical routes, hastening their own departure from the oceans, even as the steamer had swept the sailing ship into history—only faster.

Roscorla showed particular interest in their progress, and dug into the encyclopedia in the library for a map of the Indian Ocean.

"You know, Sarge," he began after supper one evening, "I reckon we're going to pass well to the east of Madagascar—hundreds, maybe more'n a thousand miles from land."

"And so what?" Langley stared blankly. "Who cares?"

"Ah-ha, my lover!" Phil broke into broad Cornish, "Tes faascinatin'! 'Ere weem be, sailing waaters unknoon to man —including usen West Contrymen!"

Langley saw he was only half-joking. "Straight up—you mean that?"

Roscorla nodded, reverting to his normal gentle burr. "Aye, Sarge. Take a gander at this map: I ask you—who'd want to sail along this track, before we came along? Not warships, nor merchantmen. Perhaps a whaler . . ." He stared at the map, shook his head, and regarded Langley with an unusually serious expression. "I'm not taking the piss, Sarge, but you're a soldier, you've got no idea of the size of all this." He tapped the map. "Thousands of square bloody miles, most of it never sailed before! Soon we could be fifteen hundred miles from the nearest human."

"Bloody good job, too! Anyway, that's nothing special; you can be alone in the middle of the Atlantic."

"No." Phil was emphatic. "The North Atlantic's stiff with ships, and there's aircraft bombing around in droves! We've had perfect weather, hardly any cloud—and when did you last see the contrail of a plane? For the next ten days, we'll be as much alone as we're likely to get this side of the grave."

Both would remember that remark.

"Come off it, Phil—you trying to give me the creeps?"

Phil grinned. "That'll be the day!"

Nevertheless, he made the Army man think. If anyone was

stupid enough to try a hijack, this period could be the time. He regarded the chances as wildly remote, but he would leave as little as possible to chance. On the morrow they would exercise action stations, and then have a practice shoot. At least it would fend off boredom.

It did rather more than that.

The company had catered for every situation they could imagine, from playing cards and birthday cakes in the deep-freeze to triplicated lubrication systems in the engine room. One store held a quantity of orange meterological balloons, fastening clips, and a cylinder of hydrogen, to provide targets. Langley's announcement was greeted with mild enthusiasm. After action stations, Colmar and Roscorla would shoot with the Adens at balloons, then all four men would try out the Armalites, and then there'd be a competition automatic shoot on the helo deck.

He noticed that Jane Harris listened with interest, and furthering his team-spirit policy, he said, "Would you like to have a go, Miss Harris?"

"Yes—with an automatic pistol. I'd like to."

Something in her manner made Phil look at her sharply. "Hey, miss, I'll bet you can handle a gun. Can you?"

"Yes—a bit," she admitted, then answered their unspoken question. "In the airline they thought it a good idea."

"Gee—a real-live pistol-packin' mamma!" The way Colmar said it, the remark was offensive.

Phil's face hardened, but Langley got in first.

"Let's hope you're as fast with a gun as you are with your tongue!"

Instantly the blood drained from Colmar's face; he fought for self-control. He glared, eyes hard, at Langley, then nodded very slowly. "Could be. That just could be. . . ."

Not for the first time, Phil thought the guy must be nuts. It was as if Colmar had been skinned alive; the slightest opposition galvanized him into ugly rage.

The shoot began with the Adens, and while proper scoring was out of the question, Langley saw that Phil was no mean shot, closely followed by Colmar. Both he and Jacens tried, but were not up to the same standard, or expected to be, especially Roscorla's. Colmar's ability was surprising, but Langley suspected that if the ship had any roll on, the sailor would be 'way out in front. Beyond doubt, at two thousand yards Roscorla would more than earn his corn.

Then they tried with the Armalites. Balloons popped and fell into the sea with satisfying regularity to all of them. On average, of the two weapons, Langley guessed Colmar had the edge; maybe not quite as good as Jacens with the carbine, but he had been streets ahead with the Aden.

Before the Browning shoot, Langley announced the prize would be an hour's overtime signed on the best shot's work sheet—and drinks on the loser. He rigged a pint beer can on the end of a cord, suspended over the stern on a broomstick. Bobbing and dancing with the ship's movement and vibration, it was no easy target.

"The firing point's the center of the helo pad," said Langley.

Jacens raised one black eyebrow. "That's kinda tough with guns we don't know."

Langley didn't answer, but produced a three-foot-square target and hung it on the stern guardrail. "Six calibration shots at that first. Anyone who hits the ship can go home. After calibration, six shots each at the can."

He went first, punctilious about his safety drill, shooting in the classic competition stance; body at right angles to the target, gun arm straight out, firing with careful precision. His test completed, he stuck paper over his tight knot of holes and nodded to Roscorla.

It was at once painfully obvious that the sailor was far less happy with an automatic than an Aden or an Armalite. Doing his best to copy Langley, his grouping was far from impressive: his first attempt missed the target board completely.

Colmar went next, strolling casually, almost arrogantly up to the firing point. After three shots in the competition stance, he shifted with lightning speed to the "gunman crouch," body and knees bent, balanced on his toes, gun held before him, level with the pit of his stomach.

51

Langley's eyes narrowed; to calibrate like that, you either had to be very good or plain ignorant. With less swagger, Jacens shot the same way, but Langley had no doubts about him. He looked around.

"Miss Harris—would you like to use my gun?"

She had been a silent spectator since the hammer of the Adens told her the exercise had begun. She took Langley's gun confidently. To him, her hand looked very frail and small. "This one's new to me," she confessed. She listened carefully as he explained about the magazine and the safety catch. He handed her a loaded magazine.

"When you're ready."

She walked self-consciously to the center of the helo pad, trigger finger flat against the guard in the approved manner. The men watched, half-prepared to dive for cover, a thought that soon went. Feet well apart, facing the target, she held the gun well up, sighting along the barrel, left hand grasping the right wrist. The safety catch snicked off.

"My dear life," whispered Phil excitedly, "proper job!"

She fired steadily; the grouping was not impressive, but Langley saw that her last two shots were a lot closer to the center, and having shot with the same gun, he recognized she had spotted the error after the first two shots. Among the congratulations, he remained silent. If she was as good as he suspected . . . He took the gun, giving her a conspiratorial smile, noting she had put on the safety catch after her last shot. She hadn't learned in a fun fair.

Then came the shoot. Langley went first, hitting the can twice. With a comical, resigned expression, Phil fired, but, beaten before he began, he missed completely, accepting their ironic cheers with a good grace. He was a gunner, not a gunman.

Colmar went next, pausing for a moment before moving to the center of the pad, breathing deeply, his face white. The rest fell silent, sensing his tension, knowing Colmar wasn't kidding. Four silent, fast steps, and he reached the firing point, dropping into the ugly, lethal crouch, the gun magically in his hand. Almost at once he fired, and fired again. Four times in less than ten seconds he hit the can as it clanged and swung. It was a brilliant display. Briefly, after the last shot, he remained frozen, then straightened up, walked back, grinning sardonically at Jacens. "Fast enough for you—Sarge?" Langley knew the crack was aimed at him.

Jane recalled her inability to place Colmar as a dog. She had been right: Colmar was a cat.

"Mighty fine, son," agreed Jacens, unmoved. "Mighty fine. . . . Say, Bill, how about the lady shootin' next?"

Something in Jacens' manner stopped Langley asking why. "Sure—if it's okay with her."

Colmar sneered: to follow that would be uphill work. Jacens was backing off.

Jane Harris obliged. Colmar outclassed her hopelessly—she'd never seen shooting like it—so she took her time, shooting carefully, slowly, and scored three hits.

Roscorla crowed with delight, and the rest joined in, clapping, including Colmar. Flushed with pleasure, she walked back and returned the automatic to Langley.

"That was nice work, lady." Jacens smiled, staring deep into her eyes. "One way an another, guess I've got my work cut out."

He strolled over in his slow, loose-jointed, casual way to the firing point, dropping smoothly into the crouch, firing instantly. Five shots ripped off at incredible speed, rewarded by four clangs from the can. Deliberately he threw his concentration away, looking over his shoulder at Jane, smiling slowly. "You want the can as a souvenir, lady?" He waited for the shake of her head, turned again to the target, took deliberate aim, and fired. The cord cut, the mangled remains of the beer can dropped into the white wake of the ship.

"Christ!" said Langley with deep emotion, "talk about how the West was won!"

Jacens ambled back. "Your pardon, ma'am," he guyed all the westerns ever made. "Yew just haveta forgive us Texans—we're nothin' but natural-born show-offs." Still smiling, he switched to the pallid Colmar. "If yew are kinda unhappy about thet last shot, son, I'd be pleased to accommodate yew with a one-shot shoot-off 'gainst a tossed-up can."

Colmar met his gaze, hesitated fractionally, and looked away, his words inaudible, but his acceptance of defeat clear.

The small scene reminded Phil of *High Noon*—except this was for real. After that display he looked at both men in a new and not very comfortable light. Up to this time, soldiers had been, to him, little more than stamping semirobots, but not now. Neither Jacens nor Colmar was slightly comic, both were accomplished killers.

Langley thought on similar lines. "Well, I've seen shooting in my time, but nothing like that! I used to think all that Wild West stuff was pure guff, but you two Yanks . . ." He shook his head.

Colmar's face was an impassive white mask, giving nothing, unwilling to admit, even to himself, that the Texan was the better shot.

"Aw, hell, no!" Jacens grinned at Colmar in a friendly way. "We Yanks is jest naturally good! I started playing with guns when I was no more than seven." He nodded toward Colmar, offering a generous olive branch. "Julius here, if he'd had my chances, he'd be 'way outta my class. When did you first grab a gun, Julius?"

Colmar replied grudgingly, "Seven, eight years back."

"See what I mean? He's a natural, yes sir!" Jacens felt he had done enough to smooth Colmar. "But that li'l lady is the real surprise packet! If she always shoots that steady, I fer one do not wish to be agin her!"

Jane smiled, hand held protectively before her face. In her own class, she was good, and had a row of trophies to prove it, but when dogs bark, mice stay silent.

Ever ready to be the butt, Phil eased the situation still further. "Well, we all know who's the lousiest shot! Come on, Sarge, time the bar was open—drinks on the loser. One drink, anyway!"

"That's a good idea, Phil." For once Langley had forgotten his beloved drill, and turning, got an unspoken reminder: both Americans had started cleaning their guns.

"Yes." Langley was angry with himself. "Yes . . . the bar opens when all guns are cleaned and stowed."

Colmar looked up from his task, giving Langley a sour

grin. The senior man's evident discomfort did much to restore Colmar to his usual humor.

Jacens declined with a shake of his head. He'd have one later. He went back on watch; the rest trooped below for the loser's drink. Jane soon slipped away to get on with the cooking, leaving the three men talking. Free from Jacens' cramping presence, aware of his own brilliance, Colmar was cheerful, lordly, happily accepting Phil's cracks about "The Ringo Kid."

Covertly watching, Langley concluded that the core of Colmar's trouble was a giant-sized inferiority complex. Now he'd demonstrated his undoubted superiority over Phil and himself, maybe he'd ease up; but it had done nothing to improve the situation between Colmar and Jacens. Langley wished the Texan had contented himself with putting the final shot in the can, but it was done, and that was that. If he'd sized up Colmar correctly, Colmar would never forgive that string-cutting bit.

Langley made a mental note to keep a careful eye on those two off-watch. Drink wouldn't start it, for Colmar seldom drank, and Jacens had a head like a rock. It wouldn't be sex; he'd swear Colmar wasn't queer, but on the other hand, there was something about him . . . Even that ill-advised crack about putting a bag over Jane Harris' head had not rung true. Silly soldier talk that Colmar repeated parrot-fashion, getting it fractionally out of context, because although he knew the lingo, he didn't speak it naturally.

It was all nebulous, intangible, and Langley did not like that sort of thought. He'd ask Jane Harris her opinion of Colmar; women were better judges than men.

Only then did he realize she had gone. He tracked her to the galley. Hot and flushed, she looked up from the oven, instinctively moving the scarred side of her face away from him.

Langley didn't even notice. "Miss Harris, it's a bit awkward, but I'd like your opinion. It could be a help to me."

Seeing his troubled expression, she relaxed. "Oh, certainly! Can't think I'll be much help, but I'll try."

"Well, it's Colmar." He spoke confidentially, quite unlike his normal regimental manner. "It's my job to keep the team together. After that shooting match, I wouldn't be surprised if there was trouble between him and Tex. Colmar puzzles me; can't get hold of him, somehow. What d'you make of him?"

She shut the oven and straightened up. "I certainly see your problem, Mr. Langley." She frowned, collecting her thoughts. "Frankly, I think Colmar is a loner. He'd dearly like to be one of the boys, yet can't make it. Mark Jacens is a real lone wolf, Colmar isn't, but from your point of view, in a pinch, Colmar could be your best man."

That surprised Langley, even as Jane had surprised herself. "You think he'd be better than Tex?"

She looked pensively at him. "It's hard to explain. Mark is far and away a better man in all respects, *and* he's tougher, more exprienced, and very probably a lot braver, but Colmar, he's . . . he's got the edge in one respect, I think. He's pushed by some inner compulsion which makes him quite ruthless." She laughed self-consciously. "Not very clear, I'm afraid, but be glad Jacens isn't the same way. If he was, he'd be ten times worse than Colmar. If you told Mark Jacens to shoot to kill, he might hesitate; not Colmar. That's what I mean."

"But what is this compulsion?"

"How should I know?" Jane Harris said sharply. "Colmar's an unusual type in my experience. He's like a cat, somehow. He's fanatically clean—I'll swear he showers and changes three times a day at least. Look at his nails sometime; he must spend a half-hour each day on them. And that's another thing—have you ever known him to touch anyone, or shake hands?"

Langley frowned, remembering Colmar's near-hysteria when Jacens grabbed his shirt. "No . . . you're right. Look, this is a bit, well . . . you know. What d'you think of him as a man?"

Jane smiled. "You mean sex. I honestly don't know, and with my face, I'm hardly likely to find out. No, don't be gallant, Mr. Langley, I know only too well what I look like. Colmar . . . I don't believe he is queer, gay, or whatever you prefer, yet . . .'' She shook her head. ''Maybe he is normal, but low on sexual drive. It's the nearest I can get. Treat him gently, allow for his touchiness, that's my advice. If you tread on your dog's tail, he'll round on you, but stop himself before he actually bites you. A cat will never let you off the hook.''

VIII

There is little to choose between one teleprinter room and another, anywhere. The company's setup was no exception. The rare layman visiting, bemused by talk of bauds, tape relay, band slips, and marks, usually found it vaguely disappointing. Air transport has shrunk the world to a mere twenty-four-hour journey, but here, in a deep basement room, anywhere on earth was only seconds away. Endlessly, day and night, the machines chattered quietly, exchanging traffic with ships in the storm-bound North Atlantic, stations in steaming Indonesia, air-conditioned offices in New York, precarious oil rigs off Africa, yet the office had all the dramatic tension of a chiropodist's waiting room.

Ten printers lined each side of the long room, all facing inward to the wide central aisle. Arranged in pairs, one machine receiving, one sending. Six pairs in each row were in regular use, spanning the globe; four were in reserve for special tasks or breakdown replacement. One of these pairs had been assigned solely to AT1, as the thumbtacked card above the position testified.

Not that the red lettering was really necessary; the supervisors might look casual, but when the in teleprinter started clattering, it got instant attention. The supervisors did not know much about AT1, but they had been told enough—more than enough.

For example, it was common knowledge among the company communicators that this radio teletype link was a lash-up, make-do affair, a technological near-nightmare to the men who made it work. Many floors up, the top brass remained in blissful ignorance of the problems, partially because they were not concerned with such low-level matters, and partially because they lacked the technical background to grasp the very nature of the problems.

From the very start, satellite communications had been planned for AT1 and its successors. That posed no problem at all: warships had used satellites for years; there were many difficulties, but that was not one, a proposition with which—ironically due to a communication failure between designers and aerial specialists—the latter agreed with.

In the early stages, critical path planning went ahead, fixing an entry time for the aerial design, which was discovered to be impracticably late.

The misunderstanding was frighteningly simple, quite beyond the comprehension of those not involved, but all too obvious to those who were. The aerial designers wrongly assumed, on the strength of a badly worded memo, that AT1 would carry a qualified servicing technician. In the blazing row that followed, they panicked, rashly agreeing to redesign and have the aerial ready for the first automated voyage. They failed.

Fortunately, the company's radio experts privately saw this coming, and AT1 had been fitted with standard HF equipment, computer-directed, before the first human-controlled voyage.

It worked perfectly; owners and insurers were satisfied. HF communications had two disadvantages: interference, human, magnetic, or solar, might garble a signal now and then; secondly, the shore-to-ship computer facility, for technical and security reasons, could not be used. The first snag was met by programming the computer to repeat all messages twice. Nothing could be done about the second, but that would anyway have little importance until there were several AT's at sea, the facility being designed to reprogram a ship when its destination was changed en route. With only AT1 afloat, this had low priority.

So the supervisors and their colleagues at the distant receiving station which intercepted and piped the signal to the center were particularly watchful, but human nature being the way it is, by July 6 they had come to accept AT1 as just another out-station. At 1155 and 2355 GMT to the second, AT1 would be up, running a call tape. Precisely five minutes later the coded signal began. Another ten minutes, and a red-painted pneumatic carrier cartridge would thump forcefully into the duty officer's basket, ten floors up. Decoded, AT1's pin on the wall-sized chart would be moved and the actual position compared very carefully with the intended position.

At 0125A—British Summer Time, one hour ahead of GMT—July 7, the duty officer performed this task. With a final approving nod at the chart, he returned to his desk and AT1's met report. This gave the barometric pressure, sea and air temperature, wind direction and force, swell, and sea-state.

He sniffed; nothing exciting there; another of those hot, airless nights he had endured many times. An experienced tanker captain, beached by an intractable ulcer, he remembered only too well—and was damned glad to be out of it. Suburban Sidcup suited him fine.

Aboard AT1 the local time was 0455, and Jacens, who had the watch, would have agreed entirely with the far-distant duty officer's views on the weather. Dawn was still the best part of an hour away; the watch stretched endlessly; even the trivial punching of the time clock was something to look forward to. He yawned, rubbed his bristly chin, poured yet another cup of coffee, and tried to think about his book, but his mind soon wandered off to other things. He walked across the citadel, absentmindedly opening the door to the foredeck with his left hand. That was an error, as a sharp stab of pain told him.

The day before, Langley had exercised action stations. Running, Jacens had slipped and fallen, spraining his left wrist. It hurt like hell, but he said nothing, which earned him a sharp reproof when Jane Harris spotted his swollen wrist. At once the professional nurse, she had ignored his protests and hustled him into the sick bay. She checked the damage with cool, firm fingers; intent on her work, oblivious to his gaze, he was free to have a really close look at her.

Jacens was tough, mentally and physically, but that face, its expression, pierced his armor. He tried to think of the most descriptive word for her expression: "sweet" fitted, but was not entirely satisfactory; it had connotations of chocolate-box prettiness, a cloying quality. He pondered, finally concluding he needed two words: "sensitive" and "tender."

Yes; both of those things and—goddamnit!—sweet. The curve of the good side of her mouth, the lips slightly parted in concentration, affected him more powerfully than her fine eyes, blond hair, or beautiful, clear skin.

She'd looked up, seen his gaze, and sharply averted her face, then resumed her bandaging, head bent well forward. That had been a tricky moment.

The tricky moment was repeated that morning after breakfast. Jane Harris had him back in the sick bay for examination. Jacens found himself staring at the top of her head.

"Don't do that." His voice was gentle. He did not have to make himself any clearer to her.

She did not answer, disturbed more than annoyed, for it was impossible to take offense. She fiddled unnecessarily with the bandage, giving herself time.

"There." She had found her professional voice. "Coming on very nicely." She turned away, tidying up. She could not pick up the challenging glove he had dropped.

"Thanks." Jacens put a lot in the word. "I'll be on deck this afternoon." He hesitated. "I'm having trouble with this book of mine; I'd be honored if you'd give me your opinion."

Jane Harris had as much insatiable curiosity as the next woman: Jacens had been as silent as a cloud on the subject of his writing; from Phil she had learned that he had said nothing to anyone, and if the Cornishman didn't know, no one did.

"I . . . I don't know." She was acutely aware he was rolling through her defenses like a panzer division. "I may be busy."

Jacens saw she did not mean to be rude. "I hope you can make it. Thanks again."

She found him in the shade of the funnel on the helo deck. He stood up, smiling. Firmly he steered her to a cushion which put the disfigured side of her face toward him. Safe behind headscarf and dark glasses, she did not argue.

She soon discovered that when it came to shyness, a reluctance to face the bright light of day, her condition paled into nothingness compared with an embryo writer. After many hesitations, qualifications, and admonitions not "to expect too much," he passed her his manuscript.

In spite of the countless millions spent these days on education, this is the age of illiteracy. The vast majority readily surrender their right of choice into the hands of TV programmers, happy to soak their brains in predigested pap. While no egghead, Jane Harris actually read books, and her reading was not confined to boy-meets-girl-over-puppy-with-hurt-foot stuff. Before she had read three pages, she realized Jacens was a notably bad writer. She read on, desperately trying to think of something to say to the anxious author.

"I haven't read many westerns," she confessed. "This character Lefty looks interesting"—she was talking fast, too fast—"and that bit about—"

He cut in. "No good, huh?"

"I didn't say that. I think there's a lot of work needed—"

Jacens shook his head. "Just give it to me, straight."

This was the first time she had talked with him alone. She had seen from the start he had personality; now she was beginning to appreciate just how much he had; there was more to him than the steady gray eyes under black eyebrows. This was a man who made his own mind up, and wouldn't change it in a hurry, not like some. . . .

"You shouldn't take much notice of my opinion; I'm no judge—I couldn't even start to write." She touched his arm, not wanting to hurt him. "For a first attempt—"

"Nope. My second."

"Oh." Jane could think of nothing to say. He took the manuscript from her and tossed it aside.

"Thanks, anyway. Leastways, it confirms a nasty suspicion I had. Guess an orphanage kid kin aim too high. Knew I'd get a straight answer from you—an' it saves me wastin' time."

"Don't give up!" Again she touched his arm. "Nothing worthwhile comes easily. You're a fighter—keep fighting!"

"Oh, sure. I won't toss the towel in, not yet." He dismissed the subject. "And how about you?" The panzer division was rolling again.

"Me?" Her heart beat faster. His fractured nose gave him a predatory look, an eagle contemplating supper.

"Yes, you—Jane." For the first time in AT1 she was addressed by her Christian name. "Can you practice what you preach?"

She did not evade the question, although no one had dared—or had enough interest—to ask it before. She hesitated, then bowed to his quiet authority, wanting to talk, to unburden herself on him. "You may think I'm sorry for myself. Partly, perhaps, but there's more to it. *I* think I'm the same person, but I've learned a six-inch scar makes a world of difference."

"Tell me." His voice was gentle.

"Don't be too sympathetic; you'll have me crying on your shoulder!"

"Anytime. But first, do me a favor; take those glasses off."

"You want a lot, Mark." His name came easily.

"Not more than you can give."

She took them off, blinking in the glare.

"That's better—no, don't look away." He took her hand. "Now, tell me."

She could not resist him, and had no wish to. For a time she was silent, thinking. "I was an air hostess; engaged." Her voice was calm, factual. "We planned to marry about seven months later. On a night stopover, the copilot rented a car, taking some of us to a swimming pool. We had a smash. He was killed. I got this; those in the back were only bruised."

"And he was—?"

She shook her head. "No. Nothing like that; just the copilot. I was concussed. It was a fortnight before I knew what was happening, and then found I looked like this." She stared at the sea. "They flew me home. The airline was kind, but who wants a hostess with a face like mine? Anyway, I wanted to hide. Nursing didn't appeal—for the same reason—frightens the patients! I hadn't much money, and only a third share in a flat. I took this job because it's not exactly a social life, and I want the money for cosmetic surgery."

"But how about the insurance?"

"None. Peter—that's the copilot—always out for a bargain, rented a car without it."

"You can't do that!"

She laughed bitterly. "You can if you know where to go. He rented it in Johore; we smashed on Singapore Island—another country." She laughed again, a hard sound. "If he'd lived, he'd have had enough trouble to last the rest of his life."

"But . . . your guy?"

"Another pilot." Her voice was flat, devoid of emotion. "He visited me twice: I knew the first time. I gave him the chance to get out . . . sent the ring back. He took it."

"Jeesus! A louse, first-class!" In anger Jacens' Texan twang deepened. "And dumb!"

Jane shook her head. "I don't blame him. Some pilots live on their nerves, off-duty, they want to relax, forget flying, bombs, hijacks. He certainly couldn't unwind with a smashed face. For me, the break was low in therapeutic value." Her tone was deceptively light.

"Do you still love the guy?" He watched her eyes intently.

"Not anymore. I understand, feel sorry for him. Once a woman feels sorry for a man, she no longer loves him."

"Waal, I kinda feel sorry for him myself—he missed the chance of a lifetime! By my book, you've got—along with a lot else—one thing no woman can do without, a kind heart. And you've got guts." His grip on her hand tightened. "We've come a long way mighty fast, Jane. Thet scar don't matter. Stop hiding—live with it! Come a week or tew, an' no one will notice it—you'll see! Later, when you've got it fixed, you'll be glad you didn't run. Take that scarf off!''

"You *are* moving fast!" She gave a shaky little laugh, hesitated, then fumbled with the knot, and stopped. "I don't know why I—"

"Yes you do, too, Jane! I ain't sweet-talking you, and you know it."

Impulsively she snatched the scarf off and did not turn her head away.

He examined her face critically. "Sure is a hell of a scar, but stateside there's a stack of surgeons kin fix it—docs who had plenty of practice with Vietnam veterans! Anyway, just as you are, I think you're beautiful, inside an' out." His deceptively casual movement cloaked his speed; he grasped her chin, kissed her lightly on the mouth, then let her go. "Okay, go right ahead an' slap my face!"

Outwardly she remained composed. "Are you just being the Southern gentleman, or are you a man trying to trap the only female for a thousand miles?"

Mark's face hardened. "Neither—an' yew say that agin, and I'll slap *your* face! I'd be a goddamn liar if I said I didn't want to make love to you, but I'm after a whole lot more than thet! If I'm a pain in the neck, say so; won't bother you agin—'cept if I see you with that scarf on!"

She studied his intense, angry face, free of any trace of insincerity. To talk of love—either way—would be ridiculous, but she realized he soon would. And how did she feel? Physically, she was attracted by his gentle strength; she felt grateful for his bold action, pushing her: with his strong support, she would not wear the scarf again—on board.

On the other hand, he could be just out for sex. There was only one way of finding out, and she had to know; loneliness has to be met and defeated somehow.

Jacens came off watch at midnight. Pale with apprehension, fearful he would misconstrue her action, Jane was in his cabin. For once in that ill-fated voyage, for two at least, the stars were reached.

65

IX

At 0015 GMT July 9, the duty officer was jerked to full consciousness by the arrival of the red pneumatic cartridge. He opened it, yawning, grimaced at its coded contents, and got down to breaking it.

AT1's midnight position was 0550 South 6046 East, course 180, speed 12.15 knots. He plotted it, checking against the predicted position.

Right on track. Bloody thing might as well be running on tram lines.

He read again the ship's met report: pressure 1001 mb, sea 15C, air 25C, wind light, variable force 1, swell negligible, sea state nil. Reading it made him yawn again. Like his Sidcup colleague, he thought the report matched AT1, damned dull.

Bloody science was ruining everything, including his career prospects. Another ten years, and master's ticket or not, he'd be seeing the sea as a beach attendant. They could stick that guard job sideways; pride wouldn't let him touch it anyhow, but more than that, the sheer, screaming boredom of it . . .

Aboard AT1 the local time was 0500. Colmar had the watch, and was well into his eighth coffee. The log had been written up—nothing to report—and he'd punched the time clock. Apart from the very faint engine vibration, AT1 might have been in harbor. Langley had paid one of his silent, unheralded visits—the bastard—half-hour back, checking his time card, the log, and the armament without a word.

Colmar grinned in the darkness. Langley would love to find fault with him, but couldn't—and hadn't enough brains to realize he could never outsmart a guy like him.

For Colmar, watches were never long; alone, he could give his imagination full rein, dreaming of endless triumphs over Langley, Jacens—particularly Jacens—and a dozen others. He had always hated authority in any form, but sergeants were his particular *bête noire*, even more than officers.

Given his nature, his failure to get the commission he had confidently expected, one-time Corporal (Ordinance Corps) Colmar's attitude was entirely predictable. Lost in his private fantasies, he bided his time. For one who could speak without thought and whose sharp bursts of rage suggested a lack of self-control, he had remarkable patience: he would get even with them, with all the wide world, everyone, everything.

Outside the citadel the predawn blackness was relieved by few stars. Only the faint reflected glow from the port and starboard lights gave a hint of light on the steel deck, dripping with dew. Astern lay the only real relief for strained eyes: diamond-cold points of blue-green phosphorescent fire flashed and danced in the broken water of the wake. Often Langley would walk aft and lean on the rail, watching for what seemed like hours to Colmar.

As far as Colmar was concerned, anyone could have his share of nature, free: he neither liked nor disliked it, he ignored it. Egocentric, he wanted position, recognition, power; deep down lay a very simple need—to be admired; and failing that, feared.

He tossed his empty paper cup in the bin and gave the horizon an all-round scan with his binoculars. Nothing in sight. Just as it should be: quiet as the grave.

But beyond Colmar's horizon there was a ship. Thirty miles astern and slightly to port of AT1, it was steadily narrowing the gap. AT1's radar held it, and the computer knew exactly where it was, its course and speed, but as it did not present a navigational hazard or a security threat, no reaction could be triggered. To the computer it was no more than a contact to be reevaluated with each sweep of the surface warning aerial.

Computers are tireless; this one had checked that particular target every four seconds, day and night, for a week. Computers are also only as bright as their programmer permits; AT1's computer had no instructions about shadowers from astern who kept their distance.

Punctual as always, Jacens arrived in the citadel at 0655, allowing five minutes for the handover. Mentally he cursed Langley's rota, designed to ensure that no man was stuck with the same watch day after day, which, with three men and eight-hour watches, was inevitable. By Langley's system, the man who had the watch to midnight also went on watch at 0700. Theoretically, this meant the man who had the 0700-to-1500 watch—with a relief for dinner—had a good six and one-half hours' sleep in the night, which, to this point, Jacens had accepted as reasonable. Even now, he had to agree that the system was fine—provided you were not emotionally involved in that time off-watch.

Jane. . . . God Almighty! How she had given herself. . . . Weary with the experience of many beds, Jacens was chary of committing himself, but again and again he told himself this was *it*. Jane was no easy lay; neither was he just looking for a cheap screw. Something that had had its tentative beginnings in Bahrein came to fruition in his cabin. If he did not love her, he was kidding both of them.

Aware of Colmar's mordant gaze, he got on with the watch-change check: logbook, time clock, armament.

Colmar stood back, watching in ill-concealed contemptuous silence.

These lousy GI's! How they clung so lovingly to all that Army crap! Going by the book; pants and shirts pressed in regulation style, just to make it look that shade more like a uniform. Bet that bastard would love a few shiny brass badges to brighten his lousy, rotten, stinking . . .

Jacens looked up from the log. "This ship half-hour back—still around?"

"Yep. Still 'way back; I'd say its overtaking us."

Jacens nodded, punched his card, official acceptance that he had the watch. "Okay."

"Okay," repeated Colmar, smiling.

His tone made Jacens look around sharply, but Colmar was just as fast. He smothered a convincing yawn. "It's me for a shower, feed, and bed. What's the chow?"

Jacens told him, wondering if it was his imagination that saw amusement in Colmar's eyes.

"Great! If our Jane performs as well in bed as she does in the galley . . . Still, that's something I wouldn't know." He turned for the companionway.

Jacens had picked up the binoculars, not watching Colmar. "Ain't yew fergittin' something, son?"

"Huh?" Colmar looked blank. "Oh, yea!" He unbuckled his gunbelt slowly and hung it on its peg. "Mustn't rile the dear old sarge, must we?"

Once Colmar had gone, Jacens relaxed. What had that young creep meant by that crack about Jane? No, he decided, Julius Colmar was just being his normal, unpleasant self; a bad conscience makes its owner unduly sensitive.

Mentally Jacens tossed Colmar aside and got on with his job, scanning the horizon. Lacking nautical experience, he could not be sure, but to him it looked as if the ship astern would pass well clear behind AT1. It appeared to Jacens that the stranger was pointing more or less straight at AT1, so assuming they were going about the same speed, the newcomer would pass seven or eight miles astern. This one apart, the sea remained as empty as it had been since they'd cleared Hormuz. Jacens relaxed.

This was the best time of the day; the sun up, but not yet at its fearful tropical power. He moved to an open window and took several deep breaths of the warm air. What a life! Beautiful calm sea, good chow, regular hours, money snowing into the bank, and Jane. Folks paid hundreds of dollars for cruises that gave nothing like the value of this one. Jane . . .

For a long time he strolled up and down, keeping an eye on the sea and the ship. Increasingly the stranger worried him. He took another long look, resting the binoculars on a window ledge; he straightened up, frowning.

Let it go another five minutes: he could be wrong.

The time passed very slowly. He spent it unnecessarily checking the empty ocean, not really worried, yet not absolutely happy. The fifth minute passed, and he concentrated once again on the strange ship; he had no desire to appear a fool. His scrutiny did nothing to allay his doubts; he reached for the phone.

"Is Bill there? Ask him to step up here, willya?"

"What's up, Mark?" Bill soon arrived, alert, regimental; he followed the Texan's pointing hand. "Yes, Colmar told me."

"When I came on, it looked as if the guy would pass well behind us. I've been watching, and it kinda looks to me as if he keeps pointing at us. Could be a mite one way or the other, but sure as hell he ain't heading the same way he was when I came on watch."

Langley took the glasses, studied the oncoming vessel closely, then grabbed the phone. "Tell Phil I want him here at the double. No, nothing much, a ship."

Phil bounded up the ladder. "You want me, Sarge?"

"What d'you make of that?" Langley handed him the binoculars.

"Well, she's a tanker, that's for sure," said Phil at last. "I'd say she's empty, small as tankers go these days, and pretty ancient. On her present course, she'll pass astern of us. What's the problem?"

"Mark says she seems to be always pointing at us, and getting closer." Langley shrugged. "Could be she's a blind bastard like the last one."

"Let's have another look," said Phil, taking back the glasses. "Yes, she's no chicken, but judging by the bow waves, she's cracking on the revs." He grinned. "If that's a pirate, they've got . . ." He stopped, looking again at the stranger, then the sun, and back to the ship.

"Okay, Phil—what's bugging you?"

"It's a bit strange, like. I mean, where's she going? We're heading south; her course is nearer southwest. Naturally," he added sarcastically, "since we're not allowed to know where the bloody hell we are, I can't be sure, but at a guess, I'd say she was going from nowhere to nowhere."

Langley and Jacens absorbed that in silence. Langley wished he knew a good deal more about the sea.

"Maybe she's going to South Africa," he said.

"Maybe she is," agreed Phil. "But why? She's full of fuck-all!"

"Could be oil down there," said Langley doubtfully.

"Oh, sure! So she tanks up and carts it off to the Persian Gulf?"

Langley didn't answer that one, staring at the approaching ship. "What d'you reckon the range is?"

"Four, five miles." He kept his gaze on the stranger. "Tell you this, Sarge, I think Mark's right; the sod's easing around toward us. I got a rough estimate of the distance between the foremast and the funnel, and I'd swear it hasn't changed."

That made up Langley's mind. "Right. Nip down and shake Colmar, and tell Jane we're going to action stations."

Phil ran, and Langley turned to Mark. "Could be a load of cobblers." He examined the ship again through binoculars, but saw nothing alarming—no guns, no activity. He turned to Jacens. "Maybe the bloke wants help, like a doctor or something."

"He can't have our Jane, that's fer sure!"

"Too right! Anyway, if he keeps coming, we'll bang off a couple of red rockets as soon as the warning lights start flashing. If that doesn't convince him, Phil can put a burst over the bridge."

"An' jest supposin' he keeps comin'?" said Jacens softly.

"We'll let him in a bit closer, another warning shot. At a mile, we give him a burst in the bows. If *that* doesn't work, that's it—alarm, radio call, hose-pipe his bridge, and smack a couple of Blowpipes into him!"

Phil and Colmar clattered up the ladder, fully dressed. As they buckled on their gunbelts, Langley ordered Phil to man the port Aden, Colmar as loader, and outlined his plan of action.

As they hurried around, closing the armored window

71

shields, the internal alarm sounded, quickly canceled by Langley. He rang Jane in the sick bay. "Remain closed up. We've got a ship acting suspiciously on the port quarter. I expect he's hoping we've got a doctor. Don't get excited if you hear us fire; it'll be a warning burst."

Phil had stripped off the gun cover, clipped in a magazine, fastened his back harness, and swung the Aden to face the stranger.

"The warning lights are flashing, Sarge!"

"Okay. Colmar, fire two rockets."

The rockets screeched into the still air, trailing smoke, to burst in a scatter of red stars. The tanker was close enough to make out details of the bows, rust-streaked, the heat haze above her stumpy, blackened funnel, and her small navigational radar aerial, rotating steadily.

"Hey, she's altering course!" Roscorla's seaman's eye spotted the movement first. "She's coming around to port!"

Mark, calmly unstrapping his Blowpipe, paused and stared in concentration at the deckhead. Port—which way was that? He turned to look.

The tanker, fine off the port quarter, was swinging slowly onto a parallel course.

"Well, get that!" exclaimed Phil in disgust, leaning back in his harness. "That twit makes the other geezer look like a veteran motorist! Did you ever see such a performance! Bloody lights and rockets banging off—didn't take a blind bit of notice. Reckon he stopped just in time, or this tub would have sheered away from him!" Neither he nor the rest realized the significance of what he had said.

The tension eased, but the team remained watchful. Jacens, cradling his Blowpipe, stood in the center of the citadel, ready to move to the best firing position. Colmar, a spare magazine at his feet, stood just in the citadel, his eyes wild with excitement, switching from Langley to the stranger and back. Langley remained stolidly by the control panel.

"Hang on," cried Phil. "What's that, right aft? Crikey, it's a bloody chopper! *Christ*!"

Even as he spoke, the helo leaped into the air. Tension

flooded back; Langley swung, stabbing the alarm button, then reached for the radiophone.

"Freeze!" screamed Colmar. "Drop it!"

Jacens moved with incredible speed, tossing the Blowpipe aside, turning, crouching, going for his gun.

The fastest man on earth couldn't have made it.

Colmar fired three times, his face deadly white, lips drawn back in a silent snarl. Jacens staggered backward; the hammer blows hurled him, off-balance, down the companionway.

Colmar swung, fired again, once, smashing Langley's shoulder. The senior guard slammed back against the bulkhead and collapsed, dropping the phone, hitting his head as he fell. Blood welled, darkening his shirt. Colmar sprang, grabbed the dangling handset, and tore it free. He paused, panting, his gun ready, swinging from Langley to the companionway, to Roscorla, trapped in his gun harness.

Even if he had been free, the sailor would have been incapable of action, fear, or thought. He stared stupidly at the killer.

"God," he croaked, "what . . . what you . . . you *done* . . ."

Colmar glanced at him, his face still set in its hideous grin. *He'd done it*! Those lethal seconds had breached the dam of his long-pent-up hatred: frightened, aghast at his own action, he also felt good, ten feet tall, liberated.

Phil fumbled with his harness.

"You stay right there, buddy!" The strange, high-pitch parody of Colmar's normal voice got through to Phil's bemused brain; survival hung on obedience to that deadly, crouching figure. "Drop your gunbelt."

As the sailor obeyed, Jane cried out; her distraught face appeared in the companionway. She stared wide-eyed, seeming not to take in the scene, even Colmar's pointing gun.

"I need help! Mark—"

"Get back!" screamed Colmar. "Get back! Show your pan again, and I smash it for good!"

She could only look uncomprehendingly at him.

"Do as he says!" Roscorla called, risking his life. Instantly the gun was back pointing at him. Jane disappeared.

"Get outta that harness and on deck—clear the helo net, and be fast!"

Roscorla freed himself and stumbled on deck, Colmar following. He picked up Phil's gunbelt and tossed it over the side, the radiotelephone handset with it.

Overhead, the pirate's helicopter buzzed impatiently; the parent ship was dropping slowly astern, edging closer to AT1. Phil worked clumsily on the net, dazed. Colmar worked too, cursing the sailor for his slowness.

At the foot of the companionway Jane worked desperately, near-blinded with tears. From the moment she had cut his shirt off, she saw there was no hope. With two bullets in the chest, the third in his stomach, it was a tribute to his tough mind and body that Mark was yet alive. She plugged his wounds, made him as comfortable as she could where he lay, waiting, knowing it would not be long. She left him once to get the morphia ampuls, but doubted if he would ever come out of shock enough to need it.

Briefly he regained consciousness, his gray eyes, no longer keen, glazed, sightless. She held his hand. "Don't try to move, Mark—don't move."

His lips moved; she bent very close. "Glad . . . we . . . we . . . met . . . beauti . . ." He did not finish the word, and fell silent, fighting for breath, drowning in his own blood. He gripped her hand, expending his last energy for her. "Gun . . . take it . . . guts." Gasping, Mark Jacens died.

Numb with shock, she knelt beside him, living a nightmare. Mark . . . Colmar . . . Her mind refused to consider what had happened, taking refuge in practical, trivial detail. She couldn't leave Mark there: people coming down the ladder would fall over him—it. . . .

She grasped his still-warm wrists and dragged him into the sick bay. The body was far too heavy to lift. Gently she straightened his limbs, lately so easy in movement, strong arms that had held her; the memory brought near physical pain. She noticed his gunbelt, the still-buttoned holster. He'd never had a chance. Anger struggled with fear as she remembered Mark's last painful message.

Without thinking, she drew the gun, glanced over her shoulder, no plan in mind. From overhead came the tramp of feet, voices, and the roar of the departing helicopter.

She glanced frantically around, seeking a hiding place. Any moment Colmar would arrive; must hide the gun. She got up, ran to the galley; the voices were louder, in the citadel, strange voices. She thrust the Browning in a drawerful of kitchen equipment. That crisis past, her mind raced, thinking ahead.

Colmar would be bound to notice, certain to collect the gun; but if she gave him the belt, holster buttoned . . . She needed a weight, something small but heavy. Frantically she sought inspiration: something weighty . . . a *weight*! She grabbed a heavy one from the kitchen scales and ran.

The prospect of a chance, however slim, made her hand shake violently as she rammed the cast-iron weight into the holster, stuffing her handkerchief on top. Buttoning the holster, she heard feet on the companionway; she let go of the belt as if it was red-hot, but remained kneeling beside the body, shaking uncontrollably.

"Okay—get outta the way!"

Colmar's voice, although less high-pitched, filled her with terror. Still kneeling, she straightened up, sitting back, her hands resting on her bloodstained thighs; she stared at the killer, his rising hate conquering fear. He stood, legs apart, in the doorway, gun in hand; briefly their eyes communicated.

Some of Colmar's euphoria had worn off; he seemed hesitant. For one weird moment she thought he was going to apologize.

"Get outta the way," he repeated. "I want that gun."

"Don't you touch him!" She hissed the words, half in earnest. Without waiting, she unbuckled the belt, keeping her hands well away from the holster, then hauled it clear from the dead man. She stood up, held the belt out.

"Don't want me to touch the boyfriend, huh? Okay, so I'm a man of feeling." He took the belt at arm's length, glanced at the holster, and grinned. "Well, waddya know? The fastest gun in the West—and he didn't even touch his shooter!"

"You . . . you bastard!" Jane spat at him, unable to stop herself; she thought that was the end. His grin froze, his eyes had a sightless look, then he blinked, and wiped his face with his hand, then the ever-ready clean tissue.

"Okay, lady. I'll remember that, when we've got a li'l more time." He slung the gunbelt over his shoulder. His grin returned. "Pity you didn't get to taking this gun, a talented doll like you!"

Jane felt her heart would stop.

"Dangerous things like this are best over the side!" His tone changed, cold, venomous. "I'll fix you before we're through! Right now, you get back to the galley; fix coffee, lots of it!" He backed away from the door. "And don't go having any fancy ideas about that—you taste it first."

Overhead, the helo had returned; Colmar hurried for the ladder. "Bill—is he dead too?" Somehow she managed to say it.

He paused, holstering his gun. "Gee! I forgot—I surely did." The fact that he could forget gave him pleasure: to shoot a man and forget it just went to show what sort of a guy he was. "No, I guess not." This self-revelation made him almost genial. "He's lying around. Come and fix him."

Colmar ran up the companionway, his twisted ego bursting with exultant arrogance. Jesus, they'd learn what a real hard man was like; he'd show them, all of them.

Langley was sitting on the deck, propped up against the empty armory, his bloodless face lined, years older. One hand held a balled-up handkerchief to his right shoulder in a feeble attempt to stanch his wound, one side of his shirt soaked, black.

For Jane the sight piled shock on shock; she examined him quickly; to dress that wound before she got him below would be a waste of vital time. She broke out the first-aid box, noticing the empty carbine rack; Langley's gunbelt had gone, too. Although her heart hammered, her fingers were steady as she tied his right hand firmly to the back of his neck, her professional mind thinking ahead to her next move; she did not like Langley's wax-yellow, gray-tinged face; certainly he had lost a lot of blood and was barely conscious.

Outside the citadel she could hear voices. To ask for help would be useless. Where was Phil? She glanced around furtively, and gasped in sudden fear.

Colmar stood outside a window, watching her, grinning.

She hauled Langley to his feet, got his good arm around her neck. He tried to help, but the arm had no strength, and his legs were like rubber. "Come on, Bill—try! Soon have you fixed up."

Somehow, half-carrying him, she got Langley down the companionway, into a sick-bay bunk. By then he was unconscious. The blue-ringed wound did not look too bad, blood still welled out, but she was relieved to see the bullet had gone right through, just above the collarbone. The wound cleaned, plugged, and dressed, she got his trousers and shoes off and tucked him in. There was nothing more she could do.

Automatically she washed her hands. Her mind, freed from its immediate task, whirled: Mark dead at her feet; Bill beside her, weak as a kitten and possibly near his end; Phil, Colmar, and God knew what going on above. . . .

Something heavy was being dragged on the deck; feet tramped. Not religious, Jane prayed fervently for Phil's safety; if he was dead, all hope had gone. Covering Mark's body with a blanket, she remembered the gun; at least Colmar had not discovered that it was missing—or had he? She couldn't be sure; he was quite capable of playing games, cat-and-mouse games. Never had she imagined, let alone met, anyone so wicked, so malignant. No, that wasn't true. Colmar wasn't so much wicked as mad.

Then she knew real fear.

X

Leaving the sick bay, she noticed for the first time the blackening, slippery mess at the foot of the ladder. Once that had been Mark's life-blood; she couldn't, wouldn't leave it there to be trampled by his crazy killer.

Cleaning the deck, she cried soundlessly, sorrow compounded with shock. She was kept on her emotional rails by the obscene practicality of her task. To clean a floor is one thing; to pour your lover's blood down the lavatory—and flush it—something else.

Wearily she looked at the clean tiles. A man had died there, a real man, and now it was as if he had never been. She realized, with clinical detachment, that her shirt and slacks were stained with two men's blood.

Staring at the clean deck, she resolved that, given a chance, she'd even the score. Her decision was not based on heroics, or anger, but fear. Not that she attempted to analyze her reasons: Colmar had to die if she hoped to live.

Making the coffee, she fought a desperate tiredness and tried to plan. She had to know what was going on, must speak with Phil—if he was still alive. It had to be a hijack, but what were they doing?

Working with the men flown in by helo, Phil had a better idea of the situation, but like an ordinary nightmare, it didn't make much sense to him—at first.

Two fueling hoses were being rigged, and he was one of the rigging party. He worked because he had to; Colmar had merely jerked his head toward a fat, sea-booted sailor who came aboard on the first lift and said, "Do as he says," and Phil had, his brain working on other things.

For a start, Colmar didn't fit his idea of the dedicated killer: he was too much on edge, and it was that that really frightened the sailor. A pro killed when necessary; but Colmar, with his sudden temper, high state of emotional excitement, and marksmanship, was much more frightening. One cough in the wrong place could, literally, trigger him.

So Phil worked, shocked and scared, but with a grudging admiration for the pirates' organization.

The helo had brought in four men in two trips, all obviously experienced tankermen, and their leader, the fat one, equipped with a walkie-talkie, certainly knew his way around AT1's upper deck. Maybe it didn't need much guesswork to find the lengths of armored hose, but he went straight to the long lockers on either side of the funnel. Meanwhile, the helo towed a line across from the tanker, which had cautiously edged closer and closer, until the gap between the ships was less than a hundred feet. AT1 held steady on course; however close another ship might get, to keep going straight ahead was the only solution the computer had.

Both searchlights had, for a long time, been flashing U tirelessly at the pirate, until Colmar, walking aft, spotted them. He couldn't resist the chance to show off.

"How about this, boys?" He yelled; then, the same deadly, blurred action as he drew and fired twice. One man nodded, impressed, but Phil saw the fat boss-man look thoughtfully at Colmar.

The lines secured, the pirate winched the fueling hoses over to her bows, where fresh lengths of hose waited. Soon both lines pulsed as the pump-over began.

Despite everything, Phil watched with interest. It wasn't exactly Navy-fashion; they took chances, the hoses not properly supported, and the pirate vessel was almighty close at times, but Roscorla guessed that the odd dent in those ancient bows wouldn't worry anyone, and if the hoses were strained and leaked, well, they were expendable.

Expendable. . . . A nasty word that dried the mouth, made

the heart thump. Outwardly resigned, hauling on lines, man-handling pipes, Phil, spurred on by the will to survive, sought any glimmer of hope, any clue to the pirates' intentions.

The head-on view of the tanker told him little; certainly old, her name had been painted out recently. He was seemingly free to learn whatever he could. The men in the pirateship's bows looked incuriously at him, conspicuous in his light gray, making no effort to hide their faces, and the men aboard AT1 used first names.

He reached the chilling conclusion that, their usefulness ended, AT1's survivors would follow Mark. What they would do with the ship was another matter, and in Phil's frame of mind a minor detail, except so far as it touched his future. Two points nagged: that job astern couldn't take even half AT1's cargo, and why hadn't they attempted to get into the computer?

He tried to talk to the men he helped, and got nowhere. Roscorla had seen little outside North European waters; these men could be Arabs, or Turks, or something: they just answered in grunts. He was surer of the boss-man; he spoke English, with a German accent.

"Coffee!" yelled Colmar. "Come and get it!"

They understood that, all right, but even then they retained their discipline. One man stayed tending the hoses, and the boss remained amidships, walkie-talkie close to his ear, one hand on an oil valve.

Jane had changed her shirt, but still looked a wreck, her eyes large with shock, her hair hanging loose. She poured coffee into paper cups, Colmar watching. He pointed.

"That's yours—drink!"

She did so, her face expressionless.

"And that's for dear old Phil—go on!"

Phil took the cup hesitantly. Jane had had a soft spot for Mark, and she was the sort of woman who'd do anything if pushed.

"It's all right, Phil." Her tired, flat statement rang true.

"Swell!" Grinning, Colmar took Phil's cup.

Jane shrugged. "There's nothing wrong with any of it—except I hope it chokes you!"

"That's the spirit!" Strangely, Colmar wasn't kidding. "I like a woman with spirit!"

"You like a woman with spirit!" she mimicked him savagely, anger overcoming fear. "*You*? You can't kid me—you're neuter, you're nothing! That gun's your penis!"

Colmar's face went deathly pale, his hand hovered over the black butt of his gun. Phil tensed himself to spring; Jane's life was a bouncing roulette ball, the bet red or black. Slowly Colmar smiled. Ever aware of an audience, he tried to drink his coffee calmly, but his hand shook. Still as a statue, Jane watched. He put the cup down, smiling like a stage villain. Without that gun, Phil would have laughed. Colmar answered her at last.

"Go ahead, go right ahead—have your fun while you can! I'll settle with you when I'm good and ready! Then we'll see!"

His words could have come straight from a B movie, but whatever the fantasies in the killer's mind, he was in a position to act them out. Phil wiped the sweat from his face, praying Jane would back off. Slowly she collected the cups and moved to the ladder. She knew that to needle him further would be certain death.

Colmar, relaxed, called after her, "And fix some chow, good chow! We eat at twelve."

For the first time he could remember that hideous day, Roscorla glanced at his watch: 9:45. Less than two hours ago, all had been normal, Mark alive. And Bill—what of him? Uncertain what to do, but determined to appear completely cowed, he paused in the doorway, looking aft. With the hoses rigged, two men were quite enough.

Had to give it to the bloke driving that tanker; of course, with AT1 steady as a rock and the sea as flat as a pond, it was easier, but to hold that old tub—

"Hey—you! Go grab a swab and clean this up!" Colmar gestured at Langley's dried blood. "Don't stay gabbing with that whore, either! And when you come up that ladder, you just say you're coming! Any sudden movement is apt to make me jumpy, and we don't want that, do we?"

81

"No," mumbled Roscorla. Passing the armory, he saw it was empty. Colmar laughed.

"Yeah—sad! All at the bottom of the ocean except those Blowpipes, and I've sent them over to . . . to the tanker. Get moving!"

Jane was in the galley, her mind in chaos, working mechanically. She jumped at Phil's entry, fearing Colmar. Filling a bucket, watching the open door, he spoke softly, quickly. "I've surrendered, given up—got it? Be back as soon as I can. How's Bill?"

Quickly, without emotion, she told him, adding, "Learn all you can, Phil—how many—and if they're all armed."

"Three of 'em. No, four. All got guns. Must go."

He worked with meticulous care, spinning out time under Colmar's watchful, jumpy eye, giving him the chance to talk. He alone had been on relatively friendly terms with the killer. He'd always reckoned Colmar odd, but he liked or was interested in people of all sorts, and Colmar had fascinated him. From Colmar's angle, Phil wasn't an ex-Army sergeant, and he was a good listener. Now that fragile relationship could be of vital importance; more than anyone else, Roscorla had an insight into the killer's twisted mind. Before the hijack, it mattered nothing; now . . . He wiped the deck clean, uncomfortably conscious of Colmar's eyes.

"My, you're real good at that—a regular mom's help!"

Phil dried the deck, ignoring the contemptuous voice. Colmar wanted to talk; let him.

"You know, old buddy, you're a creep; an even bigger creep than I reckoned. D'you think *I'd* do that?" He waited, his voice hardened. "Go on, answer!"

"No," mumbled Phil, thankful Colmar couldn't see his eyes.

"That, as our old pal, the far too late Sergeant Jacens, would have said, is affirmative! Jacens . . . he was fast—but *I* took him. You'd never have had the guts!"

Phil nodded, in complete agreement.

"Gee, if you guys could have seen your faces!" Colmar laughed, reliving his triumph. "None of you, not a single one, had the glimmer of an idea about me—did you?"

Phil looked up. "No, and I still can't get over it." He spoke with total sincerity. "Security must have checked you, same as the rest of us—and were they wrong! It beats me." He made it sound as if it was his biggest single problem.

Colmar loved that. "Security—that shower of creeps! Sure, they checked me forward, sideways, and backward, like you say—and came up with sweet zero! Shall I tell you why? *There was nothing to find!* Me, I was square and dumb, but with just one *leetle* difference, and that they missed out on! The man who set up this operation is a real planner. He looks ahead; he had a talent scout—and that guy picked me!" Colmar smiled at happy memories. "Very, very discreet; only one or two meetings—the first right there under their dirty Army noses, in my last camp! I soon saw they'd checked me out before they approached me—careful guys, guys who don't take chances! Boy, I felt good right then, just fooling those lousy crumbs who fouled up my chances of a commission. That, buddy, was real funny! So this scout sounds me out—he knows the dirty deal I get from that . . ." Colmar swore, a wild jumble of meaningless obscenities, releasing his bottled rage against the world. Phil kept the deck cloth moving, his head down.

Silence followed the outburst. Colmar wiped his mouth with the back of his hand and looked at the sailor in surprise, as if he had just appeared from nowhere. Slowly the false grin returned, and the arrogance with it.

"Yeah. I'm picked—me! They've got it all doped out. I finish my time, a few weeks, an honorable discharge and all that baby's crap! That gets me a security guard's job. You know what? Second week on the job, I'm on a payroll collection from a bank—some jerk tries a snatch!" He laughed again. "Imagine! A snatch against *me*! Guess how that one went! That really makes me; I move to tankers—as planned. Four trips. Meanwhile, I volunteer for this job—as planned. This whole goddamn operation has been planned, right down to the very last detail! I knew the time we'd be hit—within an hour—before I even set foot in Bahrein!"

Phil looked up, exhibiting more surprise than he felt.

With frightening insight Colmar jeered at him. "Sure you

want to know more—and mighty little good it'll do you! The whole operation turned on me, and *I've* done it—me! Jacens was good, but I took him! Right now there's more dough than you've ever dreamed of waiting for me—never you mind where.'' He grinned at Phil's dejected figure with contempt. ''You're a born loser, buddy. Sad . . . sad—and tough!'' Suddenly he tired of his audience. ''Go on, scram! Fix me a can of lime juice—unopened. Then give that scarface cow a hand with the chow—that's your level!'' He sneered as the sailor obediently rose to his feet. ''If you two want to cook any plans to ease you outta this jam, go right ahead! All I want is just one teeny excuse to ice both of you. It'd be a real pleasure—especially her!''

Phil knew he wasn't kidding.

With eight mouths to feed, plus tending Langley, Jane needed help. Pale and subdued, Phil went back to the galley, sickened by the realization that in the long run, their usefulness ended, Colmar intended to kill them.

They talked in whispers, asking and answering each other's questions. For Phil the only bright spot was when Jane told him of the gun; she sighed with relief on learning Colmar had ditched all the armament except the Adens, and they were useless, for their ammunition had also gone over the side.

Temporarily the thought of the secret Browning raised Phil's hopes, but the more he thought about it, the less he liked it. It would be worse than useless for him to try, sheer suicide. Keyed up, Colmar would have him before he could blink.

In a cold, contained voice, Jane said she did not think it would be difficult for her to kill Colmar. She did not have to add that she would have no compunction in shooting him in the back, but what of the rest? Even if, between them, they put all six out of action, there was still the tanker, and that had the Blowpipes, plus an unknown armament.

Colmar gave them little time, constantly ringing down for fresh cans of soft drinks, taunting, jeering at the sailor when he delivered them.

Relief came from an unexpected quarter. Colmar made one of them taste everything provided for dinner, including the salt. The fat German seaman watched in impassive silence. He inspected his steak with great care, but once satisfied, he and his henchmen got on with it, but Colmar, having sent the captive pair to the galley, kept recalling one or the other on a variety of pretexts. The third time the white-faced, tight-lipped Cornishman appeared—Colmar required a clean fork—the German spoke.

''Dot iss enuff, Colmar!'' He jerked his close-shaven head in dismissal at Roscorla. Thereafter he remained silent. Colmar shrugged, but took it.

During the afternoon, Roscorla had to help on deck. He was only too glad to be free of Colmar's constant needling. Then it was back to help out with supper. Jane had been busy with Langley, feverish and in pain. She gave him morphine and settled him down. Without a transfusion, rest was the only answer. Exhausted, she turned to the galley, glad of Phil's help and company. Now she was clear of initial shock. In fear of her life, her woman's mind still found time to mourn the man, who, if she had not loved him, had loved her.

In their brief time together, she had come to respect him, and in that one meeting on deck, now another life away, had submitted to his strength of character. Then the matter of her disfigurement had been a vital matter to her; now . . . And why had she given herself to him? Respect and affection she had had; love, no. Gratitude was partly responsible for her impulsive action, one that she certainly did not now regret. And Mark, dying, had told her to take the gun. . . . Would she have the guts to use it?

Yes. She and Phil had very little hope, and Langley even less, but if she had the chance, Colmar had none.

Phil's suspicion that the German had said something to Colmar became a virtual certainty after supper. Almost sullenly he said, ''You two. Quit fooling around with the dishes. If you want the can, now's your chance. You'll be locked up for the night.''

''What about Bill—he can't be left.''

Colmar enjoyed her anger. "Who said he'd be left? There's another bunk—you can have it!"

"Here! Jacens. . . . You can't put her—"

"Yeah, why not? She fancied him!"

Phil struggled to keep his temper. "Hell, you can't. Look, let me move him!" He made but one step before Colmar's gun appeared, as if by magic.

"Go on, buddy—just one more step!"

Locked in his cabin, Roscorla hated himself for his lack of courage, although he realized it would have been useless to resist. He sat thinking, trying to find some ray of hope. He hadn't said so in as many words to Jane, but he knew Colmar would kill them, was eager to do it, to kill anyone who had seen him ordered about, by his lights, humiliated. Why hadn't he killed Langley? Maybe he missed his aim in the citadel—for sure he'd never admit it—and later, perhaps the German had influenced him. He and Jane were needed for the time being; to shoot Langley would not help the operation, and while he was allowed to live, at least Phil and Jane could nurse the illusion that they might live.

Phil jumped convulsively as his phone buzzed. Christ! Was Colmar going on with his needling?

Jane spoke. "Phil, Colmar must have forgotten the phone; that's something. I just called to say I'm all right, and to say I admired the way you kept your temper. Don't give up hope."

Roscorla flopped on his bunk, fully dressed, thinking what a girl Jane had turned out to be: sort of bird a bloke could marry—if they had the ghost of a chance. . . . Exhausted, he slept.

Very much more tired, Jane lay awake crying for herself, for Mark. Yes, Colmar would pay. Please God, whatever else, let that be true. . . .

XI

At first light Colmar released them, sending Jane to the galley and Roscorla on deck. The sailor glanced around, shivering in the relative chill of dawn, cursing the luck of the pirates; the sea was still flat calm.

Astern, the tanker, much lower in the water, was still fueling. Roscorla relieved a red-eyed, unshaven pirate, who went below to eat. Phil watched; the tanker could not take much more. What would happen then? He tried not to think about that, and got on with his job.

This was not difficult or particularly arduous. Mats to stop chafing had to be adjusted under the thumping pipelines, relieving tackles tightened or eased. It kept him busy. With the return of the second man from breakfast, the German clumped aft, his belly bulging over his gunbelt.

"Sailor—you eat. I say so!"

Phil stretched himself, nodded gratefully to the German. His word would be an effective passport.

His jaw dropped, he stared in amazement, joy flooding into his face. Six or seven miles away on the port bow was another ship! He turned toward the German.

"*Nein, mein freund!* No. Do not hope. It no goot iss. Iss *unser*—ours." Something akin to pity showed in the tough German's face.

"Oh, Christ!" The sudden hope, so quickly extinguished, was almost too much for Phil. He turned into the citadel, slouching past Colmar, who taunted him to no purpose, his dejection no act.

But men of Phil's happy-go-lucky disposition cannot be kept down for long. He ate well, reflecting that with another tanker to come—and this one looked bigger—at least they had bought more time, and he firmly believed that while there was life there was hope.

Back on deck, he had to admire the timing and organization. By eleven A.M. the new tanker was approaching from astern, and the activity aboard the first pirate was intense. Hoses were uncoupled, capped, buoyed, and cast off; speed was reduced, and the laden tanker dropped back as the second one moved up. The helo jumped from ship to ship, men were flown in from the new arrival, and the first team, except the German, returned to their ship.

In spite of his anxieties, Phil watched with professional interest: how would the second ship pick up the hoses? Skillfully, the helo flew low, dragging a grapnel, hooking up a long bridle attached to the two trailing hoses, and towed it across the bows of the empty ship. Cut in two, winching each hose aboard was easy. By 11:30, high-seas robbery had begun again.

The German, relaxing after the hectic activity, read Roscorla's expression. "Iss goot—*ja*?"

"Fine, if the weather's right!"

"Plis?"

"Okay if der zee is flatters." Phil swept his hands in a smooth horizontal action. "But a drop of roughers"—a hand undulated—"der vind—got it? You know, storm, er, *sturm*"—he shook his head—"no bloody good— *schrecklich*!"

"Ach, you speak Cherman!"

"Not me mate—er, *nein*! *Ich bin aus Hamburg* a couple of times—der Reeperbahn—*gut* run ashore!" Phil was prepared to be buddies with the devil; whatever else, the German was also a seaman, and relatively friendly. It might help.

"*Ach—Hamburg! Sehr gut, ja?* I also Hamburg know— *fräuleins, bier*!" He laughed throatily. "But I from Travenmunde come—ve are seamen dere. You also?"

Phil nodded vigorously, pleased with the way the conversation was going. "*Ja, ja! Ich bin also in Travenmunde— der* Passat." He named a sailing ship, famous among sailors, which he had seen there.

"*Ach—der schone* Passat!" The German's expression softened, Teutonic sentimentality shone in his eyes. Abruptly he recovered, clapped a heavy hand on Phil's shoulder, shook his head sadly, and went forward.

That clap on the shoulder and the German's attitude frightened Phil even more than Colmar's ravings.

Dinner over, Colmar herded Jane and Phil into the sick bay and locked the door. They guessed he intended sleeping during the afternoon.

At once Jane concentrated on Langley. Phil sat on the spare bunk, trying not to look at the blanket-covered body on the deck, thinking.

Jane found Langley a little better, but he was still very weak. She gave him a glucose drink; between sips, haltingly, he asked her what had happened.

"Don't talk," she ordered. "Close your eyes, relax. Good; this is the situation." She gave him a terse, factual account, leaving out her fears.

Langley's eyes opened. "Listen . . . no, listen . . . important." He stopped, husbanding his strength. Hearing that faint voice, Phil jumped across, bending over the pallid face to catch the words. "Going for . . . Mark . . . bastard can't have seen . . . pressed alarm." He managed a thin smile. "Going . . . ever since . . ." Exhausted, he drifted off into sleep.

Jane and Phil stared uncertainly at each other, hope growing. A grin slowly lightened Phil's face; he grabbed her, kissing her, whispering excitedly in her ear in broad Cornish. "My robin, my robin! Good old Sarge! Colmar *can't* know! Always keeps the citadel covered—him or a thug! Just think of it—the computer's bashing out our position all the flaming time!" He kissed her again.

Gently but firmly Jane extricated herself. "Calm down, Phil! We're nowhere out of the wood."

"No, I know, but there's a chance! This alters things; we've got to be ready when a dirty big RAF Nimrod screeches over! Once they see it, they'll know the game's up—so what'll they do then?" He pounded a fist into the palm of his hand. "Think, Phil boy, think! What would I do? 'Bout the only thing is to cast off and go like the clappers. Not that that will save the sods! Yes. They'll just go. If that Jerry has any say, they'll just leave us, but not Colmar." He tried to find a bright spot. "If his wonderful boss-man says leave us—"

"No." Jane was emphatic. "Don't think that. Colmar's mad. He'd do it anyway; he *wants* to kill us. Dead, and our bodies gone over the side, there'd be no witnesses. As it is, he'll hang for murder and piracy; he has nothing to lose."

"Yes, you're right," agreed Phil somberly. "Still, there's a faint chance . . . The only thing I can think of is for us to barricade ourselves in here, hope the rest will run, and hold him off. Once he sees a bullet whistling through that door, going the wrong way, he may change his mind and go too."

"Bullets can go through that door both ways, Phil, and he's got a lot more of them than we have."

"I can't think of a better idea. To shoot it out in the open would be plain crazy. It has to be here. We'd better get some food and drink stowed in here as soon as we can. That plane could jump us anytime."

"Are you so sure they'll find us?"

"Find us?" echoed Phil. "My stars, Jane, I'll say so! There's that socking great transmitter belting out our position, course, and speed—and that's enough for a start! Then the Nimrod's got a stack of radar, can pick up a rowboat at twenty miles, never mind an object this size! Don't you worry, my robin, if that signal's on the air, we'll be found—we could be found anytime."

His confidence comforted her. "All right, Phil, I'll get some food hidden in here, and the gun—"

"Hang on! When the RAF shows up, that bunch are bound to be pretty excited, including Colmar. They don't know about the gun; there's a chance we might catch Colmar off-guard. You might have a chance to shoot. . . . Yes, I reckon we've got to stay as close together as we can, and never far from the gun. If you can hit him, we run like hell for here.''

"And you grab his gun, if you can!"

"Yes!" Phil could see it all. He went on excitedly, "I'll grab his gun, and spare ammo, if there's time." He studied her figure carefully. "I wish you could carry the gun all the time."

Jane's nerves were ragged. "Don't be a fool! Where?"

"You could tape it to your leg."

"Oh, yes—that would be very handy!" She was angry. "And supposing he decides to search us?"

"Never! Why should he?"

"There are other weapons than guns—I might have a kitchen knife in my stocking. Or you."

"Aw, no. He won't search."

"You *can't* know that!" She flared up again.

"Ssssh!" Phil glanced warningly at Langley. "Us Corns are a funny lot—no, listen, I'm not skylarking—we're not English. King Arthur, the wizard Merlin, and all that lot are ours, not yours. We're as fey as the rest of the Celts."

She shook his arm in exasperation.

"Okay, I don't claim the second sight, but I get feelings." He grinned, a flash of the old joker. "Sometimes they're even right! Colmar, now; I feel he doesn't want to come in here, and he won't search because he thinks he's too fast to be got at, and because he hates touching another human."

She nodded slowly; that partly made sense. "But why doesn't he want to come in here?"

"Well, in part, it's poor old Mark."

"Why doesn't he let us move him, then?"

"I said 'in part.' He's transferred, I think, his intense hatred for Mark to you, ever since you said he was neuter." He gestured toward Jacens' body. "He's trying to break you; that's another part, but my Celtic feeling makes me think he means to kill us in here. He's got a split mind. Part of it can't wait to kill us, especially you; the other part is scared rigid, and that part doesn't want reminding of what is here, what—

it thinks—will be done here." Speaking, he seemed free of fear, yet solemn, his eyes on something beyond the steel walls. "This is an execution cell, a tomb. . . ." He shrugged and slipped back into his normal self. "Neither Colmar nor his flaming boss can risk bodies floating; they must mean to sink AT1—without trace. This wouldn't be the first ship to be 'lost through unknown causes,' but one body with a bullet in it would blow the plot sky-high. Who knows, they may hope to pull this trick again."

"If Bill's right about the alarm—"

"I hope to God he is, but don't bank on it. I've got a feeling—"

"You and your damned feelings! Give them a rest, can't you!"

He nodded, and stayed silent, which maddened her even more.

"Go on," she hissed, shaking his arm.

"I watch Colmar like a hawk; anytime I get near that alarm button, I've seen his expression change somehow, like he had a secret joke—he's sort of expectant. Maybe he's just hoping I'll have a go. I'm useful on deck; the Jerry needs me, and Colmar has a healthy respect for the Jerry; he wouldn't dare shoot me without a cast-iron excuse—not yet. If I went for the button, he'd have one."

"Go on!"

"Thinking about it now, after Bill's news, putting myself in Colmar's place, like, I can see it's a nice idea, to that twisted mind, even amusing—but not *funny*. That's different." He frowned. "I dunno; there's something. Hey, have you checked the gun? Supposing he found it in the drawer and emptied the magazine, or put in blanks? That really would be his idea of a joke!"

"Whatever his filthy joke is, it's not that. I've checked; we've got twelve shots." She looked deliberately at the draped body; to Phil she might have been taking an oath. "If I have the chance, the first three are for Colmar." Her voice sank even lower. "It is terrible that I should think it; to stand a chance, I must shoot him in the back. He may never know what happened!"

For the rest of their afternoon captivity they tried to improve their plan and to think of other ways of surviving. Jane flirted briefly with poison, but had nothing that would act quickly. Sleeping pills in the coffee would be instantly detected by taste, even if Colmar gave them the chance.

Several times the clump of sea boots had their hearts thumping, but nothing happened, and at four o'clock Colmar released them. Jane saw that Phil could be, in part, right: the door unlocked, Colmar did not even put his head in the sick bay.

Glad to be out of the increasingly oppressive atmosphere of their prison, Phil relieved one of the pirates watching the fuel lines. Breathing the fresh, clean air, he automatically checked the sky. The afternoon was well advanced, the sun hidden in cloud, and a slight swell had set in from the southwest. He studied the sky and sea with increasing anxiety; a strong blow could be coming; it could stop the pump-over, and if that happened before the recce aircraft showed . . .

He knew the RAF had a base at Gan, almost on the equator, south of India. A Nimrod, he also knew from his service experience, could stay up at least twenty hours. Twenty hours at, say, two hundred knots, meant four thousand nautical miles; AT1 couldn't be anything like two thousand miles from Gan; if the alarm had been going for nearly thirty hours, where the hell was the RAF?

The man he had relieved returned, accompanied by the German, casting long shadows; the swift tropical sunset was near.

"Sailor—you go."

Phil looked at the sea; it could be for the last time. He shrugged, grinned at the German, moving his hand in steep horizontal undulations, looking from sea to sky. The German understood, and read his thoughts as well. Once more he clapped a heavy hand on his prisoner's shoulder. "Ve are seamen, *ja*? You are a prave man—ve are not all like dot Colmar." He abruptly changed the subject. "I tink you are right; ze wetter iss schanging. Go!"

That Jerry knew damned well what was in store, and

although genuinely sorry, wouldn't lift a single sausagelike finger to stop it. A last forlorn hope flickered and died. Still, this tanker was bigger than the first; maybe they'd got another twenty-four hours—if the weather held.

In the darkening citadel Colmar waited. "Hi, there, buddy-boy! Been working hard?"

"I think so." Phil waited; that was only a preamble.

"Y'know, I can't make my mind up about you, buddy! You act like a creep, but I ain't so sure." Contempt slipped happily into his voice. "Yeah, I guess you are a creep, but you ain't dumb—maybe." His tone changed; he sounded almost genial, "C'mon—guess you've earned a drink; the saloon, buddy."

Going down the ladder, Phil sweated; intuition and reason said no, but this could be it. No; Colmar would have to work himself up before he killed.

He stood silent in the middle of the bright-lit saloon, watching Colmar at the drinks cabinet. The killer had been busy with his gunbelt; the holster flap was hacked off, and a length of cod line secured the holster low on his thigh. Phil guessed this was all part of Colmar's fantasy, the Fastest Gun in the West. He could imagine Colmar, up there in the dark, practicing lightning draws. It would be funny if it was no more than fantasy. God knows, the bastard was fast enough before.

"What'll you have—you don't haveta sign that goddamn book!" Colmar laughed.

"Scotch." Phil kept his voice level; if Colmar suddenly refused, he'd get no pleasure from his disappointment.

"Fine . . . fine!" Colmar still smiled at his feeble joke. "Hey, switch the radio on—let's have fun!"

Phil drew a deep breath. Reluctantly he turned on the radio. "What d'you want?"

Colmar passed him a very large Scotch, taking a can of Coke for himself. "That, buddy, is the fun! Find something we both like."

Puzzled and alarmed by Colmar's malicious look, Phil obeyed. Bursts of static, music, Oriental and Occidental, snatches of guttural tongues filled the saloon. At each strong signal Phil paused, but every time met the slow shake of Colmar's head. He reached the end of the band. "What now?"

"There's two more bands, buddy. Try them."

Roscorla took a good swig of Scotch; in his state, a bottle would have no effect. The same charade was acted out with the other two shortwave bands. Nothing satisfied Colmar, yet, equally, something pleased him. "That's the lot."

"Sure?"

There had to be a trap, but Phil could not see it, and plunged. "Sure."

Colmar laughed, a mean, unsettling sound. "Yeah, you're a dumb bum!" His geniality faded, replaced by contempt, arrogance. "Okay, the party's over—go get your apron on!"

Phil put down his still-half-full glass.

Colmar had at last a flash of geniality. "No, take your drink—and one for that cow! Tell her about our little game—maybe she's not as thick as you!"

Phil left, followed by a very stagy laugh.

Jane, equally lost, had little interest, prepared to regard it as just another inexplicable example of Colmar's warped, sadistic nature.

But Phil wouldn't let it go; Colmar meant something. Washing a saucepan, he suddenly froze, shocked by comprehension. "The bastard!" he said slowly. "The—"

Jane stopped him urgently. "Tell me!"

"He made me search, not to find anything, but to see what wasn't there! Sorry, Jane; Bill was wrong; there's no alarm going out. I thought the RAF were taking their time. They're not coming."

"You can't be sure!"

" 'Fraid so. I've been in too many ships; I know that a powerful transmitter like the one we have will break in on ordinary radio reception. Colmar fixed it!"

All through supper, Colmar enjoyed his joke, grinning with triumph each time he saw Phil's wooden face. In the somber German presence Colmar said nothing, but when the Jerry left the saloon, Colmar opened up.

"Don't tell me you haven't tumbled! No one can be that

stupid—not even a crawler like you!'' He sat back in his chair, legs sprawled out, Nero taking his ease; only the can of lime juice, dangling negligently from one hand, was out of keeping. "Yeah, I fixed it! I spent one whole night watch, sweating over that alarm button, shit-scared that mother-fucking sergeant would soft-shoe up and catch me! But I made that, too! I knew it wasn't as simple as it looked, but, yeah, I got that cover off and shorted out the secondary alarm before I tackled the main one!'' His eyes glittered with triumph. "Just one leetle slip and this whole goddamn electronic jazz band would have been squarking, blowing the entire operation!'' Phil's impassive face enraged him. "If you don't believe me, go press your beautiful red button!''

Phil didn't bother. Colmar wasn't lying. Utterly dejected, he let himself be locked in his cabin. It looked like game, set, and match to the pirates. The last, ominous straw had been the bottle of Scotch Colmar had thrust, grinning, into his hands.

XII

At 0015 GMT the red cartridge shot into the duty officer's basket; automatically he glanced at the clock. Bloody train, that's all it was. He pushed aside his sketch of Sidcup's newest rockery and started decoding.

AT1's midnight position was 1502 South 6010 East, course 181, speed 12.30 knots. He hardly needed to plot it, but did. As expected, bang on course, southeast of the Seychelles, fractionally ahead of position. The Seychelles . . . He'd dreamed of starting a hotel there, but that was before the Arab-Israeli War changed the face of the world. Thankful that, for once, he had hesitated, he got back to the tricky question of placing the Alpines in his rockery.

Colmar's harsh voice woke Phil; before he opened his eyes, he realized two things: the sea had got up, and this day would see the end. The second thought brought a familiar drying of his mouth and a sick feeling to his stomach.

On deck Phil found the German very red-eyed, edgy, and with good reason. Gray, with an unhealthy suggestion of pink, the water took its color from the cloud-filled sky. A strong southwesterly wind drove a long swell, overlaid with a whitecapped sea on the tanker's starboard bow, inducing a corkscrew motion. As yet it didn't amount to much, but the sky was anything but promising.

The German hustled him aft and to work, and Phil saw why he was jumpy. The well-laden pirate had her bows so close to

AT1's stern, they rose and fell on the same swell. Tending the lines and mats, Phil thought. If the weather got much worse, the pump-over would have to stop. Obviously they wouldn't worry about the loss of fuel lines, but the need to keep the strain to a minimum forced the pirate captain to stay dangerously close; the last thing he would want was serious damage to his bows. Then there was the business of getting the German, Colmar, and the three tankermen off; Phil had served in frigates and knew something of the limitations deck movement imposed on helicopter landings and takeoffs.

He worked on, suppressing his growing excitement. If the weather got too bad for transfers, they had a faint chance: the gang aboard AT1 would be cut off. If Jane could get Colmar, maybe they'd be able to shut down the citadel. Jerry and his mates would then be in a mighty uncomfortable situation, sitting ducks for him and Jane, safe behind armor. There'd be the risk that the pirate tanker would use Blowpipes against them, but what was risk alongside dead certainty? Anyway, one thing at a time, meet that when it came.

Below, Jane could not rid herself of an insidious cloying smell, the sweetish odor of corruption, which turned her stomach. Even after a very hot shower and clean clothes, her mind insisted the smell remained. It took an intense effort of willpower to stop herself trying to kill Colmar at once, her burning hatred of the man eclipsing almost everything else from her mind. Almost, for she could not forget for a single moment that Mark's body, which she had so passionately welcomed, was now a stinking cadaver, an object of loathing and disgust. To tend Langley demanded all her self-control. He was now strong enough to sit up and feed himself, and although he had not said anything, she had to keep him well provided with cigarettes.

Phil was sent down to collect food, thankful for the chance to tell Jane how things were shaping on deck. The moment he felt sure the helo couldn't fly, he'd be back. If he couldn't get Colmar alone in the citadel, he might try to lure him down below. "We've got to play it by ear, girl. You'd better warn Bill." With sudden clairvoyance, he went on, urgently.

"Yes, Bill . . . get him out of that bunk—and Mark in! Do it! And keep the gun in your sock!"

Jane shuddered, but Phil's tone carried conviction. "Okay, but, Phil, it's *got* to be today. I can't spend another night in there."

"Don't worry," whispered Phil grimly, "Colmar's got the same idea!"

Halfway up the ladder he heard the helo arrive, and hurried to watch. The aircraft got down without too much trouble, landed one fresh tankerman, and flew off with two near-exhausted men.

Phil's excitement grew; was this the moment? They were down to four enemies now, including one very tired tankerman, the apparently untiring Jerry, who had to be on pills, the new man, and Colmar.

It all turned on that bloody chopper. The wind was still rising, and the sea with it. Wait. . . .

About an hour later the chopper returned, and Jerry and the tired man left. Now Colmar had the walkie-talkie and stayed on deck, talking frequently with the pirate. Phil could not hear, for Colmar stood downwind of him, and the noise of the rising gale whipped his words away. The motion had markedly increased; fine spray gradually soaked the small knot of men. Phil hardly noticed, trying to think of some excuse to get to Jane. Before, it had not been difficult, but now Colmar had charge of the deck, and two men had plenty to do; Colmar only watched.

Once again, the seaman in Roscorla could not help but admire the captain of the pirate tanker. If AT1 had been under human control, both ships would have come around, head-on to the swell. As it was, the pirate, clinging like a blood-sucking leech, had no option but to accept a near-gale on his starboard bow, exerting a constantly varying thrust which had to be balanced by the tanker's rudder. One wrong helm order, a second's inattention, and the whole rig could be torn out.

"Hey, you!" Colmar bawled, standing over the bending seaman. "Go fix some coffee—and be fast!"

Phil swallowed hard. This had to be the moment. He wouldn't get another chance. Five minutes, and Colmar would come to find out what the hell was going on. He'd find out, all right.

Entering the citadel, Phil gave a last glance at sea and sky. Darkness would be early, and the wind was not easing. This was it.

Jane was leaving the sick bay, an empty glass in her hand. Phil ran lightly down the ladder. He grabbed her arm. ''It's now!''

For a second she looked at him, uncomprehending. He snatched the glass from her hand. ''Come *on*—this is it!''

''How'ja guess, buddy?'' Colmar, his thin hair stuck down with spray, stood on the bottom rung of the companion-way, one hand holding on, the other gripping his gun. He moved, the ship moved, but his gun hand compensated for all movement, remaining rock-steady on Jane's stomach. ''Move! Unless you wanna die real slow!''

Overhead, a sudden burst of submachine-gun fire made the cornered pair jump.

That pleased Colmar. ''No, it ain't the Marines, only the life rafts getting bust!''

Helplessly Jane and Phil backed into the sick bay, filled with hopeless fear and anger. The gun strapped to Jane's calf might as well be at the bottom of the sea.

Colmar stepped into the sick bay; his fixed grin, half-snarl, slipped at the smell. Above the noise of the sea thundering along the ship's side, the muted whine of the wind, all heard the helicopter.

''Not much time, folks!'' Colmar's face twitched. ''Jest want you to know . . .'' In seconds, shouting wild, meaningless obscenities, Colmar worked himself up for the kill. ''Shit! Shit, I hate you all—him . . .'' With terrible speed the gun flicked around, firing twice into the figure in the bunk.

Phil jumped, throwing the glass in Colmar's face. ''Run!''

Jane ran. Roscorla slammed into Colmar, knocking him

off balance, and ran himself. The gun cracked; screaming madly, helped by the ship's roll, Colmar fell.

Phil flew up the ladder, his mind a quivering blank except for one thing: Jane needed time. He tore through the citadel, out on deck, into the growing storm, jumping for the catwalk, running desperately, crouching.

The winded Colmar took the ladder slower. He paused at the top, breathing hard, wiping blood from his cut cheek, his eyes mad with excitement. His flickering, cobralike eyes spotted Phil through the spray-dimmed window. Grunting with triumph, he ran on deck, oblivious of the spray, the tearing wind; oblivious of the other pirate, shouting frantically.

Snatching a glance, Phil saw him and dived for the guard rail and the relative safety of the fuel pipes. Colmar grinned with terrible happiness, and fired twice. The sailor threw up his hands and fell headlong among the pipes.

For several seconds, a very long time in his time scale, Colmar remained still, savoring the brilliance of his shooting. All-powerful, he bestrode the earth. Vaguely he heard a voice, dragging him back to reality.

"For Christ's sake! The helo—now!" The man ran, unaware that Colmar had swung, finger twitching on the trigger, in his direction.

Colmar's frail fantastic empire crumbled. That figure, ducking as it ran for the helo, brought realization; he had to go now, or stay—forever.

That cow—where was she? He saw the tankerman scrambling into the chopper; the sight made him run too. With luck he'd get her from the air. Crying with frustrated rage, he scrambled in. Immediately the pilot gunned his engine; the noise drowned out the wind. The pilot's gaze flickered from rev counter to the sea; he had to guess wind force and direction, deck angle; the first few airborne seconds would be critical.

Jane's anger matched Colmar's. She had taken refuge in the funnel casing, slamming the door behind her, needing those precious seconds to get at the gun. In the darkness she had torn desperately at the surgical plaster, ripping off hair and skin. Awkwardly balanced, in the dark, she had fallen as the ship rolled, dropping the gun. Clawing frantically, by the time she found it, the helo's noise told its own story. She had heard Colmar's shots, guessed, and had no thought except to kill the killer.

She flung the door open and raced for the deck. The helo was airborne, coming slowly up the port side, very close.

She saw Colmar at the same instant that he saw her, but now the tables had turned. Seated, he struggled to get his gun; she braced herself against the doorway, took deliberate aim. Filled with joy, she fired three times.

She had a fleeting image of Colmar jerking sideways, of the helo tilting, the rotor striking the top of the radar gantry and shattering. Engine screaming uselessly, the machine plunged sideways into the angry sea and was gone. Whatever else, Colmar had died. Mark and Phil were avenged, and by her hand.

Still holding the gun in her two-handed grip, Jane sank slowly to the deck, crying.

How long she spent in feminine release she could not know; gradually her sobbing ceased, and her practical nature took over. She dropped the gun carelessly; she had to find Phil: that was the least she could do. Not the man that Mark had been, he had done his best for her, and it had been enough.

On deck, gasping in the wind, she forced herself to think. Phil wouldn't have run aft; that would have led straight into the man with the submachine gun. Shivering with reaction and the chill spray, she climbed onto the catwalk and made her way slowly forward, hair streaming, praying, but with little hope.

She found him, a crumpled bundle between some pipes, and her heart sank. Dropping down beside him, she turned him over. Blood from a furrow above his left ear streaked his cheek. She tore his shirt open. Colmar had fired twice, but found nothing. Hardly daring to hope, she pressed her ear against his wet chest, but the noise of the wind made certainty impossible, and his cold spray-drenched flesh gave no hint. She laid him carefully on his side and clambered back to the citadel.

After the clean air of the upper deck, the sick-bay atmosphere made her sick. She vomited into the washbasin, spat, and grabbed the first-aid bag, pausing fractionally to look at her other patient. Langley had passed out with pain when she moved him—God, how right Phil had been!—and was still unconscious. She left at a stumbling run, glad to escape from the nauseous atmosphere, stopping for a flask of coffee before returning to Phil.

By the time she reached him, night was fast approaching. With all the care her spray-chilled fingers could command, she bandaged his head, concentrating on her task and nothing else. Wrapped in a blanket, hot coffee in his mouth—and down his shirt—Roscorla stirred. Jane worked patiently, rubbing his chest and arms, and was at last rewarded. Slowly he made the transition from unconsciousness to mental fog. One hand groped uncertainly at the mug.

"Oh, my dear life! What happened?"

Never had Jane been so glad to hear a voice, or that Cornish expression. Shouting against the gale, she told him of Colmar's end, boosting his strength. Could he move?

He grinned weakly. "Try me," he croaked.

The journey aft was painful, slow, and dangerous, and it was dark long before they reached the sanctuary of the citadel. There they rested, immensely glad to be out of the angry elements. They groped their way down to the warmth and light of the main deck, and Jane settled him in an armchair in the saloon, gave him a small Scotch, and had a much larger one herself, realizing just how cold and tired she felt—too tired to fully savor the relief that Colmar would never walk through that door again.

She roused herself, fighting the desire for sleep. A half-hour later she had Phil stretched out on the sofa, changed into dry clothing, and had redressed his wound, no more than a furrow across his scalp. Unless he had suffered what doctors called a "contrecoup"—and his condition did not suggest he had—he'd be all right. She gave him a cup of chicken soup, then showered and changed after dragging the comatose Langley into the saloon, locking the sick bay, trying not to think of that bullet-riddled body. Mechanically she ate a piece of cheese, not because she wanted it; she could not remember the last meal she had eaten, and somehow she had to keep going. Almost choking as she ate, Jane toyed with the idea of getting the men to their bunks, but decided it was beyond her strength. She made both as comfortable as she could. Tired beyond caring, she gave herself another drink and sank into an armchair, staring blankly, her brain busy with a dozen different things. Even to her untrained mind, the ship's motion had increased; Langley was fast asleep, and Phil dozed fitfully. With luck, he'd be all right in the morning; at least there was a good chance they'd *see* morning. God! She was so tired. Idly, without real interest, she wondered what had happened to the pirate. No matter. Sleep. . . .

AT1 plowed on, corkscrewing in a ponderous way through a full gale. Below decks, four bodies moved, obedient to her motion, one stiffly, grotesquely.

Nearly four thousand miles away in London, the duty officer plotted AT1's midnight position: 2012 South, 6002 East, course 181 degrees, speed back to 12.15 knots.

Still bang on track. In the next hour or so, AT1 would come around to 193 degrees, bending gently around for the cape. Given that box of tricks, it was as easy as falling off a log—easier.

The duty officer smiled, reading the met report, pitying the poor guards in that wallowing hulk in a force-eight-to-nine gale. He was far from sure he would like to be in their position, facing the sea in a black mood, in a ship controlled by a computer. All the same, they were jolly well paid.

Forty minutes after the duty officer plotted her course, AT1 shuddered from end to end. A brief flash of orange-red flame above the wheelhouse outshone the navigation lights and was gone. Ponderously AT1 smashed on in the rising sea.

Below deck, the effect was much more severe. The muffled concussion broke glass and crockery, cupboards burst open, their contents hurled on the deck, and flung the remnants of AT1's team into sudden, fearful wakefulness.

XIII

Thrown off the sofa, Phil woke on the deck. Although his head felt like a fairground roundabout, naval training had him staggering to his feet, clutching at anything firm to steady him.

Jane, on all fours, her face almost hidden in her loose hair, stared up at him, uncomprehending, her eyes bleary with sleep, "What . . . What . . . ?" She could not form a sentence.

"Quiet! Listen!" Clinging to the back of the sofa, Phil shut his eyes, concentrating. Christ! How his head hurt.

Beneath the sound of the storm, the pulsing vibration of the engines remained reassuringly regular; the ship's motion, although more violent, was unchanged, the same steady, wallowing corkscrew, the roll greater to port. Sea and swell were still off the starboard bow.

Reluctantly he opened his eyes. Jane was squatting on the deck beside Langley. "Don't know," said Phil, "but the ship feels all right, like." Langley's eyelids were fluttering. "Take care of him. I'll go and take a look."

He moved carefully, his head throbbing at every step, but his mind was working, although he felt detached, as if he were a spectator, only vaguely interested in events. Most of the lights were still burning; that gave him some comfort.

In the doorway he paused, hanging on, turning his head with caution. Jane was making the perilous passage to the drinks cabinet to get soda water for Langley, swaying awkwardly past overturned tables and chairs. The radio had been hurled to the deck, smashed. Knives and forks, sauce bottles, and jam pots clattered and rolled around.

Each step, in his state, was an adventure; in the main-deck flat he stopped again, letting his eyes do the work. In the galley he saw smashed crockery sliding aimlessly around the tiled floor; ahead of him, the computer door appeared intact. Fewer lights were working, but enough remained for him to examine the door; yes, that was okay.

Like an old man, he climbed laboriously to the citadel, stopping at the top of the companionway to give his head a break, and for his eyes to adapt to the darkness. The forward windows gradually took shape, patches of lighter darkness. Groping his way past the empty armory, he shut one swinging, banging door. It made little difference to the general racket, but the action gave him slight satisfaction, a first step in restoring order, getting some sort of control.

Clutching the watchman's stool, he peered painfully out into the night. Great sheets of spray rattled across the glass like sharp-flung gravel on a tin shack, conveying something of the strength of the storm outside, a sharp, staccato sound against the scream of the wind in the gantry, and other noises.

He switched on a wiper, and got snapshot glimpses of glittering spray flung high above the distant bows. That brief glitter told him the navigation light on the stumpy foremast was working, and on each side of the citadel the ghostly gleam of red and green.

Well, at least the navigation lights were still on. But what in hell's name was that din overhead? Something had broken loose, but what? He tried to remember what piece of equipment was above the citadel, and round. It had to be round, for it was rolling. He gave up, and climbed slowly into the wheelhouse; the noise was much louder, deafening.

Rumble . . . crash! Pause. Rumble . . . crash! Pause.

Something was rolling around on the wheelhouse roof; something bloody heavy. He wouldn't go fooling around up there in the dark, not in his state of health. Sounded like a bloody garden roller gone mad. Whatever it was, it couldn't be that important—unless it smashed the guardrail and landed on the citadel roof.

He stared out of a side window, resting his burning head on the cold glass, idly watching the cascading water on the heaving citadel roof. What had happened? Apart from that bloody racket overhead, everything seemed okay.

He glanced up at the gantry, hardly visible against the black cloud, but as the ship rolled, part of the structure swung wildly across a lighter patch of sky.

What Phil saw sent him searching feverishly for a hand lamp, his head forgotten. The light confirmed that first chilly suspicion.

All radar aerials had stopped.

"The *bastards*!" Phil cried, hitting the window with his fist in impotent fury. "The bastards!" Again he checked: he could not see an aerial which he knew was directly overhead, but if seven had packed in, he had little hope for the eighth.

Moving rather faster, he staggered down to the main deck, and again examined the computer-room door. He'd swear it had never been touched.

Maybe that was another of Colmar's skills—or one of the others'; anything could have been done while he and Jane were locked up. Colmar might have been a lock expert; he'd had plenty of time. Phil clung to the door handle, thinking. Now he knew what had been done, but not how.

On second thought, Colmar couldn't have picked the lock—his crazy vanity wouldn't have let him keep quiet about it. Someone else? Maybe, but not the German or his crew; they were seamen, nothing else. Another man, flown in while they were asleep?

What the hell did it matter? Somehow the ingenious sods had done it; no good going on about it; the real question was what did he do now?

Hanging on, he made the short journey back to the saloon. AT1's motion was unbelievably violent. In his time, Phil had been tossed around a good deal more in a frigate in the North Atlantic, but in a ship this size . . .

Jane had moved Langley, wedging him between the fixed sofa and a row of cushions. It was the best she could do. As Phil, his white face dramatic under the bloodstained bandage, clawed his way in, she got to her feet, hanging on to the sofa.

"Somehow—don't ask me how—they must have got a bomb into the computer. The radar's packed in."

She anxiously searched his pain-lined face, not fully understanding the significance of his words. Phil lowered himself gently into an armchair, splaying out his legs to increase his stability.

"Jane, fix me a drop of the hard stuff, will you?"

"It won't be good for your head."

He grinned. "I should care—it's not being very good to me!" He fished out a battered pack of cigarettes and lit one. "We've gotta *think*, Jane." Saying the words made him realize just how true that was. Ever since he had flung that glass at Colmar—and hit the sod, too—for one reason or another he hadn't considered anything more than a minute ahead.

Jane zigzagged back with a very small brandy, and left him.

He sniffed it appreciatively, then gulped it back. Right, Phil, he told himself, stand-easy's over, get down to it.

What did he know? Colmar was dead. A fact, now, of astonishingly little interest. And the pirate tanker? He hadn't really looked when he was up in the wheelhouse, but he would have been bound to have spotted any lights. Anyway, the finest sailor in the wide world couldn't have hung on in this weather. The tanker must have gone, and even if the pirates were mugs enough to hang around, waiting for the weather to ease, they couldn't have an endless supply of helos. Forget the pirate; he'd gone.

So that left ex-Leading Seaman Roscorla in full charge. . . . Start with the bang, then. As near as he could guess, the explosion had been about five A.M. Why then? Come to that, why bother at all? The second tanker hadn't been far short of full, so why not cast off and let AT1 chug on her way? It'd be four weeks before the robbery—and their bodies—were found. Wait a minute!

Phil sat up, mentally and physically. Colmar had said

something about a burst of automatic fire—the life rafts being shot up. That settled it; they had meant to sink AT1, but they couldn't have imagined that a bomb in the computer would do the job.

Phil lit another cigarette. Why did that five-o'clock bang niggle so much? Five o'clock . . .

"Have some coffee."

He frowned, nodded, and took the mug. If only he didn't feel so monumentally tired, if only his head would let up for a bit.

"And take these, Phil."

"What are they, sleeping pills?"

"No, a couple of Veganin for your head."

"That's all right, then." He swallowed the pills, sipped his coffee. "Don't slip me sleeping pills, whatever you do— a few waker-uppers might be a good idea. I've a nasty feeling Colmar hasn't finished with us yet! We've got to think."

Jane sat on the deck, holding the leg of his chair, so he could talk without turning his head. Langley slept. "Tell me. I might help, somehow."

He gave her his thoughts as far as he had got.

"You're worried about the timing of that bomb. Why?"

"Can't say, really; I mean, why not blow the whole thing up as soon as they'd finished? Why wait damn near twelve hours?"

Perhaps it was the mention of twelve hours that triggered his mind. He sat bolt upright, coffee cascading on the chair.

"Christ Almighty—the cunning bastards! I've *got* it! Look, five A.M. is thirty minutes past midnight, Greenwich Mean Time! They timed the bomb to go off *after* the midnight report had been made by the computer, which means no one ashore would even begin to suspect what was going on for another twelve hours! The last bloody tanker would have been gone—what?—say, twenty hours at least by that time. At twelve knots—with this wind up its chuff it'd be more— they'd be two hundred and forty miles away. Add the distance AT1 travels—they'd be five hundred miles clear before the shore boys even begin to suspect!"

"I see that," said Jane slowly, "but . . . then what?"

Phil tried to sound casual. "The bad weather may have upset their plans, but I very much doubt it. Colmar was right; this operation was really planned! There has to be another bomb."

"Oh!" Jane could scarcely look paler. "So at any time . . ." She did not finish.

"Could be, but somehow I don't think so. They planned to the last nut and bolt; the only hitch they hit was you! You hacked their chopper out of the sky, and I doubt if they knew you did it. Firing from the doorway, you couldn't be seen, the shots wouldn't be heard in the general noise, and visibility was lousy. To them, it must have looked as if the pilot misjudged his distance and slipped the gantry, and bing! That was it! If the bomb wasn't already aboard, and with the chopper gone, I'd have expected them to hit us with something else—for a start, they'd got our Blowpipes!"

"Could they have sunk us with those?"

He shook his head, and winced. "Can't be sure, but it'd make a helluva mess of us in the right spot. Anyway, I reckon they shoved off, according to plan. Like I said, no one ashore will have a clue anything is wrong with AT1 for another nine, ten hours. Even if everybody goes like greased lightning, I can't see them getting to us for another three or four hours at the very least—that'd be an RAF Nimrod from Gan. By the time it reached us, it'd be dark." He lit another cigarette, thinking, and had a sudden insight. "Yes, that *has* to be it! They'd time the bomb to go off just after dark, so there'd be all night for the mess to sink! All that would be left for the RAF to find in the morning would be an oil slick—maybe. By that time the pirates would be so far away they couldn't care less! Cunning bastards! If I'm right, we've got all day—a good ten hours, anyway."

"But if you're . . ."

He put his hand on her shoulder. "That's just one of those things, my dear. Soon it will be light enough for me to start looking. One thing, it should be pretty easy—no booby traps, like."

111

"D'you know anything about bombs?"

"Me?" He tried hard to sound amused. "You'd be surprised the things the Navy teaches you!"

"But where will you look? They could have put it anywhere!"

"That's a good question. . . . Where d'you plant a bomb in a tanker?" He nodded toward the bar. "Let me have another drop—please? My head feels a bit better, and it helps me to think."

In silence, she got him a second small tot.

"The only place for a bomb is below the waterline. That stands to reason. We can be pretty sure they've not got down to the engine room—the entrance is through the computer room—so it has to be forward. That's it! Where better to shove it than an empty oil tank—ignite the vapor as well!" He saw her expression. "Sorry, Jane. Got to face facts."

"But how can you work on deck in this weather?"

"That's easy—I'll get wet. As long as I can see, that's the important bit." He glanced at his watch. "Another half-hour, and it should be light enough."

"I'll get some breakfast."

"No, don't bother. I'm not hungry."

"D'you think I am?" she said sharply. "We both eat. Eggs and bacon, even if I have to fry them in a saucepan!"

Phil eyed her admiringly. "That's what I always say—first things first!"

They ate in silence. She forced herself to cram down eggs and bacon. He needed the food; what lay ahead was not appetizing, but his masculine pride would not let him refuse it in the face of her example. Two more Veganin and another cup of tea and he stood up, donning a wind-breaker.

"When you've seen to Bill, come up to the citadel and watch out for me. I may need help."

His tone was too matter-of-fact to ring true, but her tired eyes regarded him with something akin to respect. "Good luck, Phil. Be careful."

"Oh, my dear life, you can bank on that!"

"I don't know how you can be so calm."

He grinned. "I'm scared right down to my socks," he

112

confessed, "and in a funny way, I'm not. You work it out."

Alone in the citadel he paused, feeling very scared, trying to plan. Outside, spray still dashed against the windows, the ship reeled and plunged in the heavy swell, water raced across the deck, cascading over the lee side. Not, he thought, ideal weather for bomb hunting, or anything else. Overhead, the unrelenting racket on the wheelhouse roof went on and on. It was an unlikely place for a bomb, but to check would be relatively easy.

Out on the citadel roof the wind tore at him, and the spray was blinding. He climbed the ladder cautiously until he could peer over the wheelhouse roof. Much became clear.

A five-foot-long steel cylinder rolled back and forth across the wet deck, jarring against the guardrails at the end of each run. A long cutting lance, pipes, and a smaller cylinder hung over the guardrail. In one corner of the roof were the twisted, blackened remnants of a ventilator.

So that was how they did it. . . .

Careful of his throbbing head, he made his way down to the foredeck. There was more spray, but although it struck chill, it wasn't cold. The salt stung his wound, but otherwise he found it refreshing, clearing his head.

In the citadel he worked out a plan. He had to be systematic, not missing one square inch. No panic; plenty of time. Start on the port side and work forward.

For the best part of an hour he looked, not knowing what he sought. Pipes, valves, covers, the underside of the catwalk and its supports. Soaked, chilled, and slightly dizzy with all the bending, he returned to the citadel, where Jane waited, inwardly scared, but outwardly an oasis of calm. She did not ask pointless questions, just gave him coffee, strengthening him with her matter-of-fact attitude. He felt very grateful and tried to think of something encouraging.

"Weather's on the mend."

She looked doubtful; deception had no point in that context.

"It is! Wind's easing, veering westerly. We're over the worst."

"D'you want me with you?"

He shook his head. "No. You stay here. If I wave, shout, or jump up and down like, come on out."

He went back to his search, moving methodically back and forth across the deck, from the center line of the catwalk to the port side, slipping, clawing for handholds, tension growing in him like a steadily tightening knot. Nearly halfway up the port side, his training and instincts told him it had to be soon; this was the area of maximum probability. He straightened his aching back, and cheating, stared ahead of his immediate search area. Then he saw it.

Odd jobs, overtime, were part of a guard's perks. Ships need constant repainting; Langley could authorize such work. Phil had spent several hours painting and well knew how an inspection cover should look. He stared, rubbing his wet hands nervously on his soaking trousers. A few feet ahead was a cover, several nuts missing, the paint film on the rest broken. This had to be it: a spanner. He leaped onto the catwalk, waving, shouting. At once Jane ran to meet him.

"A spanner . . . spanner!" The wind shredded his words. "Adjustable bloody spanner!"

"What?"

He screamed in mindless rage, "Spanner. Christ . . . adjustable spanner!"

She was scrambling frantically, lurching, grabbing the guardrail, spray drenching her, water streaming down her face. They collided, holding each other and the rail.

"A bloody spanner—adjustable!"

"I know! Anything else?"

"Yes! Hand lamp . . . anything, tools, screwdriver— anything! For Christ's sake, hurry!"

The pain in his head did not register as he set off at a shambling run to the boatswain's store in the bows, praying desperately it would not be locked.

The motion was awful, the bows rising and falling in a vast circular motion, the noise deafening each time AT1 smashed down. Phil fought to keep his feet, struggling with the door. It flew open with the roll of the ship, throwing him off balance, leaving him clinging grimly to the handle. He staggered in, fumbling with cold sodden fingers for the light switch. The door slammed behind him.

Drums of paint had broken loose, rolling madly; paint kettles tumbling around the deck added to the din. He searched frantically, failing to find an adjustable spanner, but several ordinary ones clanked and rattled in their rack over the bench. With wary eye on the paint drums, he checked: all were the same size. He snatched one, and fought his way out. Running aft, he dropped down beside the first inspection cover he reached. The spanner fit.

At once he jumped back on the catwalk, clutching the spanner like an icon, running as fast as he dared. Suddenly he stopped, panic-stricken, cursing himself with meaningless obscenities.

He hadn't marked the suspect cover.

Phil hung onto the rail, panting, forcing himself to calm down, to think. He remembered the cover was in an inboard row, nearest the catwalk. No sweat; take it easy, walk slowly: plenty of time.

A few steps farther on, he spotted missing bolts. Sighing with relief, he dropped down, kneeling beside it.

Immediately he felt a sharp pain in his knee; he shifted his position, glancing down, and picked up a spanner identical with the one he held in his hand.

He gawped at it stupidly. How the hell had he missed it? Getting into a flat spin, when all the time there was one left by some murdering bastard.

Christ—*no*! One nut was only a couple of turns; for sure he'd have seen that; he'd tried them all with his fingers.

It wasn't the same cover. There had to be *two* bombs—at least.

The time scale shortened sickeningly.

XIV

Brushing the sweat and spray from his face, Phil felt as if a bomb had exploded in his stomach. He breathed deeply several times to ease his thumping heart and tackled the first nut. He had three off by the time Jane arrived.

"I found a screwdriver!" She knelt beside him, hair streaming, shouting in his ear. "And a thing of tools from Colmar's desk!"

"Leave 'em and bugger off!"

She saw his knuckles were scraped and bleeding. "Take it steady—you know we've plenty of time!"

He gave a short high-pitched yelp of a laugh, paused in his work, pulling her head to him. "Not anymore, we haven't!" He told her of his other find

She reacted by picking up the second spanner. He half-opened his mouth, then shrugged. It took them the best part of ten minutes to get all the nuts off; Phil sat back on his haunches, holding on with one hand. "*Now* bugger off—see if you can find the first one," he shouted, hoping she'd stay.

She ignored him, pointing at the cover. "What do we do—lift it?"

With neither time nor inclination to thank her, he nodded. "Shift around, opposite me, lift it straight up—want to look at the underside!"

In the appalling conditions, even this simple task was hard, although the two-foot-square cover lifted easily enough, proof the paint film had been broken.

"Higher," he shouted. "Get the bastard up!" He craned

116

his neck to look underneath. Nothing was attached to it. "Right—dump it!"

As the plate clanged on the deck, Phil anxiously scanned the square dark hole, and there it was: a black-plastic box, like a small transistor radio, fixed to the inside of the coaming. For several seconds they both stared.

"Doesn't look very big." Unconsciously, Jane was whispering, her voice lost to Phil in the howling wind.

"Gimme the torch!" He crouched over the hole, his fear abating fractionally. He looked at the dial setting; it should have made some sort of sense, but his brain refused to work. Anyway, he wasn't going to play with it. He shone the torch into the gap between the device and the steel it clung to, then turned the beam downward. It seemed to be lost, soaked up by the black cavern. A flicker of light came back, reflected by the surging remnant of oil swilling on the tank bottom sixty feet below, but in the dim light he saw what he sought, the wire running from the device.

Again he sat back, sickened by the smell of oil, and his own fear. "Let's have your tools," he said unsteadily.

Colmar's wallet looked more like a watchmaker's kit, but it did include a small pair of pliers. He thought briefly of simply cutting the wire, but his training rejected the idea sharply. One wire at a time: to cut both together could close the circuit. The fact that his frightened mind should even consider such a daft idea frightened him even more.

It was all quite simple, really. Nothing to it; timing device, held by magnetic clamps, connecting wire, and down there, bomb and detonator. All he had to do was remove the timer, disconnect the wires . . .

Almost casually he reached down, grasped the device, and jerked it free. He sat back, trembling uncontrollably, giving Jane a ghastly sketch of a smile.

He turned the timer over, careful not to move the dial. On the back was a small panel, secured by four screws. Somehow he got it off, scratching the metal in his clumsy efforts. Underneath lay two wires, separated from their pvc sheath. To one side, he noted the minute batteries, but decided he was too clumsy to try extracting them. Shielding the device from the spray, he wiped his free hand on his trousers and took up the pliers. He beckoned the white-faced Jane closer.

"Grab hold of that wire—and don't let go!"

He cut one wire, and paused, although he well knew the bang, if it came, would be instantaneous. Even at that critical moment some detached part of his mind registered the sharpness of the pliers and thought it typical of Colmar.

With greater assurance he cut the second wire, then sank back, head bowed, resting; to a casual glance, he might have been praying. He looked up, nodded to Jane, and took the wire from her. His smile had more conviction now; he hauled on the wire until it became taut.

"Stuck with bloody magnets, I expect!"

Jane shut her eyes as he pulled, hard. Something gave; he hauled the wire up, hand over hand, with a seaman's dexterity. The last three feet dripped with oil; on the end, a well-wrapped package, glistening black.

Phil got to his feet, steadied by Jane, and staggered across to the lee rail, clutching the oil-covered bomb in both arms. Briefly he felt it, lifted it tentatively, estimating its weight. Jane was horrified at his slowness.

"Phil, get rid of it!" she screamed.

"Don't worry," he shouted back, "safe as houses! It's plastic—'bout ten pounds of it—won't go off without the detonator, and that's electric!" He balanced himself, waiting for the roll, then heaved the bomb and wire well clear of the ship.

Jane collected the tools, and they moved slowly aft, soon locating his first bomb. Right then, Phil would have given the world for a cigarette, but dared not press his luck. Without waiting for him, Jane started in on the remaining nuts. Standing over her, balancing easily to the ship's roll, he looked down at her. She was soaked, her shirt stuck to her bent back, her brassiere standing out in bas-relief.

What a girl! Although still scared, his fear had abated slightly, now he knew what he was tackling, but her . . . Totally ignorant of plastic explosive and detonators, she remained in deep fear, but still got on with the job. He dropped down beside her.

The second bomb was a repetition of the first; the only heart-stopping moment was when Phil nearly dropped the timing device, still attached, down into the tank. That gone, they combed the rest of the way forward on the port side and found nothing. Then they worked aft on the starboard side, the wind and spray on their backs, and being the weather side, they got drenched more often. Not that it made much difference to their miserable condition.

Jane found the third bomb. Although their hands were white, water-sodden, the work went much faster, and the most difficult part of the operation was getting the oil-slippery plastic-wrapped charge across to the lee rail. As the device disappeared into the driving spray, Phil turned, grinned at Jane. Soaked, oil-stained, her hair in straggly rattails, and the scar prominent against her cold white skin, she was no Miss World, but she looked very good to him. He took her in his filthy arms, rubbed his bristly face against her cheek, and kissed her on the lips. In that moment of euphoria, she offered no resistance, her breasts soft against his chest. He kissed her again, then shouted in her ear, "Jane, you're wonderful . . . beautiful!"

Instantly she stiffened. Puzzled, he let her go, and they resumed the search. He could not see her face, but he'd have sworn she was crying. What had he said?

Another half-hour and the hunt was over. Almost light-headed with relief, he patted her shoulder, shouting that she should get below, he'd be down soon. She nodded and stumbled into the citadel without looking around.

Briefly, he thought about her. What had he got wrong? Hadn't objected to him kissing her, or being called "wonderful." "Beautiful" was where they came unstuck, literally. Maybe it was that scar; maybe she thought he was kidding her, or trying his luck? He turned and plodded forward, doing another rapid check, searching the boatswain's store, then aft again down the port side to the helo deck, and found nothing.

He was not surprised; those three charges would have been more than enough; all had been in the midships section. AT1 would have been blown open like a gutted fish, breaking its back in the process; the ship's speed would have finished the job. Not given to introspection, Phil gave the possible damage little further thought. They'd defeated the pirates; that was enough.

The immediate danger gone, he realized how cold and wet he was, and went below thinking of nothing but warmth, drink, and a long hot shower and clean clothes.

Luck, good or bad, often comes in patches. For AT1's team, this was a good patch: they'd survived, defeated Colmar and the bombs, the weather was slowly improving, and Langley was fit enough to walk, albeit with help and very slowly, from cabin to saloon.

So the late dinner was a sketchy but moderately cheerful meal. Jane allowed Langley a pint of stout, while she and Phil drank large Scotches. But beneath the veneer of cheerfulness, each had worries. Phil, the longer he was away from the deck, felt less certain about his search, wondering increasingly if he had missed anything. One bomb in a vapor-laden tank, especially in this weather, could spell curtains.

Langley's mind, at last free of drugs, thought long and hard about their dubious future, and at another level, he fretted at his invalid status and his dependence upon the other two.

Jane had a half-dozen things to worry about, but all other cares paled as the stars before the sun compared with one gruesome task which had to be tackled. The Scotches she had had—and seen that Phil had—were not celebration drinks.

Dinner over, Phil said, with a carelessness that didn't fool her, that he'd ''just take a gander up top,'' and left for one more check.

Jane soon shepherded the protesting Langley off to the security of his bunk, then cleared up the saloon, washed the dishes. All excuses gone, she went in search of Phil.

She found him on the afterdeck, still searching.

''Unlikely, but I reckoned I'd better have one more look,'' he confessed. '' 'Course, I'm pretty sure—those three would have been more than enough.'' He pointed to the two hoses that disappeared over the heaving stern. ''Have to get shot of that lot. One of those tangled around the screw wouldn't help much.''

"Is it urgent?"

"Don't suppose so. Been like that for—what?—eighteen, twenty hours. We're still moving. Why?"

"I've got an urgent job," she said quietly.

For a moment he was lost, unable to think what she meant; then he remembered.

"Oh . . . oh, yes." He managed a grin. "All go, isn't it? Okay, let's get it over."

She grabbed his sleeve. "Wait, Phil. First we work out what we do, then do it quickly."

He totally misconstrued her motive, but not the subject, thinking her a lot tougher than he had suspected. They were in the lee of the funnel, free from the worst of the noise and spray; he considered, eyeing the deck, thinking practically. The pirates had removed the stern guardrail for the hoses. He nodded. "That's favorite, I reckon."

"If you say so. We'll need a couple of blankets. . . ."

"No need for you, Jane. I'll do it; you—"

Instantly she flared up, releasing some of her suppressed tension. "Don't be a fool! That body's been in a steel box for four days at seventy-five degrees! It'll take two of us to move it—or do I have to spell it out?"

Phil saw intuitively she had to talk of "it," and recognized the nightmare in which she had lived. "Sorry, Jane. Whatever you think."

"I'll get the blankets, you find some rope." Her tone had softened. Phil was a strange character; superficially a good-natured no-account nonentity, yet he had insight, vision. But for that weird flash of his, Langley would be dead too. "I'll be waiting for you in the saloon."

And he got that one, too. "Don't put any water in mine."

They needed it. For both, an age seemed to pass before they emerged, staggering under their dreadful load, into the fresh air, Jane pale as wax, Phil's face a greenish tinge. In silence they carried the body aft, and wasted no time.

Her responsibilities at an end, Jane appeared to sag, staring at the indifferent, rolling sea. Phil took her arm. "Come on,

Jane. That wasn't Mark; he went when . . ." He shook his head. "Let it go. Forget *that*. Remember Mark the man—a real man."

"He was a man, all right." Jane looked straight at Phil. "Don't get it wrong; Mark meant something to me, yes, but I didn't love him, but he'd got something. I'll remember him."

Phil broke the silence. "Yep. Mark was great. Wish I could be like him."

She cast a valedictory glance at the long wake, vanishing into the murky horizon. Mark had finally gone. For her it had not been love; gratitude was nearer, but if he had lived, if he had meant what he said, and she felt sure he did, with his dominant personality . . . Who could tell? But Mark had gone, and she mourned his passing. She turned to the silent Phil, who, sensitive as ever, had stood back.

"Mark was a man." Not religious, she felt the need for something to be said, and she must say it. "He was fearless." Her voice was loud, steady, fighting the dying storm. "Scared of nothing under God's sun. Yes, a fearless man . . . and gentle." She fought for her composure, turning from the dead to Phil. "He was fearless; you are brave. That's a lot harder."

"Jane . . ." he began uncertainly. She knew the tone and cut him short.

"No, Phil! Do whatever you have to do with the hoses. I must . . . clean up. After that we'll have a drink."

He saw that her smile was overbright, that tears could not be long delayed. "Okay," he said briskly, holding her up mentally, "the washing machine will have to work overtime on my stuff!"

They met an hour later in the still-rolling saloon, both dirty and sweating. Jane smelled strongly of antiseptic; she had been scrubbing.

Phil, once again smeared with oil, poured two large Scotches. For a moment they stood facing each other, swaying to the roll. He raised his glass, guessing her thoughts.

"Here's to Mark—a bloody good shipmate." He hoped she realized that was the highest honor a sailor could pay another.

"Mark . . ." she echoed, her throat tight. They drank, and Phil diplomatically busied himself with the bottle. They took the second drink more steadily.

"You know, Phil, the awful thing is, I can't be certain—already—how he looked." Her voice trailed away.

"Let me tell you something, my dear." Phil was unusually serious. "You think that now, but if you're warm and breathing in forty years' time, and Mark happened to be down the street, fifty yards away, and walking in the opposite direction, you'd know him instantly. That's the memory that matters."

She looked at him strangely, nodding in agreement. "Yes, you're right." Her smile was less forced, the twisted mouth forgotten. "I'm beginning to think you Cornishmen are a bit odd."

At once he was into his broad Cornish. "Ah, my robin! An' let me tell 'ee somthin' else! Youm look at the clark! Reckon weem beaten they pirates and they piratical bombs!"

Phil changed the subject: the less both of them brooded on that problem, the better. "Pity the radio's busted. Might have given us a clue." He examined the wreckage briefly. "Yep. It's proper smashed, that." He finished his drink. "Better stop there, otherwise this'll turn into a right session! It's Mrs. Roscorla's little boy for the shower and another change."

Along with the sweat, oil, and dirty clothes, both sloughed off some of their fear, anger, and sorrow of the past hours. The drink took the edge off their immediate fears, carrying them through the first hour of darkness, which Phil had predicted as most likely for an undiscovered bomb to detonate.

Getting supper ready, Jane took refuge in the comforting normality of her work. She did not want to think of the past or the future, and with AT1 heaving around, she needed her wits about her.

Phil hung around the galley, theoretically helping, but in

fact just as anxious as she was not to think too much. Inside, his nerves still jangled like strings in a broken piano; he needed company and drink.

Only when Langley appeared in the galley did they remember his existence. Jane covered up by saying that she thought it would do him good to sleep, but Bill Langley didn't entirely believe her. He'd been lying on his bunk, wide awake for over an hour, and knew damned well that neither Phil nor she had been near him.

Phil got him into the saloon, fixed him a drink, and brought him up to date with the situation. Langley's irritation grew as he watched the sailor's frequent trips to the bottle, yet felt he could say nothing.

Jane had prepared a good supper, and although she barely ate at all, Bill soon saw that the Scotch she had was by no means her first. He ate stolidly, inwardly angry that Jane had to cut his meat up for him, his resentment growing at the easy chat—Phil made the whole bomb-hunt episode a joke—born of a shared experience in which he had had no part. It wasn't his fault, nor, he admitted to himself, was it theirs.

He had done little but think all day, and he took a certain grim satisfaction, at the end of the meal, in breaking up their dialogue. What he had to say was sobering and disturbing.

XV

The failure to receive AT1's midday position report, while unsettling, was not regarded as alarming. The Communication Center said sunspot activity was kicking hell out of HF communications; it was possible they had missed the tanker's signals, although it struck them as unlikely.

The duty officer, told of the situation by 1210 GMT, was inclined to think the communicators' "unlikely" was no more than the communicators' union closing their ranks, unwilling to admit they had goofed. He rang the shipping super, reporting his view that the radio boys were trying to blind him with science, adding that the last report from AT1, at midnight, had shown the tanker on course, on time, in a force-nine gale.

The shipping superintendent, knowing very well that his bosses knew his views of automated ships and that if he overstated the situation they would think it no more than wishful thinking on his part, stuck to the duty officer's report when informing the managing director.

The managing director, about to leave for an important lunch, rang the chairman, already eating a solitary meal. The chairman immediately rang the duty officer and got it all over again from him, and, unable to think of anything more constructive, ordained that they would wait for the next report time. If nothing was heard, every button in sight was to be pressed, including his. He then returned to his smoked salmon and hock, hardly tasting either.

Not worried, he was not happy. Of course, AT1 was all

right, but he liked to know where his six-million-pound ship with its five-million-pound cargo was. Any malfunction, and the insurers would jack up future premiums, and God knows, they were enough already. . . .

The time was 1225 GMT, July 12.

By way of a preamble, Langley said that his military training had taught him that, in a new situation, the proper course was to make an "appreciation" of that situation. So far as he could, he had done this, but there was information he needed; they could provide it.

Lack of sleep, the fearful tensions of the day, and drink were all affecting Phil; while the words got through, the general drift of Bill's remarks did not. He stared, a little glassily, his mind free-wheeling. No less tired, mentally shot, and tipsy, Jane, with innate female toughness, remained very much more on the ball. She saw Bill was reestablishing himself as the boss; that was fair enough, but she thought he might have shown a little more tact. Her stare was far from glassy.

For instance, went on Langley, had Phil noticed if the navigation lights had been on all day?

Phil was not that far gone: he said he had failed to notice, and that he'd also failed to write up the log or punch his time card.

Aware that he owed his life to the sailor, Bill let that go, but reverted to the lights. "I'll bet you'll find they were. Think, Phil," he said earnestly, "the computer, the radar, all that is obviously u/s, but the engines, the light, everything else isn't affected. Everything's the same—except the computer's no longer in control."

Phil laughed carelessly. "So we're stuck with this course and speed." He sat up, realizing what he was saying. "Jesus Christ! What the hell have I been thinking about?"

"Bombs," said Jane accurately.

"Yeah, bombs. All the same . . ." The effect of this thought upon the sailor was powerful. No longer tired, carefree, or tipsy, Phil got up, found the encyclopedia, and returned to his seat, sweeping the table clear with no regard for the crockery.

"Know anything about navigation, Sarge?"

"Not this sort."

Phil shrugged. "Oh, well, s'pose I'll have to do the best I can. Jane, my lover, can you find a ruler and pencil?" Waiting, he stared gloomily at the map. "There—a bloody great ocean big enough to drown Africa in, all on a page not much bigger'n a bit of bog-paper—and I'm no flaming Captain Cook! Ah, thanks, my robin. Fix me a drink, willya?"

Langley looked as if he might comment, but Jane's cold stare stopped him.

Oblivious, Phil muttered to himself, counting on his fingers, doing small sums in the margin of the map. "It comes to this," he said at last. "I've assumed we've been heading due south ever since we cleared the gulf. Don't think I'm far wrong, either. Secondly, I've assumed we've been doing a good twelve knots—the pilotage office said we'd average twelve-point-something. Twelve knots multiplied by twenty-four hours makes two hundred and eighty-eight nautical miles; add on a bit for the point-something and call it three hundred." He grinned. "Specially as that equals five degrees of longitude. My dear life! It's a bit of luck we're running due south, otherwise I'd be proper buggered!" He glanced again at the map. "By my reckoning, we're somewhere east of Mauritius. Anytime now, we ought to come around to a southwesterly course."

"Ought to," said Langley, "but we bloody won't, will we?"

Phil shook his head.

"So what, then?"

Jane watched their faces anxiously. This was men's talk, for once vital.

"Well, if no one took any interest in us, we'd keep churning until we hit some bastard thing—like Antarctic!" Phil tossed his pencil on the table. "But that's a daft idea. The RAF will be screeching around the ocean already; no report went out at midday—that's four-thirty our time." He consulted his watch. "They've had five hours; the RAF will be on the job right now."

He was wrong.

Fortunately for their peace of mind, none of them suspected the truth. Certainly Jane and Langley were comforted by Phil's quiet confidence in the Royal Air Force, but the pessimistic Langley had another point: out of control, AT1 was a deadly menace to herself and other ships; they would have to keep constant watch.

"What ships?" said Phil belligerently. "And what do we do about it—jump up and down? Colmar was a thorough bastard; he even ditched the distress rockets!"

Langley muttered.

"Look, Sarge—I don't suppose there's another ship within three, four hundred bloody miles! I've *told* you; we're way off any route to anywhere. I mean, you look at the map yourself, use your loaf. And every minute we get farther away. This ocean is a bloody great expanse of nothing!"

Jane intervened before Langley could think of something to say. "Neither of you is working tonight, anyway. Phil's right; there's nothing we can do. We all need sleep—even you, Bill; AT1's just got to look after herself for the night."

The duty officer's room was unusually crowded by midnight. The shipping superintendent was there, trying unsuccessfully to look as if he just happened to be passing; the managing director, grand in full dinner dress, paced up and down the room, trailing blue clouds of cigar smoke, and making no secret of his edginess.

The duty officer just sat; this could be his chance to show the top brass his executive ability. He had done all his thinking in the past three hours. The communication boys had been on top line ever since midday, and secret instructions had gone to all the company's ships to keep a special watch for a distress call at any time, and for this next vital routine period in particular. Working on the assumption that the worst had happened, he had his signal already prepared: one word to the Communication Center and it would be on the telex to the Ministry of Defense, backup for the telephone call he would make.

None of the men spoke, each busy with his private thoughts. The one thing they had in common was the clock. The second hand swept up to midnight, precisely, and the duty officer's heart beat faster. He'd told the T/P room to call the moment they heard the tuning transmission, due five minutes before the hour. As far as he was concerned, that was *it*: he had no doubt at all that AT1 was in trouble, but he held back. A few minutes wouldn't make any difference, and if AT1's timing had gone slightly off, he could look a real Charlie.

At five minutes past the hour the phone rang. The managing director froze instantly, glaring at the duty officer. The super remained staring impassively at AT1's red flag on the wall chart.

Listening, the duty officer was careful not to look at either of his superiors. "Understood. Yes. . . . Keep checking. Report back again in ten minutes." He addressed himself to the super's broad back. "Nothing heard." Already he was lifting a second phone. "Communications supervisor? Open the envelope marked AT1 and send the signal in it at once. Report time cleared." He returned to his first phone: "Ministry of Defense—extension 6116."

"Hell and damnation!" said the managing director, and hurried out.

The super took out his pipe and filled it slowly, resisting a terrible desire to race after the managing director, shouting, "I bloody told you so!" He stared at the duty officer; doing his stuff all right, but he'd been watching too many old war movies. . . . Pity that split-arse accountant wasn't around. . . .

0020 GMT, July 13. In the Joint Services Plot, Ministry of Defense, the duty RN and RAF officers studied the company's call for help with professional detachment. The Navy man turned his attention to the vast wall chart of the world, twenty feet high, tended by a Wren on a track-mounted ladder.

"Liz, special-situation marker in position twenty-twelve South, sixty-zero-two East at 0005 Zulu, twelfth—yes, I mean twelfth—July. Course one-eight-one. Got it?"

The Wren repeated his instructions, and another esoteric symbol was added to the chart, but unlike some, the red shape had a great deal of space to itself.

"Looks like a job for your intrepid birdmen, Jock. We've nothing handy. A Nimrod from Gan should soon find it. Bet the bloody thing's only blown a fuse!"

The RAF officer frowned. "Very likely, but Nimrods don't grow on trees. Nearest one's in Cyprus." He tapped his teeth with a pencil, thinking. "I'll ask the South Africans to help."

"The Springboks? They've only got Shackletons; there's some pretty big distances involved."

"They won't have much time on task," admitted Jock, "but with luck, it should be a straightforward trip, no swanning around. We know the intended track to the nearest inch; all they'll have to do is to fly up that track till they find it. Piece of cake." He reached for a message form. "But just in case, I think I'll get that Nimrod moving."

At 0320 GMT a SAAF Shackleton rumbled into a murky sky, its crew somewhat less than delighted. Met said they could expect eight-tenths cloud down to two thousand feet all the way, a nasty crosswind, and plenty of rain squalls. They got it, enduring a long, bumpy ride, dipping down through the overcast to check all likely radar contacts. After five and a half hours of boring discomfort they reached the last known position, and had found nothing. The plane descended to five hundred feet, flogging around for an hour on visual search, working steadily along the tanker's intended track, flying low to the farthest point the ship could possibly have reached. They saw nothing on radar or visually, and heard nothing on the HF and VHF frequencies.

Maritime Headquarters, Silvermine, concluded that the Shackleton had either missed AT1 (possible) or the ship had sunk (improbable) or AT1 was not on its proper course, 195 degrees (probable). With memories of the *Torrey Canyon*,

MHQ did not care for that last solution. If AT1 *was* off course, it could be heading straight for the African coast and a far greater environmental disaster than *Torrey Canyon*. MHQ ordered the weary Shackleton to spend the rest of the mission checking to the west of the track, the danger zone from their point of view.

But AT1 had not altered course from 181 to 195 degrees. At one point in the flight, the SAAF aircraft had been within two hundred and twenty miles of the tanker, but had been too low to pick it up on radar.

The Shackleton's final negative report really alarmed the South Africans, and soon after, London. As night closed in, the SAAF issued a navigational warning: all ships and aircraft were requested to report any trace of AT1.

It was this warning which alerted the world's press; sensing "drama on the high seas," they jumped at it. ZOMBIE LOOSE IN INDIAN OCEAN and WHERE IS THE ZOMBIE? were much-used headlines. The company's public-relations branch were driven nearly mad, sandwiched between a plague of reporters and a tight-lipped, angry managing director. Only the shipping superintendent extracted any pleasure from the situation. Studiously silent, he took great pleasure in nodding politely to the chief accountant whenever they chanced to meet.

The South African Air Force and the Ministry of Defense, London, conferred, both now very anxious to find AT1, if for different reasons. London said a Nimrod had been staged from Cyprus to Gan and would be in the search area by dawn the next day, July 14. The SAAF said, in that case, they would put up two Shackletons at first light, concentrating on all possible approaches to the eastern seaboard of South Africa, west of 42 degrees east.

MOD, London agreed, confident that the much more sophisticated Nimrod would succeed where the older Shackleton had failed. Tactfully, they did not mention their intention to repeat the SAAF search from the beginning.

July 14. AT1's team woke, all feeling much better for a good night's sleep. Phil was up first, his last lingering doubts about another bomb dispelled. He went up to the citadel, glanced cheerfully at the sea, noted with pleasure a break in the clouds, and returned, waking Bill and Jane with a cup of tea, a big smile, and the news that the weather was getting better and better all the time. Breakfast over, Jane had them both in the sick bay, dressing Phil's head wound first, for he was impatient to be on deck. This would be the day, if not of rescue, of their location.

On Langley's orders he daubed HELP in green deck paint on both sides of the funnel. It didn't strike him as particularly useful work, but fretting over what he regarded as his failure in the past few days, Langley was mighty touchy. If it made him happier, why not?

While he worked, Phil kept an alert eye on the sea and sky. A slight westerly swell was all that remained of the storm, but the brassy tropical sky did not return, replaced by a thickening, dismal blanket of low cloud. Not ideal search weather, he thought, but a Nimrod's sensitive radar just couldn't miss a thing the size of AT1. The thought of the RAF's difficulties did nothing to dampen his spirits: things were looking up; his head hurt, but that was mainly due to Jane redressing it. And when he remembered how they had been fixed the day before . . .

How on earth had he found the nerve to fool with the bombs? Simple, he told himself, no bloody option. Bit of luck he'd known something of explosives. Daren't let on to Jane just how little that something was: one afternoon helping prepare wreck-demolition charges, plus his basic gunnery course.

Langley, pale and grim-faced, came on deck, his first visit in five days. Watching Phil humming happily to himself, he wished he could feel half as confident. He moved away, not wanting to talk, and inspected the smashed hose lockers, the undefended helo pad, the oil-stained afterdeck, and the wrecked life rafts.

What a shambles! He'd done everything according to the book—and this was where it got him. Should have seen Colmar was bad news, right from the start.

"Cheer up, Sarge—the RAF'll be along anytime now!"

Langley repressed a wave of irritation. "And just supposing you're right, what can they *do*?"

"Well, I dunno. Up to them, like. Anyway, it'd be a start. One quick gander at us, and they'll see we're light in the water, and it won't take a great brain to guess what's happened." He pondered on the question. "Here, I've got it, Sarge! You seen those inflatable hovercraft?"

Langley shook his head.

"Yes—that's it!" went on Phil with great enthusiasm. "There's these hovercraft, see, built for rescue work. Inflates when it hits the drink. Gotta small engine with a fan to push it, and to provide lift. Put one of those down, well ahead of us, drop a couple of blokes alongside, they get in, start up, cruise alongside us, we take 'em aboard—and there you are!"

Langley was not overimpressed, and secretly, neither was the sailor; he could see all too many snags. For a start, what was the chance of the aircraft having an inflatable hovercraft aboard? And the blokes who dropped would have to be full-time heroes.

Langley said curtly they'd keep watch throughout daylight hours, and walked slowly back to the citadel. It didn't strike him as all that warm on deck.

That observation started a very uncomfortable train of thought and sent him in search of the atlas.

If Roscorla's figuring was right, they were well over twelve hundred miles south of the equator, heading straight for the Antarctic, and the southern hemisphere's winter.

The Nimrod flew eleven hundred miles south from Gan, arriving punctually at dawn, over AT1's last known position. Their flight plan called for a meticulous search along AT1's intended track, and fifty miles each side of it, out to the "farthest on" position, then a low-level sweep back, if nothing was found, looking for something the aircraft's radar would not show, an oil slick.

In not very favorable weather, the outward leg was flown

with no result, and Gan informed. The low-level search began.

Neither RAF Gan nor MOD London viewed the aircraft's report with excessive disquiet. One or two officers with long memories started talking about the tanker *Ennerdale*, which had struck an uncharted pinnacle or rock in the Indian Ocean in June 1970 and sunk. The odds against a tanker finding yet another deadly needle in the same vast haystack seemed astronomically remote, but as time passed, the theory gained increasing support. Approaching the original start position, the Nimrod reported nothing had been seen. With uncharted rocks in mind, MOD considered the most likely answer was that AT1 had gone off track after its midnight report on the twelfth, and between then and midday had hit something, or at very least, suffered enough damage to put all radio out of action.

Acting on this assumption, the Nimrod was ordered to do a circular search from the last known position, out to a radius of two hundred miles, investigating anything, including wreckage, and to go on doing it to the aircraft's prudent limit of endurance.

After twenty-two hours airborne, and with nothing to report, the Nimrod landed at Gan. The SAAF Shackletons had also had a fruitless day, but even these negative reports had value. The "rock-pinnacle" theory could be discarded. MHQ, Silvermine, and MOD, London, agreed: AT1 had to be afloat somewhere. Something had happened after 0005, July 12 to send AT1 wildly off-course. The company's experts had nothing useful to offer, reluctantly agreeing that if the computer had gone haywire, the ship could be heading in any direction.

At once a navigational warning fo the entire Indian Ocean was issued, and the press reached new heights of frenzy, rehashing the stories of the *Marie Celeste*, the *Waratah*, and the *Flying Dutchman*.

And all the time, AT1 steamed steadily south. The Nimrod had got within four hundred miles of her at one point. By midnight July 14-15, the tanker was 600 miles off-course, nearly 900 from its last reported position, and 2,100 miles from Gan.

Fresh air-plans were made. After essential servicing, the Nimrod would conduct a circular search out to the PLE. The SAAF, recognizing the heat was off most of their coastline, would shift, covering the area south of the Cape of Good Hope.

XVI

July 15. Still confident, but less inclined to say so, Phil was on watch in the citadel at first light. An hour later, after breakfast, Langley relieved Phil while he ate, and when the sailor returned, did not seem disposed to go below. Not for the first time they went over the hijacking, and Phil suddenly remembered the cutting gear left on the wheelhouse roof.

Langley showed little interest. "What did the bastards want that for?" he said morosely.

"I haven't got around to looking closely, but it's a bloody long cutting lance. They must have known there was a protective grille of some sort inside the exhaust-vent trunking, and used it to burn a hole through, so they could lower the bomb down into the computer room."

"Cunning sods!" commented Langley. After a pause, he went on in a very different tone, "Here—d'you know anything about that sort of gear?"

"Me? No, but the computer's bitched—"

"Bugger the computer," said Langley warmly. "I'm interested in the cutting gear. What's to stop us using it to cut a hole in the deck? If we're lucky, we might be able to get at the steering, maybe the engines!"

"Yes?" Phil was less than enthusiastic.

"Yes! At least we might be able to stop this bastard!"

"We'd look bloody silly if we stick a white-hot torch into an empty fuel tank," objected Phil.

"There can't be fuel tanks on the other side of our cabins!"

"No-o, but—"

"No bloody buts! I'm no sailor, but it stands to reason if your parachutists leap out of the sky, they'd stand a better chance if this contrivance is going dead slow—right?"

Reluctantly, Phil nodded.

"Right! You get the gear off the wheelhouse roof and down on deck; I'm going to have a look at the encyclopedia. Must be something about blowtorches."

Searching for a rope, Phil saw that the idea had its good points. Burning holes through bulkheads when you hadn't the faintest idea what lay on the other side did not appeal to him, nor did Langley's scheme for getting at the steering, but reducing speed was another matter, for a private worry of his was what would happen if they hit really bad weather. At least three-quarters empty, AT1 was in no shape to buck through a force-ten-plus at twelve knots. In his Navy days, he had seen what really bad weather could do to a frigate at speed; splits in bulkheads, upper-deck gear ripped out and tossed over the side, boats smashed—and frigates were ten times stronger than AT1. In his opinion, the tanker would buckle in the middle and break in half, or fold up like sodden cardboard—or both.

By the time he had it all down on deck, Bill was back. "It's just a matter of getting the mixture right." Confidently he examined the gear. "Connect that lead to the big bastard. Here—why d'you suppose they disconnected it?"

"Perhaps there's a deposit on the bottle, Sarge." After a quick look at Langley's expression, he added quickly, "Probably meant to ship the lot back to the second tanker, but the weather bitched it."

He dragged the gear around to the lee side of the funnel, and for half an hour experimented with it, as directed by Langley, finally achieving a realistic-looking flame. They tried it on a battered hose locker, and managed to burn a hole through it.

Inwardly, Langley was very excited, but kept himself in check. "Okay, turn it off. If your bloody RAF doesn't show by four o'clock, we'll have a go."

"*My* bloody RAF?"

Langley grinned, for the first time in days, better-tempered now that he had a plan and was in a position to exercise his authority once more.

Nothing had happened by four o'clock to break the unending monotony of empty sea and sky, and Langley had Phil lug the cutting gear down to the cabin passage. Jane was posted to watch in the citadel.

Phil, although very dubious about the enterprise, couldn't argue; deeply disappointed and depressed by the failure of the RAF to show, he got on with the preparations, Langley fussing, certain that if he only had two good hands, he could make a better job than the sailor.

He pointed at the bulkhead at the end of the cabin passage. "We'll try there."

"Suppose we cut an electric cable and start a fire?"

"Aw, wrap up!" Langley relented. "Okay, get an extinguisher, if it worries you that much."

Wearing sunglasses, they tried. Scorched-paint fumes soon had them coughing. Phil made a shaky vertical cut six inches long and crossed it with another horizontal cut, then bashed the center of the cross with a hammer, bending back some of the metal. He peered in, shining a hand lamp as best he could, Langley, in a fever of impatience, holding the roaring lance.

"Can't see a damn thing."

"Here, let me!" Langley thrust the lance into the sailor's hand. "Hold that bloody torch steady." Equally baffled, he straightened up. "There's no oil, anyway. Come on, get cracking!"

A few minutes later, the flame changed color. "You touched the taps, Sarge?"

" 'Course I haven't!"

"Give 'em a twiddle, then. The mixture's gone wrong." Ten minutes of cursing passed before they discovered the cause; one cylinder was empty.

"Fuck it!" shouted Langley. "Of all the lousy, rotten luck!" He stamped off to the saloon. Phil dismantled the equipment, not sure if he was glad or sorry they had failed, and went after Langley.

138

He found him struggling with a can of beer. "Yes, I know—breaking my own bloody bar rules! Open this, will you?" He tossed the can to Phil. "This bloody arm of mine!"

Phil opened two cans, and they drank in gloomy silence. The sailor had nothing to say, and the soldier was too full for words.

"Sod it!" exploded Langley. "Aw, let it go . . . let's have another."

Phil recognized that the blowtorch episode was officially forgotten, and felt it safe to get back to another subject. "I'd better relieve Jane if we're to get any supper."

"Hang on a moment, Phil." Out of character, Langley was pleading. "We've *got* to think of something, can't just sit on our arses! Haven't you any bright ideas?"

Phil shook his head. "Don't think I haven't tried, Sarge. I still think—"

"Yeah, I know. . . . I tell you straight, I don't go much on our chances. I had a look at the map; if your figuring's right, we must be somewhere off the Cape of Good Hope. Good Hope—that's a flaming laugh! The RAF'll be skating up and down, looking where we ought to be, while we're hundreds of miles away and still going!"

"Give 'em time, Sarge. The RAF's not a bunch of Charlies. I've worked a lot with Maritime Air, and they're bloody good, but you've got to give them a chance. They've got a hell of a lot of ocean to cover. They need time."

"You go on about time," said Langley irritably, "but how much have we got? I dunno if it's my imagination, but it struck me as a bit parky on deck."

"My prickly heat's got better." Phil grinned, changing the subject. "We'd better ditch these cans. Jane'll do her nut if she finds we've been sipping ale while she minds the shop."

Once again, the air search produced nothing, except in a negative sense. The shore authorities were now certain AT1 was not in the sector from the northern tip of Madagascar down to the cape. Time had run out in this area; AT1 would have hit the coast somewhere, and a hundred-thousand-ton object, moving at fifteen miles an hour, had to leave some trace. One hundred and twenty degrees of the circle centered on the last known position were now eliminated.

This assessment brought little comfort to the company or the insurers, reducing the company's public-relations officer to the ultimate admission of defeat in his trade: "No comment."

MOD's interest in AT1 had escalated fast, particularly in the Royal Air Force section; now they were only too aware that the world's press was breathing down their neck. What had started as no more than a welcome break from routine had become a major challenge.

During the day, a second Nimrod was hastily staged out from the U.K. to Gan. At dawn, the SAAF would have two Shackletons searching south and west of the cape, and the two Nimrods would split the remaining 240 degrees between them. AT1 had to be found, and very soon.

But in the SAAF MHQ at Silvermine, Cape Province, they had one worry. If the met forecast was right, airfield visibility could be bad: the Shackletons might not get off the deck.

July 16. Langley was up well before dawn, breaking another of his personal rules—smoking before breakfast. In the last hour of darkness, he had finished writing up the log as best he could, back to the traumatic moment when Colmar . . .

He shook his head, as if to rid himself of the memory.

This was a hell of a mess . . . and every hour the chances of survival got less. Perhaps it was all for the best: even if he got out of this, they'd never employ him again, even if his shoulder did mend properly, even if he could stand the sight of a ship again. And he'd never be able to pay off the debts that bitch had run up. God! Life was a strange caper: a week ago his chief problem had been how to keep his hands off Jane; now he couldn't care less.

In a descending spiral, his thoughts plunged lower and lower. No seaman, he took little notice of the dark clouds banking up on the southern horizon, or the rising swell. His thoughts struck bottom; he even extracted a certain twisted satisfaction from the totality of his personal disaster.

Hopeless. Another forty-eight hours, and even Phil would lose his maddening bloody optimism. This contrivance would career on until it hit the Antarctic continent: Phil had said that himself, one of his weak jokes that would come true. Already it was chilly; sunrise was later, and sunset earlier. Not even a bloody boat, a raft, or anything to make a raft with. Wouldn't be much use, even if they could make a raft. . . . Rafts . . .

The word started another, practical train of thought: back in his basic training, before his first trip in a crewed tanker, there had been a brief mention of life rafts. Langley hadn't paid much attention, but he dimly remembered some chat about survival equipment; the bloke had mentioned distress beacons.

Immediately his somber thoughts vanished, swept away by the prospect of action. He snatched the phone off its hook, his hand trembling with excitement. Jane and Phil were to come up to the citadel at the double.

They arrived in less than a minute, but Langley still glared impatiently. "There you are! Get out and search the life rafts for a survival pack; there may be a radio. Get cracking!"

They started on the port raft, shivering in the cold morning air. Phil concentrated on clearing away the shattered container, less enthusiastic than Langley, because he hadn't thought of it. Heaving one piece over the side, he noticed the sea and sky and paused to take a longer look, incurring Langley's anger.

"Get on!"

Phil jerked his head to the south. "Don't go much on that lot, Sarge. We're in for another drop of roughers." Impatient sergeants were as nothing compared to the power of the sea.

"Sooner we finish, the better, then!"

Jane, on her hands and knees, stopped groping in the mass of orange fabric, proffering a broken black plastic box the size of a brick. "What's this, Bill?"

Langley took it in his good hand; triumph and disappointment mingled in his voice. "Yeah; that's it—and look at it! Of all the lousy luck, the bastards have to hit it! Phil—the other raft."

Impatiently Langley ran, the sailor following, leaving Jane still ferreting in the remains of the port raft. A sudden squall sent hail rattling and bouncing around them. Langley hardly noticed it.

Phil dug into the mess with renewed energy, half-hidden in the tangle of rope and fabric. He backed out, holding an identical box. "How about that?" It appeared to be intact.

To Langley it was all the treasure of the Incas. "Great!" he said with reverential softness. Jane came running, hailstones stuck in her hair; she had a half-dozen distress flares. "Good girl! See if you can find some more in this one."

In the relative warmth of the citadel, Langley gloated over their finds; Phil had caught some of his enthusiasm. Cursing his own incapacity, Langley let Phil examine the device.

In three languages, a metal plate stated: "Distress beacon—121.5 mhz. To operate, extend aerial and put switch to ON."

"Can't say fairer than that," commented Phil. He carefully drew out part of the telescopic aerial. "A bullet's chewed a bit off the aerial, Sarge. Reckon we'll need to fix a splint on it."

"Surgical tape and pencils!" snapped Langley.

"Um. That would do."

"I've got some knitting needles," volunteered Jane. "Would they be any good?"

"Yes, be fine," said Phil.

"Yes, a good idea!" Langley spoke with surprising warmth.

Encouraged, Jane asked what made it work. To her it looked far too small to be any good.

"Oh, miniature batteries. Sort of things you get in posh watches or hearing aids—mercury whatsits," volunteered Phil, guessing wildly.

"That's a thought," cut in Langley. "Have a look in the other one. Perhaps the batteries are okay."

Phil removed four chrome-steel pellets from the broken set and passed them to Langley.

The senior guard contemplated them in the palm of his hand. "If only we knew how long they last." He wished he'd paid more attention in his training days.

"I think they said at least twenty-four hours. Much less would be as useless as a spare prick at a wedding." Too late Phil glanced apprehensively at Jane, but she was far too absorbed in this slender hope of survival to notice his lapse into navalese.

"So we should have power for forty-eight hours." Langley was really talking to himself. "Forty-eight hours, and it's VHF, so it's line-of-sight reception."

Phil nodded in agreement. Servicemen knew about VHF. "We used to reckon on a surface range of eight to ten miles for a boat set."

"An aircraft would do a hell of a lot better than that. Your RAF plane at ten thousand feet would pick up the signal at a hundred miles, easy."

"Except he won't be that high, Sarge. Nearer three thousand, or less, for a search. Fifty to sixty would be more like it." He brightened up. "Tell you what: we could bump the range up by shoving the beacon on the radar gantry."

"Bloody good idea! We'll do that. We'll run it in daylight hours only." After the incident with the blowtorch, Langley didn't intend wasting any energy. "You get cracking, Phil, dish the aerial up, and let's get it going."

Down in the saloon, Phil said to Jane, "A wee dram before we start, hey?" Without waiting for an answer, he poured two Scotches.

"Phil, d'you think this beacon will help?"

He shrugged. "It won't do any harm, that's for sure, and it'll keep Bill happy. Personally, I think the RAF will find us, beacon or no beacon."

"D'you think that, or feel it?"

Phil's puzzlement gave way to faint amusement. "Oh, you mean the old Celtic stuff! No. I've got both feet firmly planted on the deck: the fly-boys know their stuff, and the Nimrod's a bloody good plane."

"Oh." Jane was disappointed, preferring his "feelings" to his thoughts.

Phil laughed at her expression. "Aw, come on, my lover! Don't worry, your old Phil will look after you!" He slipped an arm around her.

AT1 rolled slightly more than she had done since the storm; the atlas slipped off the polished table.

"He-oops—here we go again!"

Skillfully Jane disentangled herself. "I'll get the needles and tape."

An hour later Phil returned from the gantry, flapping his arms and stamping his feet. "Fixed and working, Sarge. If it's all the same to you, I'd like to switch it off before it gets really dark. It's no picnic up there right now, and it'll be blowing a bastard by nightfall."

"If it's that bad, do it when you think fit. And don't just switch it off, bring it down. Not going to risk that going overboard."

"And that goes for me, too!"

Throughout the day, tension slowly mounted. For the first hour or so that the beacon was working, Langley stared expectantly at the cloud-banked sky, but when nothing materialized, he sank back into his old silent gloom, answering questions in monosyllables. After dinner, Jane saw him in the cabin passage, staring at the cross-cut in the bulkhead, as if toying with the idea of tackling the hole with his one good hand.

She felt increasingly in tune with Bill. If not frightened, he was clearly deeply worried, which summed up her feelings, too. Phil's easy "don't-let-it-get-you-down" attitude was harder and harder to take.

In fact, Phil felt far less happy than he admitted; standing his watch in the wheelhouse, he thought of little except the search aircraft and constantly scanned the lowering sky. He knew very well that the cloud conditions, the frequent rain or hail squalls, and the decreasing visibility ruled out any hope of a visual contact, but the knowledge did not stop him trying. Finally, he could no longer kid himself; it *was* getting colder. That was chilling, mentally and physically.

He recovered the beacon as the last feeble light of day failed. Even the simplest task up on the gantry was hard and dangerous. The wind had, he estimated, increased to a force-eight southwesterly gale, and was still rising. AT1, lightened by the loss of so much of its cargo, rolled and pitched in a much quicker tempo. One false step on the gantry and he could be hurled off into the sea or down to the steel deck, forty feet below. He stowed the beacon carefully in the empty armory, and went below, shivering, making straight for the Scotch.

Untying the soaking towel he had worn as a scarf, he grinned at Jane. "Don't have to bother about my prickly heat anymore, Jane." He clutched at the back of the sofa as the ship lurched. "That's a big 'un—and plenty more where that came from!"

"Oh, shut up, Phil!" She stuffed her knitting down the side of her chair and staggered out of the saloon.

"What's got into Jane?"

Langley stared disapprovingly at the size of the sailor's drink. "Maybe she finds your cheerfulness hard to take."

Phil looked at him in blank surprise, aware that Langley had not expressed his opinion, but was clearly of a like mind. He laughed shortly. "Well, get that! If that's all, I can soon add my bit to the general gloom." His voice hardened. "F'rinstance, seeing as I'm not the blue-eyed boy, maybe you'd ask her."

"Ask what?"

"To grab a spare blanket and do a rapid conversion job, like cut a hole for my bleeding fat head, make a poncho, like. I bloody near froze on that gantry." He poured another drink, half-hoping Langley would comment. Getting no answer, Phil zigzagged across the saloon, picked up the atlas from the deck, wedged himself professionally in an armchair, and concentrated.

Outwardly, Langley remained impassive, indifferent, smoking another nonroutine cigarette, staring at nothing. Jane banged about in the galley, annoyed with herself for being annoyed with Phil, but in her tense state, unable to do anything about it.

Finally Phil dropped the atlas back on the deck and stood up, balancing effortlessly, grinning at his drink.

"And what does that mean?" Langley wanted to know, although he hated asking.

"Mean, Sarge? Nothing cheerful, if that's worrying you. If I'm right, and if you've ever wondered what the Roaring Forties were like, now's your bleedin' chance!" He gulped the rest of his drink.

The ship hesitated, trembling, the after end whipped uncomfortably. "Feel that?" said Phil unnecessarily, his grin strained. "Stuck her nose in a bigger one—and there's more coming! The old windjammers used to get in this stream and belt around the world! We have to be bloody different. We have to go the wrong way—and we're going too bloody fast!"

XVII

In the Combined Plot, Ministry of Defense, London, the staff were trying to make bricks with very little straw. They, and the company, were puzzled by the tanker's silence on the International Distress Frequency: 2182khz is by no means first-class for long-distance work, but a range of a thousand miles at night is not unreasonable. All search aircraft had listened to this frequency, and shore stations bordering the Indian Ocean had given it special attention since the alarm had been raised, backed up by ships in the area. The company disclosed that AT1's radio set was sited in the citadel, well away from the computer, so that not all eggs were in the same basket. Some sort of disaster must have happened, bad enough for both radios in computer and citadel to fall silent. Were the guards all dead? Both sets out of action? Worst of all, had AT1 sunk? Each question only raised a dozen others.

The two Nimrods got nothing except the virtual certainty that further vast tracts of ocean could be ruled out. The plane operating in the southern sector of the search area might have established contact despite the bad weather, but in the middle of its task, a civil airliner reported an oil slick southeast of Mauritius, and Gan diverted the plane to investigate. The aircraft backtracked eight hundred miles, and found a very small patch of oil and no wreckage. The pilot decided it had nothing to do with AT1 and went back to his search, but even a Nimrod cannot burn up an extra sixteen hundred miles without noticing it; the plane was forced to return to base, its search pattern incomplete.

Farther south, it was a frustrating day; the met forecast proved all too accurate, and the SAAF Shackletons were unable to fly.

The emotions in London ranged from deep pessimism in the company's headquarters to black depression among the insurers. The RAF, if not worried, was getting close to it. Through the foreign secretary, the minister of defense asked the U.S. and U.S.S.R. if they, by any chance, had a satellite which might have observed the southern half of the Indian Ocean. The United States answered smartly: sorry, not a chance; nine-tenths of the area was currently shrouded in cloud. The Russian embassy said the request would be passed to the appropriate authorities.

Elsewhere, the pirates, slightly puzzled that no trace of their victim had been found, listened to the newscasts with increasing hilarity. Fifteen million U.S. dollars were in the bag, and the way events were shaping, they'd be able to pull the same trick again.

The fat German laughed along with the rest, comforting his conscience with thoughts of his share. In his Alpine retreat, the man who conceived and controlled the operation smiled in cautious satisfaction. The hard-drug trade wasn't what it had been, but the worldwide network of dummy companies, export-import agencies, had been ready-made for disposal of the oil haul. Another week, and the evidence would be beyond trace, the fuel discharged, the ships on their way to the scrapyard—and at a good price, too. He gave his mind to the severe splendors of Johann Sebastian Bach. Neither he, nor the German, nor anyone else gave a moment's thought to Colmar.

By suppertime the acrobatics of AT1 were sufficient to spoil Langley's invalid appetite, and reduced Jane to pushing the food around her plate. Phil made no comment, determined after Langley's remark to say nothing. In spite of his increasing worries, he could still spare time to feel hurt at Jane's attitude, and, naturally, blamed her. He gave added offense to both by eating heartily; they watched, unfairly, almost hating him.

148

He had more on his mind than queasy stomachs. Of a seafaring breed, trained in wild northern seas, he realized what they did not—that if the weather got much worse, AT1 would be in real trouble. What had vaguely bothered him as a possibility was rapidly becoming concrete reality.

Roscorla knew the tanker was going suicidally fast. What oil the pirates had left was in the forward tanks; he knew that by the sluggish motion of the bows. In essence, AT1 was a hollow tube with a weight at each end; oil forward, engines aft. In that condition, eight knots would be comfortable, ten just acceptable if the owners were in a hurry and were prepared to pay for upper-deck damage, but twelve-plus . . .

The tragedy of humanity was summed up in that lurching, heaving saloon: lack of communication. Phil ate cheerfully to show he wasn't worried; Jane and Bill watched in hostile silence, not understanding.

Blindly, AT1 plunged on into night like an untamed horse feeling the bridle for the first time. Uncontrolled engines, obedient to the computer's last command, produced power for 12.15 knots, the locked rudder directing the ship ever deeper into the Roaring Forties.

The cheerless meal over, Jane clawed her way in silence to the galley. Phil waited hopefully, but she did not return, going straight to her cabin. Another half-hour of brooding silence, and Langley left, annoyed with himself that he now lacked the moral courage to lock the bar, well aware that Phil knew it too.

Alone, the sailor shrugged, taking no pleasure in his moral victory. He poured himself a final tot, drinking it slowly, swaying with the motion of the ship in the middle of the bright-lit, empty saloon, staring vacantly at a picture, a reproduction of a Spurling clipper ship, all sail-set, bowling along on deep-blue sea in bright sunlight.

Concentrating on the motion of the tanker, it was some time before Phil was aware of the picture, and when he finally had it in focus, he scowled.

Look at it; all bloody lovely. Bet it wasn't so bloody lovely to be in. That bastard was no cruise liner, full of overfed sods, middle-aged women grabbing their last romance. All the same, I'd sooner be in her than this elongated bathtub. Christ! Feel the way the stern waggled, like a bitch in heat. If only there was some way of slowing down.

He had a final tot to make him sleep. It did him little good; for two or three hours he lay awake, listening to the working of the ship. New sounds, strange creakings and shudderings, told him the hull was fighting dangerous stresses; now they were relying on the designer's factor of safety. Less dangerous, but very ominous, the sullen boom of the near-empty hull, as successive, tireless rollers crashed and broke against it, sounded like the knell of doom. At last he slept, exhausted, but needed no alarm clock to wake him at dawn; one particularly violent leap catapulted him into full wakefulness. He was glad to struggle up to the citadel, away from the endless echoing hollow booming, the fearful whipping of the stern.

That first bleak light revealed an uninviting scene. Long, gray-green spray-veined mountain ranges of water, forty, fifty feet high, came blindly on from the southwest, smashing with malignant, mindless fury against the shivering hull; the blunt bows rose and fell sluggishly in the familiar circular motion, each crashing descent the herald of a cloud of spray that tore aft, to be lost down the screaming wind.

Shivering with cold, he clung on, unsure which was worse, to be below and listen, or to be up top and watch. He zipped his breaker, wrapped a towel tightly around his neck. Rigging the beacon would be a chancy business, but now he was as keen as Langley to have it working; time was running out; no hope, however faint, could be ignored.

In average conditions the job would have taken little more than five minutes; it took twice that to fight his way up to the gantry, where the wind, tearing and howling in the radar aerials, was deafening. He finally dropped back on deck forty-five minutes later, soaked and exhausted. Langley greeted him in the citadel.

"Fixed it?" The sailor's condition meant nothing.

Phil nodded, not minding Langley's attitude, aware that, but for his arm, he would be prepared to go aloft himself. "Yep. Should be okay."

"Should be? *Should* be!" Bill was very much the

sergeant. "You ought to be bloody certain!"

Phil recognized that Langley's temper stemmed from strain and sleeplessness, but he had his own worries.

"Sarge, I'm the flaming sailor around here! We're dealing with the sea, not a bloody parade ground. Nothing's certain! I've done the best I can, and if you're not—"

"Okay, okay," replied Langley wearily. "Sure you've done your best. Sorry, Phil. All this is getting on my tits."

The sailor mopped his face, hanging on with one hand. He grinned. "That has to be today's understatement."

Langley managed a grudging and very faint grin. "You better dry out and eat."

Phil nodded, glancing at the sea. "Funny thing, doesn't seem so bad in daylight, but Christ, it's bad enough." He staggered toward the companionway. "What's for breakfast?"

Langley's frail goodwill shattered. "I didn't bother."

Jane hadn't bothered either, but had cooked for the men. Phil's popularity sank to a new level when he ate sausages, bacon, and eggs—including Langley's. Afterward he helped with the perilous task of the dishes.

He detected it first. "Big 'un—hold on!" He grabbed a pipe with both hands, Jane gripped the faucets. Both swung sideways with the sharp deceleration, the deck thrust upward under their feet, whipping crazily. Phil lost his footing; only his hold on the pipe saved him from being flung across the galley. Plates jumped from the rack, smashing on the draining board and deck; a cupboard burst open; cans rolled and bounced around, and the dishwater leaped out of the sink, drenching Jane.

"God, how much longer! This can't go on!"

Phil got his balance back as the motion eased, and tried to comfort her. "Think nothing of it; we just hit a patch of cobblestones!" He looked at the mess, then at Jane. "Stick it out. Won't be long now."

"For God's sake, don't go on about that plane coming! Even if it did, what could it do?" Her red-rimmed eyes were near tears. "There's no plane coming."

"Oh, yes, it'll come, don't you fret!" He put an arm

around her, still holding on with the other. "Crikey! You're soaked! You go and get cleaned up—I'll sort this lot out."

But Jane stayed; together they restored order. As they finished, AT1 hit another big wave, but this time the cupboard was locked, the remaining dishes stowed.

He gave her a wink. "We'll make it, my lover. You get changed."

Gripping the doorway, she smiled at him, forgetful of her leering mouth. "You're a good sort, Phil, but you know we can't go on like this, can we?"

"My dear life! I've been in worse weather than this, and in a frigate a fraction of our size!" He did not add that he wished he was back in the frigate. "AT1's as steady as a rock, compared with my last ship."

His jaunty air vanished as she left, well aware this couldn't go on. Sure as hell, some frames must have buckled already; each heavy sea would work remorselessly, extending the damage until something gave, and that would be the end of all their problems, even if the entire Royal Air Force was circling overhead. Still, it hadn't happened yet, and he never met trouble halfway. He fought his way into the saloon, relieved to find the bar cupboard intact, and poured himself a drink.

To this moment he had thought no further than the ship being located; the problem would then be in other hands. "They" would do something. Now he recognized that "they" might not be able to help. Ever ready with a platitude, Phil told himself that "the Lord helps them that help themselves," and got down to it.

As a first move, he decided to try to find, very roughly, where they were. Wedged in a chair, trying to ignore the fearful motion, he studied the atlas. His earlier sums gave the estimated run for twenty-four hours as a little less than three hundred miles; five degrees of latitude. He had not seen the sun for two or three days, but felt sure the course was still south. If both guesses were right, AT1 had to be forty-three or -four degrees south. As near as he could judge from the map, the Antarctic continent roughly followed the line of the sixty-fifth parallel.

Forty-four from sixty-five left twenty-one. Five degrees a day . . . In little more than four days they'd pile up on the shore.

Less. This was winter; there'd be ice, well before that final, fatal moment. He traced the wavering line marked "extreme limit of pack ice": the very way it was mapped conveyed something of the cartographer's uncertainty. If they were dead out of luck, they could be in that in a couple of days. Supposing it was at night . . .

Phil put that thought aside; two days, the way they were fixed, was a mighty long time. The rescuers—what could they do, and what could the team do to help?

For a plane to drop a life raft would be a waste of time, even if it landed on AT1. If it dropped in the ocean, it would be just as useless. To abandon ship with the ship doing fifteen miles an hour would be as good as suicide: they'd be bashed against the side, probably dragged under, never mind the injuries they'd collect, leaping forty feet into the water at that speed. If they jumped off the stern, the screw would mince them.

Phil concluded he wouldn't care to jump off a moving ship anywhere, anytime, and certainly not AT1, even in a flat calm. Anyway, what of Bill and Jane? She might stand as good a chance as he did, but Bill, badly weakened, wouldn't have the ghost of one. He discarded the whole idea; whatever else, they had to stay with the ship.

Four days to be found *and* saved. But how? He could think of only two ways: a couple of parachute technicians, plus cutting gear, would have to land on the ship and get at the engines; or, best of all, a helicopter.

Phil hardly knew which was the least practicable. Just supposing men with the necessary skills existed, and were on the spot, it would still be incredibly risky. Miss the ship, and they'd have had it in a big way, and a broken leg or two would be easy to come by in landing on a pipe-covered deck. And what good would that be? As for the helo idea, that was fine, except the problem of where the helo could come from. Few helos had a range more than three hundred miles; the nearest airfield could be five or six times that distance from AT1.

Hang on. . . . Maybe there was one stationed at one of these Antarctic scientific stations!

At once his spirits soared, only to dip sharply at his next thought: he couldn't see choppers flying in blizzards, and no one in their right mind would keep a chopper on the ground in the Antarctic in winter; it would be a useless embarrassment, needing constant attention—and what for, in near-total night?

Perhaps their only hope lay in another direction; perhaps they'd run into steadily thickening pack ice and grind to a halt, the propeller churning away until the fuel was exhausted.

The thought brightened him up again. Yes, that had to be the answer: all they'd have to do would be to sweat it out until an icebreaker arrived—after the RAF had found them. He'd go over this with Bill.

Langley shared none of the sailor's optimism. Clinging on with his good hand as the ship reeled and plunged, he shouted above the sounds of the storm, "You're a bloody ostrich! Don't try to kid me—we've had our chips!"

July 17. As more possibilities were eliminated, the shore authorities were coming rapidly to the same conclusion as Langley. If AT1 was still afloat, it had to be heading south. As time passed, and the possible "distance traveled" of AT1 increased, other countries had joined in. Military aircraft of India and Pakistan scoured the subcontinent's coastline; Indonesian planes checked the western seaboards of Sumatra and Java. Only two possibilities remained: either AT1 had inexplicably gone to the bottom, leaving no trace, or she was heading deeper and deeper into the desolation of the Antarctic Ocean winter.

The RAF worked on the latter assumption. One Nimrod, briefed to recce the "farthest on" position the tanker could have made to the south, lumbered into the air with a maximum fuel load, faced with a minimum trip of 5,500 miles. The flight plan called for a high-level transit—to conserve fuel—to the search area, south of 35 degrees south. From there on the aircraft captain would have to use his own judgment about search patterns and heights; the weather he would meet was just another unknown factor; the indications were that it would be bad.

The "indications" proved only too accurate. At 35 south the aircraft made a steep descent from 32,000 feet, bumping through successive cloud layers down to 5,000 feet, a relatively clear stratum. Below lay endless thick gray cloud. Experimentally, the plane dived again, but finding nil visibility down to 1,500 feet, climbed back to 5,000 and settled down to a blind radar search, the radio operator listening out on the HF and VHF distress frequencies.

Hour after hour the search went on, the radar operator and the navigator splitting the scan watch between them, a boring yet exacting job, calling for high concentration.

On the assumption that AT1's computer had gone haywire, the search was not a simple matter of flying straight along her possible track. Without the computer's compensatory action, wind, sea, and currents could all have pushed her off-course; a very wide area had to be covered.

"Fifteen minutes to PLE." The captain's laconic announcement brought relief and disappointment. The prudent limit of endurance marked the turning point in the mission; the search would go on, but the plane would be heading for home.

The radio operator stretched, yawning. Any minute now, the skipper would give him a signal for base. He stopped, his mouth still wide open.

In the headphone tuned to 121.5 mhz he heard a very faint, broken-up signal. For several seconds he listened, excitement growing. Beyond doubt it was a distress beacon: SOS repeated three times, followed by a four-letter group, followed by a five-second dash. At the third repetition, he had got the four-letter group. He had no need to check his brief; the group was AT1's international call sign. Forgetting procedure—this was, after all, the radio equivalent of Stanley and Livingstone's meeting—he broke in on the intercom.

"Skip, I've *got* the bastard!"

Ten minutes later the radar operator had a large contact at

extreme range. For two more minutes the Nimrod hung on, evaluating and classifying the contact: yes, a ship, large, heading 180 degrees, estimated speed 12 knots.

Five minutes beyond PLE, the plane turned, climbing, its crew jubilant. They had done their job.

AT1 had been located in position 4450 south, 5820 east.

XVIII

The Nimrod's flash report had a powerful effect in many parts of the world. In London the initial feeling of relief was quickly overlaid with dismay. Maritime HQ, South Africa, felt very relieved, and the Australian government, preparing to search their west coast, was glad, but for sheer depth of emotion, the pirates eclipsed all. The boss, high in the Alps, after a brief vitriolic tirade, concentrated on his commercial defenses, his chief concern that whoever else might suffer, he would not. His subordinates afloat were even less happy: at first they had clung to the hope that AT1 was no more than a floating tomb, but that hope went overboard when the news of the radio beacon broke.

And while the report revived a sagging news story, filling radio and TV with a rehash of events, backed on TV and in the press with some highly inaccurate maps of AT1's location, MOD London and the company grappled with the second problem: rescue.

Calculations soon showed that AT1 had not deviated from its last known course and speed, allowing for drift, and it seemed fair to assume the tanker would go on holding its course. The company's computer center reran AT1's program in several different ways, feeding in known parameters, such as winds and currents the vessel must have encountered; they gave the computer's opinion that the ship-borne equipment had failed shortly after 1200 GMT July 12.

The Combined Defense Plot staff thanked them politely for information that neither impressed nor interested them.

Their far less abstruse calculations had produced one simple, chilling fact. As someone succinctly put it, AT1 would run out of water in seventy-four hours.

The small group of officers in the Combined Plot stared at the wall chart in silence. The chief of naval operations spoke briefly to his duty commander, both looking at AT1's "special situation" marker, now moved to the new position west of the uninhabited Kerguelen Island. Apart from a ship marker a long way southwest of the tanker, the whole area was empty.

His chief gone, the duty commander sat down, reached for a signal pad, and started writing. His RAF colleague knew better than to interrupt that tricky operation, and strolled over to the Wren plotter.

"Who's that, Liz?" He nodded toward the small black marker.

She had no need to consult her movements list. "*Guardian*, sir. Ice-patrol ship. She's on passage from the Australian Antarctic base at Mawson to the Falklands."

The RAF officer stared meditatively at the chart, gauging distances. The Wren, who had been doing her own calculations, broke in. "Not very good, is it, sir? *Guardian*'s no flyer. Fifteen knots is her top speed."

"It's not good at all, Liz," agreed the wing commander, drifting back to his deck, thinking.

The duty commander had finished; already the signal was on its way to the Communication Center. He slid a copy across to his colleague.

HMS GUARDIAN   FROM MOD (NAVY)

FOR INFORMATION MHQ S.A.   IMMEDIATE

PROCEED WITH ALL DISPATCH TO ASSIST AT1 LOCATED 0700Z IN POSITION 4450 S 5820 E COURSE 181 SPEED 12 KNOTS. FATE OF FIVE CREWMEN UNKNOWN. COMPUTER U/S AND RUDDER PROBABLY JAMMED AND SPEED CONSTANT. DISTRESS BEACON ACTIVE ON 121.5 MHZ. NO OTHER TRANSMISSION HEARD. RAF/SAAF COOPERATION MAY BE EXPECTED. 2. REPORT PRESENT POSITION FUEL STATE AND INTENTIONS.   =0815Z

"That covers it," commented the wing commander. "For us, it's a hell of a way from Gan; I'm going to stage a Nimrod down to the cape and ask the SAAF to maintain surveillance in the meantime." He wafted the signal back. "D'you think *Guardian* will make it?"

The naval man shrugged. "I wouldn't put my life savings on it. There's so many unknown factors. The crew could be dead, anyway." He sat back, staring at the bright-lit chart. "Can't understand why we haven't heard a single cheep out of her. With the R/T set sited well clear of the computer room, what disaster could put both out of action, yet not destroy the ship? It's a pretty tall order that *both* should go, unless there were two separate disasters—one to the computer and the other, later, to the crew. If they're all dead, well . . ."

"Um," said his colleague. "If the tanker should turn out to be another *Marie Celeste*, think your lads can save her?"

The naval man sounded irritated. "Give us a chance! This is a life-saving mission right now; once *Guardian* gets contact, she'll have to play it by ear. The first problem is whether *Guardian* can damn well reach her!" He picked up a telephone. "The owners can prepare a brief: *Guardian* will need all the dope she can get, *if* she gets contact with that box of tricks."

Three hours later the ice-patrol ship's red-flagged answer was on his desk:

MOD (NAVY) FROM: HMS GUARDIAN
INFO MHQ SOUTH ARFRICA IMMEDIATE

1.   YOUR 0815Z. PROCEEDING MY 1000Z POSITION 6015 SOUTH 4855 EAST SPEED 12 KNOTS. FUEL STATE 70 PERCENT. WIND WSW FORCE 8 SWELL HIGH SEA ROUGH VISIBILITY POOR TO NIL IN SNOW SQUALLS. SOME SEA ICE.
2.   WEATHER DOMINATING FACTOR. ANY FURTHER DETERIORATION WILL MAKE CHANCES OF INTERCEPT MINIMAL.   =1045Z

"Doesn't sound overoptimistic, does he?" said the wing commander.

The duty commander grunted. Privately, he thanked his personal gods that he was not stuck with the job. He had served in polar waters and knew the fury and hell of the dark winter seas, the conditions which cannot be described, only experienced. Momentarily he pictured *Guardian*, plunging to the rescue, AT1's last frail hope.

"No," he replied at last, "and I don't blame him."

The tension in the saloon on the night of the seventeenth was so strong as to be almost visible. Paradoxically, had it not been for the violent motion of the ship, violence would certainly have erupted among the survivors of AT1's guard. At one level, the motion apart, life was as normal as it had been when they sailed. They had plenty of food, the saloon was comfortably warm, they had a library of a couple of hundred books, and the cassette player was there, if wanted.

But like the humans, the player stayed silent, the books remained unopened, except the atlas, which Phil stared at, as if wishing would change the picture. Tensing inwardly with each whipping motion of the stern, he hardly took in the map. Jane knitted mechanically; Langley just sat, brooding.

By unspoken agreement the drinks cabinet remained open. From time to time one or other of the trio made the dangerous journey to refill their own glass, indifferent to the rest. Jane had offered once to fix Langley a drink, but he rebuffed her with a surly grunt.

The incident angered Phil. Miserable bastard. . . . He wondered if Langley had suffered some brain injury when Colmar shot him. Certainly he had never been the same since. Phil remembered the way Langley had appraised Jane's figure in the early days; it hadn't been hard to guess the thoughts having a good time in Langley's mind; now he couldn't even be civil.

He turned his attention to Jane. No doubt about it, she was making out better than either of them. Funny, he hardly noticed that scar now; a smashing bird, kind, gentle—and brave.

Langley got up, shuffled awkwardly to the bar, generously

160

refilling his glass, and staggered out of the saloon without a word.

"He's a miserable devil these days," observed Phil.

Jane glanced up from her work, her face pale, tired. "You can't blame him. He's the boss, but through no fault of his, any real work that has been done since the shooting has been done by you. He feels he is a failure. If you add that to our situation . . ." She shrugged.

Phil got up, moving over to her. "Just now I was thinking what a real marvel you've turned out to be. As a woman, I reckon you've got the lot. If we get out of this jam, it'll be thanks to you."

Even in a force-twelve gale it was pleasant to hear, until she remembered another man.

"No, Phil. Don't go on. I know you mean well . . . Here, get me a drink, please."

He obeyed, wondering yet again what caused her abrupt change of manner. Every time he got close to her, there was this sudden turn-away, and he'd swear she wasn't just giving him the cold shoulder. There was something, somebody. Somebody. Call him—it had to be a him—X; some figure in her past life. That scar hadn't been forever; she must have had men around her like wasps around a honeypot; no, later than that. It had to be Jacens—and how could one be jealous of the dead? Very easily, especially when life was a fast-wasting asset.

Once again, AT1 plowed into a big one, breaking his thoughts. He clung on, experiencing once more that sickening motion, as if he had jumped fast, up a row of steps. Somewhere below his feet he felt a different, almost squashy movement: something had buckled. He waited apprehensively, but the feeling did not come again. And if it did, what then? The only choice they had was where they died— below deck or up top in the full violence of the storm.

Phil let that choice go. Either they saw the dawn or they didn't. He poured another large drink, and wiser than Langley, did not risk spilling it, drinking the neat Scotch where he stood.

None of them undressed. Langley lay on his bunk, his good hand gripping the bed frame beneath him, staring at the deckhead. Jane, equally sleepless, felt sick, but fear was the main ingredient. Only Phil, expertly wedged by knees and backside between the sides of his bunk, got off quickly, helped by Scotch and his temperament. Many affirm that if nothing can be done about a situation there is no point in worrying about it; he was one of the very few who really believed that proposition.

The ship plunged on; by two A.M., even Jane and Bill, totally exhausted, dozed fitfully.

At half-past four, all three were jerked into fearful consciousness by a new sound, a terrifying loud screeching, bumping noise which overlaid all else. Phil was out of his bunk and on the ladder before the other two had their feet on the deck. He reached the front windows in the citadel, heart pounding.

The noise went on, endlessly renewed high-pitched shrieks, like a derailed train with the brakes on, bumping over the ties, a sound that set the teeth on edge.

In spite of the bitter cold, the sailor sweated, waiting for his vision to adapt, but strengthened by one realization: the ship's motion had eased. AT1 still rolled and pitched, but the heart-gripping whipping of the stern had stopped, although the wind tore with undiminished ferocity outside the relative calm of the citadel.

Langley stumbled up the companionway, closely followed by Jane, both clumsy in the darkness.

"What's happened?" Bill yelled above the din.

Phil didn't answer. He had found a hand lamp and was cautiously easing himself on deck through the lee door. An icy gust swirled through the citadel, chilling Bill and Jane, who found time to think of the thin-clad sailor. She shuddered at the screaming of the wind tearing at the gantry and aerials, a sound suddenly damped as Phil slammed the door.

Outside, he gasped at the cold; his healing wound felt like frozen fire, his face burning, stinging.

Jane and Langley could hardly see him through the obscured windows. Cursing, Langley got the wipers working; they glimpsed his misshapen figure, leaning against the storm, trousers flapping as he staggered and slipped along the lee guardrail. For what seemed an eternity he stayed, stopped, hunched over the rail. Jane prayed. If Phil went . . .

"Taking his bloody time," Langley shouted above the continuing din, but Jane hardly heard, his voice drowned by the awful screeching. They saw Phil move forward, his lamp waving erratically. "What's he on about?"

The sailor turned, his lamp flashing blindingly in their eyes, but by its light they saw snow, not rain, slanted across the heaving deck.

Jane shivered uncontrollably with fear and cold, gritting her teeth against the noise, watching with anxiety the progress of Phil's bobbing light, bright then blurred through the window, cleaned by the wipers, to be instantly obscured by snow.

They heard rather than saw him half-fall, half-stumble inside, accompanied by the demonic screech of the wind and a flurry of snow, cut short as he slammed the door.

"Well?" Langley was shouting.

By the light of his lamp they saw him brush snow from his face.

"For Christ's sake, what is it?"

His bloodless lips formed the word with difficulty.

"Ice!"

XIX

"Ice?" Jane echoed the word in stupid amazement. Phil motioned both of them closer; huddled together, conversation was possible.

"Nothing to worry about." He spoke with overelaborate unconcern. "It's only two or three inches thick. Expect the gale's blown it this far north." Both watched his face in the dim light, trying to guess his true belief. He cupped his hands, blowing into them. "Bloody wicked out there. Talk about brass monkeys! Jane, how about some coffee with rum? I'm fair perished."

At once Jane hurried below to the hellish noise in the galley, less terrifying now that the sailor had so calmly explained the cause. They could all do with rum and coffee.

Langley grabbed Phil's shoulder. "Now, tell me straight —what d'you reckon?" He had to shout in the sailor's ear.

Phil shouted back. "Maybe the ice is a bit thicker, but honest, I do think it's been blown north. Makes a lotta noise, and there won't be a scrap of paint left on the waterline"—he moved closer, watching the companionway—"but if that's all we've got to worry about, we're laughing."

"What d'you mean?"

"Well, if, along with this stuff, there should happen to be an iceberg . . ." He let it go at that. "Still, it's an ill wind and all that; at least the ice has damped the sea down. I'm going below to warm up and give Jane a hand with that coffee."

Langley nodded, thinking of icebergs.

To even try to sleep in all that racket would have been pointless, and the brain-battering noise drove them all to the citadel, to spend the rest of the night staring helplessly out at the slanting snow.

Shortly before dawn, as suddenly as it had begun, the noise stopped. In the slow-growing light, three haggard faces, devoid of all expression, looked incuriously at one another. Roscorla roused himself first; at least he had something to do.

"Well, thank Christ for that." He rubbed his still-singing ears. "I'll get the beacon fixed. Jane, how about some grub? Lashings of bacon and eggs and fried bread when I get back, hey?" He clamped a brotherly arm around her shoulders, shaking her gently. "Cheer up, my robin. Take a tip from your dear old Phil, fix us all a bloody good meal, including yourself. Plenty of fat—Eskimo grub."

"How he can be so, so . . ." said Jane after he had gone, shaking her head slowly. Langley wasn't listening.

AT1 still rolled viciously, but the movement was nothing like as bad, and Jane had no difficulty in preparing the breakfast Phil wanted. Langley refused to leave the citadel, and while he munched huge egg-and-bacon sandwiches in solitude, Jane and Phil ate in the saloon, but this time she did not take offense at his hearty appetite, eating quite well herself. The meal over, she began clearing away. The food had done her good, but she felt, and knew she looked, a wreck. With the tension eased and daylight offering some hope, and better weather, she felt so tired.

"Leave all that, girl. You go and get your head down for an hour or two. I'll get through this little lot." He grinned. "Who knows—might even have a bit more bacon. Go on, shove off."

"Oh, Phil, sure you don't mind?"

Phil was through the dishes and had an extra couple of rashers spluttering in the pan when the phone buzzed. What Langley said made him start for the door; he stopped and went back, made a hasty sandwich of the bacon.

Langley was in the wheelhouse. He pointed. "There."

Phil took in the bleak, monochrome scent. Snow covered the tanker's foredeck; by contrast, the still-lumpy sea looked

165

almost black. Visibility was patchy, much of the horizon blotted out by snow squalls, but in the direction Langley pointed, he could see two or perhaps three miles; distance was difficult to judge in the flat, lifeless, and shadowless light.

About two miles distant was a long straight-sided, flat-topped island, bigger, much bigger, than AT1. Phil studied it through the binoculars.

"Yep, that's an iceberg, all right, Sarge. Still, no sweat. We're well clear of it." The berg was to port, and the still-strong wind would keep it moving away from them.

Langley did not answer; he had nothing to say: the implications of that monster were all too plain. AT1 was only a counter on a gigantic snakes-and-ladders board, Fate throwing the dice. Lose, and no painted tail awaited the helpless ship, but the bottom of a freezing sea. Much worse, no ladders of salvation showed.

Both men scanned the horizon, forgetful of planes, their thoughts contracted from ultimate rescue to immediate survival.

July 18. Ashore, the RAF and SAAF, at least, were happy. To locate AT1 was now little more than a navigational exercise, one that an SAAF Shackleton had solved by midday.

Flying conditions below 5,000 feet were bad for seagulls and impossible for man's clumsy flying machines. The plane circled above the dense overcast, holding AT1 on radar and the distress beacon on VHF. Twice the pilot tried to get lower, but finding no break in the murk at 2,000 feet, had to climb again; altimeters are not that accurate. He hoped at least that the crew of the tanker would hear him, but in fact they did not. Outside the wheelhouse the strong-to-gale-force wind effectively blanketed the engine noise. Patiently the plane circled, looking for a break in the cloud, sending hourly position reports. At midday AT1 was at 5226 south, 5744 east.

The news media wrung the last drop of drama from the situation, mostly concentrating on Jane's predicament. For a time, her picture, one taken before her accident, in press and on TV made her familiar to millions, sharpening the jaded palates of a news-satiated world audience, half-eager for the *frisson* of shock which the news of AT1's anticipated end would bring. Sharp news editors across the globe had quickly appreciated that her picture "personalized" the impending disaster, boosting sales and TV ratings, bringing happiness to many a newspaper office and advertising agency.

Smiling faces aboard *Guardian* were few and did not include the captain's. The weather could be much worse, but the unwelcome top weight of her iced upperworks had the ship rolling like a drunken pig. Each time she dug her bows in, half-seen green seas crashed thunderously on the forecastle, smashing in tireless fury against the bridge structures. Before the AT1 order had been received, the upper deck had been placed out of bounds; now, at the best speed the ship could make without breaking up, to venture on deck would have been suicide. The ship shook, plunged, and rolled; below decks, icy water had got down a ventilator trunking, flooding a mess deck. Men cursed, crockery smashed, adding to the din. Thus far the human cost was only two broken limbs and a chronic shortage of sleep; the ship, too, was paying tribute the sea exacted. The port sea boat had gone, smashed beyond recognition, no more than bits of timber dangling on the end of ropes. Upper-deck lockers had been ripped with frightening ease from their welds; others had been twisted, bent into grotesque shapes. Above all, the steady accretion of ice added to the roll, increasing the sickening loll as the ship rolled to leeward, just another nagging worry for the captain.

But at this moment he and the navigating officer were concentrating on AT1. Clinging to the chart table, they evaluated the tanker's probable drift, their own progress, and the hazards they faced to reach her. Fog and icebergs could radically affect their calculations.

"Allowing ten percent for the unknown, with luck, I estimate we'll be within a hundred miles of her by midday, sir."

The captain studied the chart. "What time's sunrise and sunset?"

"0829 and 1540, sir."

"So if we have the luck, we'll get about five hours of reasonable light, if the visibility improves and if this damned weather eases."

The navigator nodded diplomatically. There were altogether too many "ifs" for his liking.

The captain felt the same. "We can only try. I've put it in my night orders that short of major structural damage, speed is to be maintained." He looked once more at the lengthly signal from MOD, the company's crib on AT1. "Tell the first lieutenant I want all officers and chiefs off-watch in the wardroom for briefing at 1645."

"Aye-aye, sir."

"And tell the chief engineer I'd like to see him in my sea cabin as soon as convenient."

Woken by her alarm clock, Jane was back in the galley by midday. The sleep had done her good, but she still felt as if she could have slept for a week.

Having started a massive stew in the pressure cooker, she went in search of Langley, insisting he go down to the sick bay. Reluctantly he left the deck.

At least his wound was progressing satisfactorily. Basically a fit man, Langley was replacing his lost blood, and the wound itself was healthy. Jane moved his arm through a variety of positions, happy to have something other than their present predicament to occupy her. In that professional frame of mind, she told her patient that in an emergency he could use his arm, but otherwise he was to keep it in a sling.

For the first time in a long while Langley genuinely laughed. "I can use it in an emergency? If I happen to miss out on the next one, you let me know. I think . . ." He stopped short. Both men had agreed there was no point in adding to her worries with news of the iceberg.

"You think what, Bill?" She paused in her clearing up.

"Well, nothing. I mean, I think this is one long emergency."

"You know very well what I mean. Send Phil down; I'll have a look at his head."

The sailor was much less reluctant, almost bouncing into the sick bay. She redressed his wound, replacing the bandage with a large strip of plaster.

"You were very lucky, Phil. Another half-inch, and you wouldn't be here."

"My old ma always said I was. Said I'd die at a ripe old age, surrounded by a large, sorrowing family."

"Let's hope she's right."

"Certain!" He got up. "Thanks, Jane, we'd have been right up the creek without a paddle, but for you." He took her hand. "Jane, if we get out of this—"

The phone buzzed.

"My dear life! Every time I—"

Jane interrupted. "Bill wants you in the wheelhouse."

"Did he say why?"

"No. Just 'send Phil up,' that's all."

"Bet he's run out of cigarettes again. Ah, well, better go." He did his best, convincing neither of them.

Langley's face was the color of putty, his voice high-pitched. "Look!" He thrust the binoculars into the sailor's hands, pointing with a shaking hand.

The gray light, devoid of contrast, gave no sense of distance. At first Phil thought it was the horizon; only when one end, clear of a snow squall, showed, did realization hit with all the sickening violence of a kick in the stomach.

Dead ahead lay a vast iceberg. Even as he stared, horrified, fresh snow threw a cloak over the scene.

Langley looked at Phil. "My God, what can we . . .?" He fell silent, aware of the futility of his question, and their utter helplessness.

Phil had no ready answer. As the snow swept away to port, he looked again. In spite of the chill air, sweat ran down his face; he struggled to keep his voice calm. "Can't tell how far off the bastard is; could be two miles, or ten." His lips drew back in a false grin. "Pray for ten."

Like the first berg, this one was flat-topped, straight-sided. It stretched from ten degrees to port to dead ahead, its outline blurred, its fearful bulk almost lost in snow.

"We must tell Jane." Langley wanted to do something, anything.

"What for—get her as twitched up as we are?"

"She's a right to know. Perhaps we could get on top of it."

"Don't talk bloody rubbish!" snarled Phil. "If we hit that, we're not going anywhere except straight down."

"She's got to know!" Both men glared wildly, seeking relief in a row, a fight.

Jane settled the question by arriving with coffee, her surprised look changing swiftly to alarm. "What's happening?"

Phil turned wearily away, not knowing what to do or say.

Langley managed to speak. "There's an iceberg up front. We . . . we may hit it."

She seemed to shrink; her body bent slightly, as if under a heavy load. Almost incuriously she looked ahead, not trying to see. "Oh," she said in a dull tone. "Oh. Have we got . . . got long?"

"Ask Phil," retorted Langley savagely, "he's the bloody expert."

But the steam had gone out of Phil: he didn't want to fight anymore. "Can't tell. Fifteen minutes to three-quarters of an hour."

"And . . . and then?"

Phil shook his head irritably. Angered by responsibility thrust upon him, his answer was unusually brutal. "Why ask me? If you've ever driven a car at fifteen miles an hour into a concrete wall, you'll know more about it than I do." The snow had cleared, giving a better view; he concentrated on that, not Jane's expression.

For her, his simile was far worse than he could know. She stared blankly at his back, put down the coffee, and went below.

With a shaking head Langley poured two cups. Half his mind refused to accept that in half an hour he would almost certainly be dead, drowned, but his more elemental level knew, his heart thumped, gearing his body for what must

170

come. "Think we'll last long, Phil?" All animosity had gone.

His concentration lost, the sailor swore; he lowered the binoculars. "What—in the sea, like? No. Toss-up whether shock gets you, or you drown." He was remarkably casual. "Five minutes, and you've had it." He glanced around. "What's Jane up to?"

Langley shrugged. What did it matter? Jacens' gun was around somewhere; a bullet in the head might be a better way out.

Jane returned; she had brushed her hair, tying it in a ponytail, and put on lipstick. Around her shoulders hung a blanket; she carried a bottle of Scotch, three glasses.

Phil recovered first, and he smiled admiringly. "That's the stuff, Jane—never say die!"

Her brave attempt to appear composed dragged Langley from his somber thoughts. A small, grim smile lightened his lined face. "I thought England had given up making your sort."

Stiffly, unsmiling, she handed him a large whiskey. Langley half-raised his glass. "Here's to you."

Hearing nothing from the sailor, he looked around. Phil was concentrating on the iceberg, once again visible and closer. "What d'you say?"

Phil did not answer. Langley's overstrained temper flared, but Jane put out a restraining hand. They both drank.

Shaking with excitement, breathing hard, Phil lowered his glasses. "Sarge, tell me when one minute is up."

"Why?"

"For God's sake, don't bloody argue!" screamed Roscorla. His gaze fixed on the berg, he wiped his brow with the back of his hand, rubbed both palms on his trousers, and resumed his watch with the binoculars.

Langley hesitated, but noted the time.

Jane fought down a surge of hope. Once before she had seen the sailor like this, when he tackled the bombs; shaking uncontrollably, then steady as a rock.

"Twenty seconds to go," said Langley laconically. Even

this trivial task was better than just waiting.

All three were as statues, the silence broken only by the moaning of the dying wind.

"Time!"

"Okay . . . another minute from now!" With difficulty Phil looked away from the berg. "Look, don't get too bloody excited, but I'm taking rough bearings on the nearest edge of that bastard. It's tracking from right to left. . . . There's just a chance . . ." He dared not say it.

Now Jane and Bill stared, wanting and not wanting to look. Visibility had improved considerably, and the distance had shortened frighteningly. They had no idea of the iceberg's size, but it appeared vast. Jane thought of that concrete wall, and shut her eyes.

"Time!"

His voice hoarse, unsure, Phil said, "We've got a chance." Openly he prayed. "God, give us a chance. . . ."

"Here." Langley passed Phil his drink. The sailor drank it as if it was iced tea, and held the glass out for more. Jane slopped Scotch in, watching in terrified fascination the advancing berg.

Phil returned to his observation, lining up the sharp edge of the ice monster with the tanker's bows and the top of a catwalk stanchion. Repeatedly he checked, almost as if the action would have some practical result. Jane was near-screaming at his grunts, muttering, and moaning, his sharp movements; then he stood up, no longer shaking.

"It's going to be a bloody close shave, but—"

"Shut up!" yelled Langley. As ready for death as he ever would be, in a curious way he resented the intrusion of agonizing hope, and wanted to destroy it. Phil's silence forced him to go on. "Even if we don't hit, the underwater part'll rip the bottom out!"

"Not this one—you're thinking of a pinnacled berg. This is tabular!"

"Aw, shut up—what the bloody difference?"

"Enough to save us!" shouted the sailor excitedly. "See those straight sides, the flat top? Pretty much as it was when it broke off from a sodding great ice sheet. Water's in the end, the bastard'll get top-heavy and capsize; *then* you've got a pinnacled berg with the underwater chunk broader than the top!''

Langley did not answer. He'd screwed himself up and would stay that way until their fate was decided. Jane dimly grasped Phil's argument, but was chiefly moved by his excitement. To her, collision was inevitable; the evidence of her eyes contradicted Phil's opinion, and her mind was too paralyzed to make a judgment.

Phil shrugged, wrenched open the frozen wheelhouse door, and ran out onto the citadel roof to get a better view. He looked intently, ran back, slamming the door, shivering, and grinning. He drained and refilled his glass.

''Ten minutes and we'll know who's right!'' Now he was certain, free from the fear that still gripped his companions. He gave them both a drink-tinged grin. ''If I'm wrong, don't speak to me again!''

But for all his confidence, he too fell silent as AT1 steamed blindly on, and the berg loomed larger and larger, a vast dirty-white mass. Jane and Bill clutched the rail convulsively, their knuckles white, bracing themselves.

Disturbed by the tanker's approach, a small group of sea birds took flight from the top of the berg. For the first time the watchers had a yardstick by which to judge the monster's size, and those half-seen dots, swooping and soaring between ship and berg, gave sudden depth to the picture.

''God Almighty!'' said Phil softly, reverently, overwhelmed by the size and majesty of the iceberg. Then he was off, running out on deck, sighting along the ship's side to the nearest edge of the berg.

''We'll make it . . . we'll make it!'' he yelled, waving to his companions. ''Come and see!''

But neither Jane nor Bill moved.

XX

For them, the last half-mile lasted a lifetime, Langley gripping the rail, his face a mask. Jane tried to look away, but could not do it, staring wide-eyed, her heart thumping painfully, her mouth dry. Phil stayed on deck, unconsciously leaning to starboard, as if to pull the ship away from the berg by his nervous tension.

With sudden, sickening speed the time scale changed. To Jane and Bill, the iceberg appeared to rush down upon them, a towering cliff only feet from the bows. Involuntarily Jane cried out.

"It's okay!" yelled Phil. "We'll clear by twenty yards, easy!"

She was dimly aware of the sailor shouting, but his voice was lost in the sudden thunderous roar of the seas breaking against the weather side of the berg. Great clouds of spray mounted slowly up the sheer face, giving some hint of the titanic power of sea and berg. AT1 appeared to be moving at fearful speed, sliding past great sea-carved caverns, vast black mouths, gaping menacingly, the hollow reverberant crash of waves within, the voice of the monster.

Langley's toes curled in his boots as he waited for the long, shuddering crunch as the bottom was ripped open like tinfoil. Phil had quickly overcome his awe for the berg, confident that the tanker would miss it, yet seized by the irrational fear that AT1 would alter course and smash her stern in passing. Shivering with cold, he watched the gap between the berg and the ship's stern.

God! It was less than twenty bloody yards . . . nearer fifteen. Come *on*! Widen, you bastard. . . .

He straightened up, relaxing, grinning at the two in the citadel. He felt very cold and realized he had been drenched by spray.

In the citadel the thunder of the sea ceased as if a loudspeaker had been switched off. For another ten, fifteen seconds Langley waited, unmoving; then his shoulders sagged, he turned away, not wanting to see or be seen. "Christ . . ." His voice was shaky, uncertain; he fumbled clumsily for a cigarette, spilling matches on the deck.

Jane paid no attention to him, Phil, or anything else; she turned, stumbled over her dropped blanket, ignored that too, and disappeared below.

Phil returned, slamming the door shut, and headed straight for the Scotch.

"Ah! Just enough for a tot each!" He drained his in one gulp, looking aft at the iceberg merging steadily into the gray mist. "Well, bugger that for a game of darts! Reckon that bastard was well over a hundred feet high and best part of a half-mile long! Fantastic . . . fan-tastic."

His jaunty manner did something for Langley; he took his drink, regarding it briefly before drinking, his face expressionless.

Both men watched until the iceberg was lost in the dim gray mist.

"Yes," said Phil once more, "fantastic."

Langley found his voice. "Yeah. Like as not, there's more of 'em loafing."

"I know that," replied Phil quickly, "but let's take 'em one at a time. Main thing is we've survived."

Langley's anger boiled over. "Who are you trying to kid—yourself?" He hated the sailor's ability to bounce back so fast. "We've *had* it!" He stabbed at the matchbox, breaking the match. "Since you're so bloody sure, you keep watch for that bloody plane. I'm off!"

Phil did not reply. Alone, he picked up Jane's blanket and slung it around his soaked shoulders, scanning the bleak scene ahead.

Perhaps Bill was right; maybe he was kidding himself, but not that much. If they weren't sighted in the next twenty-four hours, Bill would find out what a despondent bastard *he* could be.

In the empty saloon Langley dropped into an armchair, totally exhausted, yet unable to sleep, reliving that last two minutes before they cleared the berg.

In her bathroom Jane knelt over the water closet, violently sick. She struggled slowly to her feet, shaking with weakness, and confronted the mirror; a pallid face with swollen eyes and smeared lipstick stared back, until vanity, that great stiffener, came to her rescue. She rinsed her mouth, feeling light-headed, detached, almost as if she stood outside herself, watching. She undressed carelessly, dropping her clothes anywhere, and stepped into the shower.

For the best part of an hour Roscorla stamped up and down the citadel, getting colder and colder as the power of the Scotch and the short winter day both waned.

Face it mate . . . two hours of light of sorts left. But two hours is two hours; the RAF could still come. Right now, a bloody great Nimrod could be running in. . . . Also on the good side, the wind's dropping fast, and the swell, and the visibility's a whole lot better—what more could they want?

His mind had a ready answer. They wanted bloody Batman, and soon.

He shied off that thought, concentrating on yet one more all-round scan, working systematically on sea, then sky, in ninety-degree sectors.

Which was why the first warning he had was by sound. At first he rejected it as some internal vibration, but the sound grew, rising and falling in the spasmodic gusts of the dying storm. He stopped his search and stood very still, his head on one side, listening.

Sounds just like a bloody engine. Stupid; can't be that. Must be going out of my tiny mind. Could swear it's a chopper.

Galvanized by a feeling of real shock, he leaped to the ladder and was in the wheelhouse in seconds, scanning the sky. The sound was stronger, steadier. Frantically he wound a window down, heedless of the biting cold. Now he was sure; he'd heard too many helos to get it wrong.

He saw it. Two or three miles away, low, heading straight for the tanker, its warning lights occulting, a helicopter.

Shaking with excitement and cold, he stared, doubting his eyes, then ran to the ladder, almost fell down it, and reached the top of the companionway, yelling at the top of his voice.

"Bill . . . Jane! We're saved! Come on, my dear life, *come on*!" Shouting incoherently, he tore across to the citadel door, struggling to open it, cursing, laughing, then out, up on to the catwalk, waving, cheering.

The helo was close, losing height; he could hear the harsh slapping of the rotors as the pilot adjusted pitch, and he prayed for the pilot, his skill.

Jane and Bill shot out of the citadel, kicking up snow, slipping, waving frantically, shouting. Ahead of the hampered Langley, Jane scrambled up beside Phil, impulsively grabbing him around the waist, waving her free arm, eyes shining.

The helo banked sharply, the tail swinging, presenting itself broadside on as it cruised slowly up the starboard side, abeam of the trio of waving figures.

"Oh, dear Christ, a . . . a Wessex!" Choked with tears, Phil could say no more, pointing.

On the dark-blue fuselage, two very emotive words for the sailor stood out sharply in white: ROYAL NAVY.

Phil was near-mad with excitement. He kissed Jane, shook her, and pointed again. "Tes my lot! Look . . . look at bloody that!"

Briefly the aircraft hovered, then shot ahead of the ship, to drop back on the port side. Its door on the starboard side slid open. With tear-blurred eyes Phil saw the familiar olive-green flying suit, the white bone-dome of the crewman who waved, then sat nonchalantly on the floor, legs dangling in space as the machine edged over the ship. The crewman took the lowering line, attached a bag, a gloved hand gesturing to them.

Phil ran forward, disregarding the ice and snow underfoot.

The helo must have plenty of room, must keep clear of the gantry. The bag swayed down; at the second attempt, Phil grabbed it, swiftly casting off the line. He dropped the bag, spread his arms, and gave the "up" signal. At once the plane banked, climbing. A final wave, and the door slid shut. By the time they reached the citadel, freezing, the helo was a fast-retreating black shape, soon lost in the low cloud.

"What's he doing?" Langley said aggressively.

"Don't you worry"—Phil wrestled with the bag—"*he* knows what he's doing? Bloody Fleet Air Arm, mate—the boys who fly when the birds are walking! He'll be back." He got the bag unzipped. Inside was a walkie-talkie radio and a note:

GLAD TO MEET YOU, DR. LIVINGSTONE. WILL RETURN AT FIRST LIGHT. IF WEATHER FAVORABLE, WILL LAND ON. IF NOT, WILL WINCH YOU UP. ONLY ONE SUITCASE EACH, PLEASE, PLUS ONE BAG FOR SHIP'S PAPERS, ETC. SET WATCH ON THIS RADIO AS SOON AS YOU SEE US. DON'T GO AWAY.

SHIP'S FLIGHT. HMS GUARDIAN.

"What does he mean, 'don't go away?' " Still bemused by events, Jane frowned.

Phil laughed, the first really cheerful sound aboard AT1 for many days. He grabbed her around the waist, waltzing her across the citadel. "Ah, my robin, my bird! It's a Navy joke—a lovely, silly, marvelous, stupid Navy joke!" He stopped, his head on her shoulder, sobbing.

Jane spent a busy evening. In his excitement Bill had waved with the wrong arm, opening his wound slightly. After she had redressed it, and while the men showered and packed their bags, she cooked a large supper of steak, eggs, and chips. Aided by several cans of beer, the meal was the happiest event of the voyage. Their relief was immense, but only Phil regarded them as saved. The sight of any helo would have had almost the same effect—but not quite. Like any ex-sailor, he was prepared to curse and swear about the

Navy, but deep down he had a pride in, and a respect for, his old outfit's professionalism.

Although Jane knew the volatile Cornishman's optimism, she took comfort from his absolute assurance, but she wished the helo had lifted them off, and said so. Phil dealt with that very sharply. There were a dozen reasons, but the most likely one was fuel. As to ice, said Phil, dropping a cube in Langley's after-supper whiskey, the chopper would have had a damn good look ahead of AT1. No, there was nothing to worry about.

Langley took the drink, far less confident. He stared at the glass, thinking; his gaze narrowed; for the first time, he saw the ice cube, almost submerged.

"Christ!" He glowered at Phil's surprised expression. He couldn't complain; he always had ice in his whiskey; it wasn't Phil's fault, or his own, or anybody's. He scrabbled in the glass, tossed the cube into a dish, and gulped the Scotch. "I'm turning in," he said shortly, not inviting comment on his action. "Thanks, Jane. Good supper." With the briefest of nods to Phil, he left.

"Well, get that!" Phil scratched his head. "Poor old Bill's still twitching!" He saw her troubled look. "Don't tell me you are too? Aw, come on, you can't be!"

"Of course I am! We're so close to rescue from this awful nightmare. Time and again there's been some dreadful disappointment. Now we've got to face this night—"

"Don't be silly, Jane! Time and again we've had a hell of a lot of luck. We're still here, and out there"—he jerked his head—"there's one of my old mob, and she's got the one thing we need, a chopper. No, we're practically home and dry."

"Don't say that—it's flying in the face of Providence!"

He grinned. "I did say 'practically.' Aw, come on, my robin, just look at me—a born coward who gets the shakes at the slightest sign of trouble, and am I sweating? No!" He moved to Langley's chair, closer to her. "Cheer up! Your old Phil knows—*feels*—we won't crunch up against anything!"

Jane, nervously tracing circles on the table, remained unconvinced.

XXI

For all his confident air, Phillip Roscorla was up by six
A.M., a good three hours before first light. He bustled around
making tea, and found that Jane was already up and that
Langley's bunk was empty. He took Langley's mug up to the
citadel, humming discordantly to himself. AT1's motion had
diminished to an easy, gentle roll.

The citadel was bitterly cold; dimly he made out Langley's
heavily muffled figure. "You're up sharpish, Sarge." Phil
was bright and cheerful. "Brought you a cuppa."

Langley grunted his thanks, not mentioning he had been
up all night.

For a time both men stared out into the blackness, one full
of confidence, the other deeply fearful that the feeble gleam
of the forward navigation light would give bare seconds'
warning of another ice monster, towering over them, and
then . . . He could not get the image of the berg of the
previous day out of his mind; never had he dreamed of such
terrifying strength.

Jarring unwittingly on Langley's nerves, Phil said
brightly, "Well, this won't buy the baby a new hat. I'll nip
down and see how the grub's coming on. Going to be a long
day; got to have a good stoke-up."

Langley would have preferred to stay in the citadel, but
pride would not let him show just how fearful he was, and he
too went down for breakfast. He could face anything on two
legs, but the last half-mile before they shaved past the iceberg
had completely unnerved him. For him the meal was

purgatory; he ate, tasting nothing, unable to concentrate on anything but the fearful picture in his brain. It was left to Phil to take the lead.

"First light can't be more'n an hour away, Sarge," observed the sailor. "We'd better get our bags on deck, hadn't we?"

"Er, yes. Yes."

Phil glanced sharply at him. This was not the old Langley; now he was a bundle of nerves—and if he was any judge, the bundle could split open anytime. "Okay, then"—he was very diplomatic—"if you like, we'll do it as soon as we've finished, and if you'll take the watch, I'll lug it all up top to the helo pad. Or do you want me to keep watch?"

"No, I'll do that." His sharp reaction told Phil all he needed to know.

Phil shifted the baggage, and on his final trip told Langley that there was a good deal of ice on the pad. "Best have a go at shifting it, Sarge. Me and Jane on broom and shovel, if you can hand on to the torch."

It proved a wicked job. Wearing their thickest clothes, topped with the ponchos Jane had made, they scraped and swept. Their bodies were warm enough, but the cruel wind cut their faces, and their teeth ached with every breath. Half an hour was enough; they retreated to the citadel for coffee and rum. By the time they resumed, the first thin light, secretly so blessed by Langley, had come. The foredeck took shape, the bows visible.

Another fifteen minutes and they had the worst off; a thin film remained, but nothing could be done about that. With the coming of the dawn, Jane and Langley revived like flowers in water. At Phil's request, Jane cooked another breakfast, but light or not, Bill preferred bacon sandwiches and coffee in the citadel.

Over the meal, Jane wanted to know what Phil thought the Navy would do, and how soon, questions he could not answer any more than he could fly.

"Don't worry, Jane. I don't say the Navy's never failed—'course it has—but I do say there's damn few times its failed for want of trying! The chopper'll be back soon; what happens then, I haven't a clue, but the chances are you'll find yourself sleeping in the captain's cabin tonight.''

She got it wrong.

Phil laughed. "No! Most of the older ships, like *Guardian*, have two cabins for the old man; a proper one, like, and a pokey affair close to the bridge, 'cause at sea the old man's watch on, stop on if needs be. He can't be in two places at once—so there you are.'' His tone changed. "Jane, if I'm right, this could be our last time, well, you know—together, like. I won't say what I want to say, but I think you know.''

He badly needed a shave, his hair a mess, but the eyes revealed the man and his sincerity. "Yes, Phil, I know.'' Her voice was soft. "Thank you.''

"Thank me!'' His manner changed swiftly, back to the clown, aware this was not the moment. "Boot's on the other · foot, as they say. Well, I'd better get up there.''

"Yes.'' She hesitated. "He's in a bad way—mentally, I mean.''

"I know that. I've got a strong suspicion he didn't turn in at all last night. Funny, really. Who'd have guessed, back in Bahrein, that the female would turn out to be the strongest of the bunch?''

Langley was hunched on the stool, staring at the sea ahead. Cigarette ends littered the deck, more eloquent evidence of his state than any words.

"Won't be long now, Sarge.'' Phil cast an eye at their expanding horizon. "Um. Not bad. Sea's calm. Let's hope the visibility holds.''

"Too bloody right,'' said Langley fervently. "Reckon they'll be long?''

"No. Expect they launched the chopper while it was still dark, but there's no point in reaching us before light. Flaming mad to try a landing with no deck lights or navigational help—and on a strange deck. But before they get here, bet they'll take a gander at the sea ahead of us.''

Langley nodded; that made sense.

Phil was on the point of telling his senior not to worry, but realized in time that that remark could cause an explosion.

Langley had lost a lot of his taut edginess as the feeble winter light grew, but it was obvious his self-control was very tenuous. Everybody had their Achilles heel; weakened by his wound and a sense of failure, Langley had found his. Only training and discipline held him together.

"How about some of Jane's coffee—mit der rum? It's bloody cold up here."

Phil stopped, listening, concentrating. "Hear anything, Sarge?"

"Yes." Langley was frightened to speak. "Yes . . ."

Rising and falling with the wind, they heard the deep hum of an engine.

"The radio!" cried Langley. "Switch the bastard on!"

Two, three minutes passed; the noise grew louder, passing the point of any doubt, but they saw nothing.

"Christ Almighty!" Langley was not blaspheming. "Where is he?"

Answering his Prayer, they heard a voice.

"AT1, AT1—this is your friendly neighborhood helo. Do you read me? Over."

It was the first voice they had heard from outside for ten days, a breath of fresh air in the fog of their claustrophobic world. Langley fumbled frantically with the switch, but the time lost restored something of his old regimental self.

"This is AT1. You are loud and clear. Over."

"AT1, you are loud and clear. I am coming in to lower one passenger. Are there any snags? Over."

Phil grabbed Langley's arm. "The aerials, and the surface in dicey."

"This is AT1. Watch out for our whip aerials—and the deck has a bit of ice on it. Over."

"Thanks. We'll watch out. Please have someone on the pad to assist our passenger. His baggage will come down first. Over."

"Roger. Wilco."

Shivering with cold and excitement, Phil was on the pad well before the Wessex arrived. He waved as the helo moved alongside, the pilot taking a good look at his target. Crab-like, the helo slid sideways, over the tanker, the door opened, and the crewman lowered a heavy bag, followed by the passenger.

As the man came in reach, Phil grabbed his feet, his legs, then his waist, steadying the well-clad figure as his feet touched the icy deck. The line slackened, the man freed himself from the encircling strop, and waved.

Up went the lowering line, the helo climbing, banking sideways. Phil caught the whiff of paraffin, till then no favorite smell. The helo shot ahead, lost to his sight. The whole operation had lasted less than two minutes.

With more enthusiasm than discretion, Phil slapped this first arrival from the outer world on the back. "My dear life, are we glad to see you!" He was near tears. "Come on, let's get out of this flamin' cold!"

The visitor grinned, his face almost hidden by his flying helmet and an impressive tawny beard. "In a minute. Let's have a look at this deck first." He surveyed it rapidly, scuffing the thin ice with his boot. "It's certainly big enough, and the builders tell us it'll take a loaded Wessex."

Phil had picked up the bag, almost dancing with impatience.

"Okay, lead on."

Bill and Jane waited, equally impatiently. Suddenly Jane felt her old inhibitions return. In the past few days she had been quite unconscious of her face, not now . . . No, she would not run; Mark had been right. Poor Mark . . .

Langley grasped the stranger's hand, pumping it in a very untypical manner. "God, we're glad to see you!" The man nodded, smiling politely, but getting across a certain reserve. He wanted to get on. Langley hastily made the introductions. The visitor's face was fractionally still as he saw Jane's scar, but that was all.

"I'm Carter—weapons electrical officer. Very briefly"—he clearly meant that—"what happened?"

Langley's answer was a masterpiece of brevity.

"We were hijacked. One of the guards was a hijacker. He's dead, so is another guard. Most of the cargo's gone, the computer's wrecked, so is our radio."

The officer's eyebrows shot up, but he had no time for chat. "I see. . . . Is the computer room open?"

"Nossir."

"Um. Well, I'll take a look." Phil led him down, and Carter examined the door carefully while Phil explained what had happened. "At least the door doesn't look deformed." He dug in the recesses of his flying suit, producing a signal. "Let's hope it still works; it's our only chance of getting to the engine room."

He set the combination and pulled at the bolt handle. Nothing happened, but at the second attempt the lock worked. The bolts were very stiff, but they got the door opened. Phil shone a hand lamp; one glance was enough.

"Christ!" said Phil; the officer whistled. They entered cautiously, crunching over broken glass and mangled metal.

"This has to be the most expensive junk heap I've ever seen," observed Carter. "Well, that's that. Press on, the door to the engine room is somewhere."

Less strong, that one had been blown off its hinges. They moved along a short passage, shifted the remains of the door from the top of a ladder, and descended two decks to the engine room, hot and noisy with the clamor of the tireless diesels. Carter took the lamp, flashing it around until he located the local control panel. Phil found a light switch. As far as both men could see, nothing had been damaged. Carter gave the thumbs-up sign, pointing upward. Back in the citadel, he called the helo.

"Charles, this is James. Relay this to the ship: Hijack. Computer and radio wrecked, but engine room intact. Suggest engineer officer and chief mech join. Three survivors aboard. Over."

"Roger, James. Wait one."

Carter put down the walkie-talkie, then frowned with annoyance as he saw Langley's sling. "Damn! Sorry, I forgot, but I'll get the helo to lift you out."

"Not necessary, sir," said Langley stiffly. "Miss Harris is a fully qualified nurse."

"Still, you ought to see a quack."

"Nossir. I'll stay until we all go."

"Go? It's not that bad—yet." Carter explained. "We've been mulling over your problems for the past thirty-six hours. Your safety is the first consideration, but we'd like to save the ship too, if we can. The captain said that if the computer should be beyond my expertise"—he grinned—"we would have a stab at reducing the ship's speed. That's why I called for the plumbers."

"James? Charles here. From the ship; approved. Ends. What d'you want me to do?"

"What's it like ahead? Are we running out of water?"

"Not so far. No sign of ice for the next forty miles."

"Good." Carter looked at Langley. "Any stores you need?"

"No, we're all right, but we don't have much in the way of tools."

Carter nodded, thumbing the radio switch. "You can go home, Charles. En route, warn the E.O. to bring his own spanners. And tell my P.O. to load a kit for me, including an Avometer. When you get back, I'll land you on. The deck's okay, but a bit icy, so no fancy stuff."

"Roger. On my way."

The Navy's casual approach shook Langley; he did not care for all this "Charles-James" stuff—until he realized that less than fifteen minutes had elapsed since Carter had landed. Casual or not, they did not stand around.

And Carter kept moving. Jane appeared with coffee, he thanked her, but did not take time out to drink it, moving on to the steering system, taking sips while listening to Phil, who explained the setup as far as he understood it. In the wheelhouse he examined the stout steel cover over the instrument panel.

"That looks too tough a nut for us. What's in there?"

"Gyro compass repeater, log indicator, engine controls, fore and aft anemometers, and wind-direction indicator." Phil rattled it off.

Carter looked at him with new interest. "You have to be a sailor."

"Yessir. Ex-leading seaman—most of my time in frigates."

Carter grinned at him. "You really jumped out of the frying pan into the fire!"

Phil grinned back. "I got married; the wife nagged me to get out. I did. Six months later she ran off with a bloody car salesman!" He shrugged. "End of story."

Carter made sympathetic noises; it was a tale as old as the hills. "Anyway, you being Navy is good news. Are you prepared to stick with this job?"

"What, now, like?"

"Yes. If Langley and Miss . . . er . . . Harris want out, we'll ship them over to *Guardian*, but it would be a help to have someone who knows their way around this thing."

"I don't think Bill Langley will go, or Jane—that's Miss Harris—either."

Carter slapped the top of the cover. "Okay; fine. No point in wasting time on this lot. I suppose there isn't a magnetic compass in there?"

"No, only the gyro repeater."

"And the master gyro smashed." Carter grimaced. "Still, if Engines can solve the speed problem, we should be able to steer this sea cow somehow. London says the changeover from manuals to automatic steering is in the computer room. . . . Can you give me a hand to trace the wiring?"

"Sure, sir."

Jane found them crunching around on the debris in the computer room. "Mr. Langley says the helo is in sight, and can you tell me how many there will be for lunch?"

Phil smiled to himself; now it was "lunch."

"That's very kind, Miss Harris." Carter tried not to look at the scar. What a waste! She must have been a real little raver. . . . He smiled. "Anything will do—a sandwich, perhaps?"

Jane was shocked. "Oh, no! Would you mind steak and kidney pie?"

"Marvelous!" said Carter raptly. He saw Phil's sardonic expression when she had gone. "What d'you expect me to say, yuk? Our chief cook would slay me—his pies are out of this world."

"Ours are out of the deep-freeze, but Jane's a good cook.

In fact, she's a damn good kid all around.''

Carter, concentrating on the wiring, said, ''That's a hell of a scar she's got. How did she get it?''

''She's never said. She was pretty shy at first, headscarf and glasses all the time, but that's the one thing; this affair has got her over it.''

Carter glanced at his watch. ''Better get ready for the helo. You had any deck-handling experience?''

''Only with light stuff—the old Wasp and the Lynx.''

''That, my boy, makes you the most experienced man in sight. You're chock man, okay?'' They ran for the companionway.

''One slight snag, sir, no chocks. The civvy jobs have skids.''

''Oh, yes we do—two pairs in my bag.''

Carter brought the heavy Wessex down on the center spot without trouble; Phil raced in, head well down, deafened by rotors and engines, and chocked the wheels. AT1's roll was very slight, but with ice on the deck, no chances could be taken. The two new arrivals jumped out and unloaded their gear. Carter climbed up for a shouted word with the pilot. He returned looking thoughtful.

''You lot are packed, ready to go?''

''Our bags are in the citadel.'' Phil looked anxious. ''Trouble, sir?''

''The pilot says the weather's getting thicker up ahead— and fog could mean ice, a lot of it.''

''How far?''

''Right now, about forty miles.''

''Oh, well.'' Phil was relieved. ''The engineers should have plenty of time.''

''Yes, but reducing speed only delays matters. The steering's another problem. And I learn our met man has dreamed up a depressing forecast. He's expecting another strong blow from the west.''

''That's all we need! What you going to do, sir?''

''Not me, laddie—up to the captain. He's pushing the old girl as fast as he can; hopes to be with us in a couple of hours. Ah, James is ready.''

The helo left for another recce to the south before returning to *Guardian*. Thankfully Phil and Carter retired from the freezing cold of the helo pad to the warmth of the computer room, taking the tools with them. They worked, Phil holding wires and lights, happy to be without responsibility; judging by Carter's pithy remarks, he had problems.

An hour passed, and Phil was horrified to find it past midday. Still the engines rumbled remorselessly on at the same even tenor.

"Taking their time down there, aren't they, sir?"

Carter came back reluctantly from contemplation of the multicored cable. "What? Oh—Engines knows his stuff; he's stuck with some pretty novel machinery. One wrong move and we get a loud twanging sound. Still, as you say, time is fleeting."

Langley looked in. "The helo's gone back to *Guardian*. Pilot says it's thickening up fast up ahead, and he's relayed a message for you, sir, from the ship. Said you'd understand."

"And?"

"It's one word: 'expedite.' That's all."

Carter grimaced. "Which means get a bloody wriggle on. I'll see Engines."

With a wealth of Welsh expressiveness, Engines said they had only two pairs of hands, etc., but action might be expected in fifteen minutes. If, however, they fancied a shower of blue sparks in the computer room, he'd be happy to oblige right away.

Ten minutes later, the sound from below told of his success. After one fearful moment, when the noise increased, it ebbed steadily to a distant murmur.

Engines peered into the computer room, wiping his hands in slow satisfaction on a rag. "Okay, James boy?"

"Not bad," conceded Carter. "What are we down to?"

"Not knowing, can't say, but you've got revs for a fraction less than five knots."

"Well, it buys us some more time," observed Carter, intent upon his bunch of wires, "and I need all the time I can get."

Jane announced that "lunch" would be ready in ten minutes.

"Just time for a jar," said Phil hopefully.

"We'd better eat in two watches. You go first, Taffy."

Phil and Jane ate with the engineer officer, Phil enjoying himself hugely, recounting their story. Jane liked his modest account of his bomb-disposal efforts, but blushed when he praised her part, not least her shooting.

Not given to self-analysis, she was surprised to find she had no second thoughts about killing Colmar. As Phil told the story, she saw again in her mind's eye Colmar flung sideways by her shot, hitting the pilot, causing the crash. She felt sorry for the pilot, nothing more.

Langley, Carter, and the chief mech had a much more sober meal. Langley's account was much shorter, and the telling made him gloomier than ever: for him it was a recital of his personal failure.

On watch in the wheelhouse, Phil's euphoria drained away. In the past hour the weather had got thicker; he hoped the helo pilot's idea that it presaged ice was wrong. He took some comfort from the speed reduction, but less from the increasing swell setting in from the west.

God! What an awful chunk of ocean—ice, fog, snow, and bastard wicked gales.

"AT1, AT1, this is *Guardian*. How do you hear me? Over."

"*Guardian*, this is AT1. You are clear but weak. Over."

"AT1, you also. Report situation. Over."

Phil had more than a suspicion the order was for Carter, but reckoned the bloke had earned his grub. "AT1 here. Speed down to about five knots. No steerage as yet."

Guardian wasn't satisfied. "Tell Lieutenant Carter to speak. Over."

The captain told Carter that *Guardian* would be alongside in fifty minutes. If repairs could not be completed by that time, the tanker was to come down to bare steerage way. *Guardian* would pass a tow to the tanker's bows and haul her around to a safer course by brute force. Assuming there was no power on the forward capstan, Carter should have all available hands up there to get the hawser aboard.

Phil winced as he listened. It sounded simple, but was nothing of the sort. Barely two hours of thin daylight remained; fog could clamp down any minute, and they could have a full gale before morning, all complications to a tricky operation even in ideal conditions.

The engineer officer got the speed down to three knots, and although the roll was nothing by previous standards—or what they might expect—the reduction did nothing to improve it.

Carter, before returning below, studied the swell carefully. With an icy deck, more than a five-degree roll each way would prevent the Wessex landing.

The captain called again. If the engineer officer was satisfied that the chief mechanic could handle the engines, he was to return with a verbal account of AT1's misadventures. In the same lift, extra clothing would be flown in for Carter and the chief. No further flights could be expected except in an emergency; if the stewardess wanted to get out, this would be the moment.

Jane's response was a firm refusal, motivated less by courage than the prospect of facing so many strangers. Fortunately for her peace of mind, she could not know her name and face were known worldwide.

Twenty minutes later the helo arrived. Carter decided against landing the Wessex, so down came the stores— clothing and spare batteries and a boat compass—and up went the E.O.

On time, out of the gathering mist, HMS *Guardian* appeared. Phil blinked at her unfamiliar bright-red hull; unlike most war vessels, ice-patrol ships wanted to be seen. Phil called the saloon, and Langley and Jane came up, feasting their eyes on the sight. Langley thought she looked very small, but in the face of the sailor's enthusiasm, said nothing.

Once again the radio crackled into life. Hands were to be on the forecastle to take the tow in ten minutes' time. Carter led the party, muttering to himself about the impossibility of getting on with his work. Jane was laden with flasks of her now famous fortified coffee, and Langley went to operate the walkie-talkie. Bringing up the rear, he noted sourly that the chief mechanic, a large, black-bearded man, showed great solicitude for Jane, taking her arm and one of the flasks.

Guardian slid alongside, rolling easily in the growing swell, barely twenty yards of the tanker's starboard bow. Deserted forward, well-clad figures were intensely active right aft.

While they waited, Jane served out coffee, and wanted to know what they were going to do. Phil felt some of Langley's frustration when the chief mech explained, one arm around her shoulders, his hairy face close to hers as he pointed.

With the warning whistle from *Guardian*, they took cover. The Coston gun banged, the line snaking across from the helo deck to the tanker's bows, quickly gathered in by Phil. Hauling in the two-inch manila attached to the gun line was easy, but next came the heavy towing hawser. Although the ice-patrol ship got within ten yards, it took their combined efforts to manhandle the thick, freezing rope aboard and over a bollard.

Innocently, Jane thought that would be all, and was wrong. A second hawser was coming. They labored again, clumsy with cold, the short winter day fading by the time they finished their back-breaking task.

Guardian wasted no time. Even as Langley barked "Both hawsers secured" into the radio, the Navy ship had begun to move away, slowly increasing her speed a few revolutions at a time, her course diverging only one or two degrees from AT1's long-held 181 degrees.

The party watched anxiously as the hawsers rose dripping from the sea; an error of judgment could be disastrous. AT1's bollard could be ripped from her deck like rotten teeth, or the hawsers might part; there were no spares.

The ropes tightened, groaning as the stress wrung the last of the seawater from them. Carter watched from the bows, his eyes streaming with cold, looking for that slight slackening in the hawsers which would tell that the tanker responded. Seemingly an age passed; the water under *Guardian*'s stern boiled white, the ropes were bar-taut, vibrant, and then he saw the lines dip fractionally, marking the minute easing of tension.

With infinite caution the Navy ship edged one, two degrees to starboard, her captain learning the complex balance of forces by trial and very little error. Towing a ship ten times one's own size is not for the inexperienced, but to turn the ship towed while it still moved under its own power with a jammed rudder involved a lot more, including danger to the towing ship. Tugs have capsized, a remote possibility with *Guardian*, but Carter noted the tall, thin figure of the first lieutenant standing beside a large sailor, who leaned on an ax, ready to cut the tow if necessary.

Carter reported all well at his end and received permission to get his team back under cover. Flapping their arms, stamping their feet, the party got quickly back to the relative warmth of the citadel. Glancing at *Guardian*, now little more than a group of blurred lights, Jane remarked that it had got dark even earlier than she had expected.

Carter and the chief mechanic smiled, nodding agreement, but said nothing. Old Antarctic hands, they realized that more than night hid the ship: AT1 was in the ice fog. The swell, unremarkable as yet, served sinister notice of bad weather to come.

If *Guardian*'s radar detected heavy ice, she might be forced to cut loose and order the tanker to stop engines. In which case AT1 would drift helpless before the storm, hopefully, as fast as the threatening ice. Neither Carter nor the chief doubted that they would be rescued, but it would be a mighty hairy operation for all concerned. Neither man mentioned this to AT1's team.

But the Navy captain, backing experience and judgment against a host of dangerous problems, refused to be stampeded. With frightening slowness *Guardian* inched the vast bulk of AT1 around. The captain stood where he could see his tow, feeling the response of his own ship through his body, backed up by an endless succession of quietly spoken reports from the officer of the watch.

More than Jane or Bill, Phil had some grasp of the

difficulties, but was quite happy to leave all that to the *Guardian*'s Old Man; that was what captains were for. After all, paid nearly as much as a suburban bank manager, he was only responsible for a hundred and forty lives and thirty million dollars' worth of ships.

XXII

Even as they thawed out, they had little time to consider the big step to safety that had been taken. Tired though he was, Langley realized it more than the rest. Minute by minute, inch by inch, they were being literally dragged from the jaws of icy hell; hazards still lay ahead, but surely they would not fail now? Langley had known and faced fear in diverse ways; walking down a Belfast street, sweating with the certain knowledge that a well-armed dedicated sniper lay ahead, sweating in a very different way in the steaming Borneo jungle, with the imminent threat of death from a poisoned dart no less lethal than a burst of automatic fire, or on United Nations detachment, stoically enduring mortar fire and rockets in Cyprus. All this, to him, was as nothing compared with his fear of the ice, the unknown.

Surely they could not fail now? Yes, he told himself, oh, yes . . .

Lieutenant Carter tactfully consulted the soldier about the watch-keeping rota. He, Phil, and Langley would split the wheelhouse watch between them; the chief mechanic, on call at all times for engine-room duty, would assist Carter with the steering repairs and rig emergency lighting in the computer room.

Carter, who recognized an exhausted man when he saw one, contrived the watches so that Langley would have a solid night's sleep, then hurried below to get on with the steering, assisted by Roscorla.

But of all, Jane was the busiest. With two extra men

aboard, she had to do something about their accommodation. To this point she had had neither the time nor the inclination to tackle the dead men's cabins; now she had to.

She began with Jacens'. She pretended to herself that it was no more than cleaning out a room after a patient, but the flimsy defense soon failed. Packing his pathetically few belongings, she wept. Mark, already growing shadowy, seemed such a lonely figure; no photographs, no letters, only that sad, wretched manuscript. For a mature, attractive man to have so little did not make sense; somewhere in his life there had to be a tragedy that had set his feet on this final, deadly path.

The only personal effect she found was a small, battered, and chipped plaster rabbit, its Disneyesque expression nearly rubbed off. What had that meant to him—a child, a memory of a fun fair, a moment of happiness with a woman? Wife?

Briefly she held it in her hand, certain he too had held it in just the same way. She wanted to keep it, regretting that she had never taken a photograph of him, regretting that she had nothing except memory. With sudden resolution she thrust the memento in his bag, it might bring a message of comfort to someone. . . .

The packing finished, she made up the bed with clean sheets, dusted and polished until no trace of Mark Jacens, not even a fingerprint, remained. Her task ended, she ran from the cabin to her own, and for a time was alone.

She tackled Colmar's cabin with a totally different sort of reluctance. One step into his cabin, and the smell of his after-shave lotion brought back, with awful clarity, his smooth face, the cold eyes, inhuman eyes, devoid of humor, compassion.

She found his grip in the hanging cupboard, and with one swift movement swept all his considerable toiletry into it with a clatter. He too had little else: company-issue clothing, a few western paperbacks, but she did not find that surprising. She opened a drawer, scooped out the neatly arrayed shirts and underwear, stuffing them in the bag, anyhow. If Bill had not warned her the police would want it all, she would have tossed the lot over the side. To even touch his clothes, clean as they were, was physically repugnant to her; the very neatness made it worse. Colmar the cat, a neutered cat.

Impatient to be finished, she wrenched the lower drawer under his bunk open. For a second she thought it empty; she stared, puzzled by the familiarity of a small black box. Why should she recognize it? Then she spotted the cable.

The sudden shock of recognition drove the breath from her body as if from a physical blow. She snatched her hand back, wide-eyed in disbelief and gripping fear.

In the silence of the cabin, she heard it *ticking*.

The faint, deadly sound shook her into life. She screamed, again and again.

In the computer room, Carter and Phil jumped convulsively at the terror in her voice. Both dropped their tools and ran.

Jane struggled to her feet as the naval officer crashed in. "There! Ticking!"

Carter had no time for thought, only action. The black cable ran to the back of the drawer, terminating in a shapeless lump, taped in the corner. He grabbed it, forcing himself to slow down. Apparently calm, he eased the pencil-shaped detonator from the plastic explosive, pulled the lump loose, and got to his feet. Phil was unceremoniously bundling the shocked and trembling Jane out.

"Get her into the saloon," ordered Carter sharply, "and grab a fire extinguisher. Don't touch the detonator; it could go anytime." In the passageway they met Langley, startled.

"What the hell—?"

"Demolition charge." Carter kept his professional calm. "The detonator's still live. Leave it." He pushed past the senior guard. "I'm ditching this."

Barely a minute later he was back in the citadel, the plastic explosive gone. Outside, the cold had been intense, but in the darkness Carter sweated.

Descending the companionway, he heard the sharp pistol-shot crack, and found Phil, pale, but grinning; an acrid smell of scorched paint filled the air. The drawer was buckled, and a small hole had been torn in the bottom. "Well, a miss is as good as a mile," observed Phil with synthetic cheerfulness.

"Yes," said Carter flatly. "Stow the extinguisher; we'd better get back to work."

Phil gave him an admiring look. " 'Fraid we can't allow that, sir. We've a custom in this bastard; anyone who finds a bomb buys drinks all around."

Carter smiled thinly. He could certainly do with one. "Okay, you know the form: a quick one."

Langley and Jane were already drinking. Langley finished his and left hurriedly.

"I'm sorry I screamed like that, but I didn't recognize it at first, and to *hear* it . . ."

"You did absolutely the right thing, Miss Harris," said Carter soothingly. "To yell blue murder was, as we say, the appropriate action."

"Thing I can't get over," put in Phil, passing drinks, "is why the bastard didn't go before."

"Luck. Probably that fellow—what was his name? . . ."

"Colmar."

"Colmar, didn't wind the clockwork fully. It ran down, and the jerk when Miss Harris opened the drawer started it again."

"Luck," said Phil meditatively. "Yes . . . well, it's the one thing none of us can do without. Here's to you, sir."

"Here's to all of us," replied Carter, and drank.

"To think that bomb has been there all this time!" Jane shuddered. "There may be others!"

"No." Langley had returned, smiling grimly, angry that, once again, he had had no part. After his time in Northern Ireland, bombs held little terror for him, not compared with icebergs, anyway. "I've searched Colmar's cabin; that was the last."

Phil gave him another Scotch.

"There can't be any more," went on Bill. "It's asking too much that a second charge should have failed to detonate. My guess is the pirates provided the makings, that murdering swine Colmar had a bit of plastic left over and a spare detonator, and stuck it in his cabin.''

Carter drained his glass. "I hope you're right—and I think you are. If you should turn up another one, tell Phil. I must get on.''

The rest took the hint and got back to work. Phil and Carter found that the chief mechanic had emerged from the recesses of the engine room and was fixing temporary lighting in the computer room.

"Oh, hello, sir! I was beginning to wonder where everybody had got to.''

The laughter which greeted his remark left him very puzzled. If he hadn't known better, he'd have sworn the pair of them smelled of Scotch.

A half-hour later, AT1's motion had changed. Jane and Bill did not notice it, but the sailors did. The chief, in the computer room; Lieutenant Carter, head-down in the steerage electronics in the engine room; and Phil, flitting from point to point as Carter directed, all felt it.

Sent to test a wheelhouse connection, Phil told Langley, "We're moving around, Sarge.''

"How d'you know?''

"Feel it, Sarge! Don't you notice? We're beginning to pitch. Not much, but it's there. *Guardian* must have lugged us around a good fifteen to twenty degrees. Bloody good-o!''

"They've said nothing—''

"AT1, AT1. Lieutenant Carter, please.''

Phil grabbed the handset in a buoyant, whiskey-assisted mood. "Lieutenant Carter right now is arse-up in the steering compartment, three decks down. Over.''

"Very well. Tell him that the captain requires a progress report on the steering. Over.''

"I will tell him, but I happen to know he had been delayed. He had to defuse a bomb.''

"*What* did you say? Say again.''

With great enjoyment, Phil did.

"Roger.'' The voice remained impassive. "In future, all

bombs are to be reported at the earliest convenient moment. Out.''

Anyone can take the rise out of the Navy once; few do it twice.

After so many shocks, fears, and dangers, it seemed to the survivors of AT1's team that Christmas had come. Certainly the sea was rising, and aboard *Guardian* anything but happiness reigned, but as far as the tanker's trio were concerned, that was the Navy's business. The knowledge that the ship was no longer heading south raised their spirits, which got a further boost shortly before eight P.M. when Carter, very dirty and getting tired, reported to his captain that he had cut out the wrecked computer and was ready to go ahead with a test of his direct link with the steering.

He learned, in return, that the tanker was roughly on a course of 300 degrees, pointing in the general direction of South Africa. The confirmation of Phil's guess was greeted with enormous relief; even poker-faced Langley thanked God audibly.

There followed strict instructions for the conduct of the test. It would be unwise to cast off the tow until everyone was satisfied the steering worked. Carter's tinkering—as the captain put it—could result in one of two new states: either it worked, or it freed the rudder. In the first state, fine, but if the rudder merely flapped free, AT1 could be, in one way, in a worse condition, unable to hold any course. In which case, said the captain, the tow would have to go on until the steering was made to work. The test would start in ten minutes' time.

Carter, who knew his captain, could read between the lines. The Old Man hadn't said a lot of things: nothing about the weather, nor about the difficulties in casting off the tow in the dark. The only simple way to do that would be to cut the hawsers, but if the tanker's steering failed again, there'd be nothing to tow her with. On the other hand, for AT1 to be able to cast off, the hawsers would have to be slack, and to do that *Guardian* must slow down, and that, with a hundred-thousand-ton tanker under shaky control coming up behind her, in the dark, could scarcely appeal to the captain of a three-thousand-ton ship.

But if the steering worked, that was what he intended to do: Carter felt he must have some powerful reason.

In ten minutes they were ready. Phil stood by the wheel, staring glumly at the boat compass, placed conveniently on the deck. In his private opinion, it was a sheer waste of time, with all the surrounding steel, it would be hopelessly inaccurate.

Langley held the walkie-talkie, wooden-faced and silent. While he did not understand the finer points, clearly this would be a critical moment.

Jane's position was beside the galley phone, leaning out of the door, ready to relay messages from Carter or the chief in the computer room.

"AT1. Captain speaking. Connect up steering when I give the order. Do not, repeat not, touch the engines. Pass to Lieutenant Carter, who is to acknowledge. Over."

Langley passed the message to Jane, made her repeat it, and she ran to Carter, who nodded. "Say, from Carter, 'acknowledged.' " He was tense, unsmiling, but the chief gave her a comforting wink.

, Satisfied with the communications, the captain checked another point. "Who will be on the wheel?"

"Tell him Leading Seaman Roscorla," said Phil with some pride.

The captain greeted that news with perceptible relief. "Pay attention, Roscorla, when the connection is made, keep your hands off the wheel—it may fly around—then take it very steady. Without a rudder indicator, I know it's hard, but I don't want more than two degrees of helm either way. If you feel you've got control, bring the wheel amidships and wait. Understand?"

"Yessir!"

"Very well. Connect!"

The message was swiftly relayed: wheelhouse to galley, galley to computer room.

Carter took a final look. "Switch on, chief."

The switch slammed down; both men looked apprehensively at the loosely hanging cables, smothered with insulating tape. "Well," said the chief after a few tense seconds, "can't smell anything burning."

"I'm going down to see." Carter headed for the engine-room ladder.

"For Christ's sake, be careful, sir—there's a lotta volts charging around down there!"

In the wheelhouse Phil had three fingers resting on the hub, trying to sense the first sign of movement. The wheel stirred, and his hand came back as if burned. Lazily the spokes rotated one way, paused, then reversed direction. Phil gingerly took a light hold of the wheel, getting the feel, trying to remember how it had felt, a lifetime back, when AT1 sailed from Bahrein. He gripped the spokes more firmly, and gently eased the wheel a fraction to port and held it there, his heart thumping, for five, ten seconds. He released his hold, the wheel spun back. Catching it, he made the same test to starboard, and with the same result.

Phil gulped, fully alive to his responsibility. Once the tow was cast off, they'd be on their own with a vengeance.

"Tell the Old Man I reckon it's working!"

If the captain was relieved, he did not say so. What course, according to the boat compass, was he steering? Two-thirty-five, said Roscorla. The captain told him the true course was three hundred degrees, and to remember that the sixty-five-degree error applied only to this course. He was to remain on that heading until further orders. Lieutenant Carter was to be found and report.

Carter hurried to the set and was told that if, after one hour, he was satisfied his repairs would hold up, the tow would be cast off. Meanwhile, the steering-control switch was to be constantly manned.

During the hour, Carter had a badly needed shower and changed, then took over from the chief mechanic while he cleaned up. Anxious about supper arrangements, Jane sought and found them, both in white polo-necked sweaters and navy trousers; with their large beards and weatherbeaten faces, they reminded her of old tobacco advertisements.

Carter told her supper would have to be a pretty mobile

feast. If all went well, he and the chief would soon be required up forward, casting off the tow—maybe some soup, sandwiches, and her famous fortified coffee?

Jane firmly rejected the idea. Soup and coffee, yes, but something more substantial in between, like steak. She would cook it when they were ready. No, no trouble at all. Involuntarily she smiled, and instantly turned her head, and left quickly.

"Sad, that, you know," said the chief, shaking his head. "They ought to be able to do something."

Carter nodded. "Certainly is a mess." He turned to more immediate problems. "Come on, chief; fifteen minutes to go, time for a final check of *our* botched-up job."

Ten minutes later the inspection was completed. Carter sighed. "Can't say I'm exactly proud of it, but it works. If it holds up for forty-eight hours, maybe I can get some of my lads over to make a better job of it."

"The way the sea's getting up, I think we'll be bloody lucky if the chopper can get off the deck in the next two days."

"That's what I like about you, chief, always the ray of sunshine!"

On time, Carter reported himself satisfied, and at once got the order to prepare to cast off. With Langley to man the radio, the Navy men went forward, into the Antarctic night, a freezing journey along the icy catwalk, not made easier by the blaze of light from *Guardian*, which blinded them as the tanker's screening bows dipped, followed by pitch darkness as the bows rose again.

Guardian had two searchlights on; one lit the towing hawsers, the other AT1's bow. Armed with crowbars from the boatswain's store, they waited impatiently, the chief kicking the eye of the rope on one bollard in a futile attempt to make it more pliable. At least it helped to keep his circulation going.

None of them peered over the bows; to do so would only blind them and invite frostbite. Carter thought the Old Man was more than welcome to this evolution; he could guess the tension on *Guardian*'s bridge as the speed was reduced. The hawsers had to be slack to get them off the bollards, and to watch the bluff bows of the giant tanker inching nearer would test any skipper's nerve and skill. As *Guardian* slowed and the line slackened, so the strain came off the towing ship, tending to increase her speed, but to reduce speed sharply would be to invite disaster. In *Guardian*'s engine room, the chief engineer juggled with the throttles, cursing AT1.

Langley yelled, "Slip!"

The Navy men sprang into action. First one, then the second frozen hawser was levered free, sliding like sea serpents through the fairleads, down into the dark water.

"All gone!" shouted Carter, and Langley repeated the message.

"From *Guardian*. Very good. Return to wheelhouse and report on arrival."

"Okay. Acknowledged."

Thankfully, they headed back. "My bloody oath," said the chief, combing frozen breath from his beard with his fingers, "what a bastard!"

Phil, bowed with responsibility, hardly heard him, concentrating on his steering. Langley stared at the patrol ship's receding lights, rising and falling in the darkness, and went down for a hot drink.

"*Guardian*. Carter here. Am now in the wheelhouse."

"Roger. Hold your present course, and increase speed to six knots."

"Thank Christ for that," muttered Phil. "She's a right cow at this speed."

The chief mech ran down the ladder. "What a carry-on—from umpteen below freezing to umpteen above!"

Soon they felt the increased vibration in the wheelhouse. They had revolutions for six knots. Carter told his captain.

"I am taking station one mile off your starboard beam. I hope we will have a quiet night, but the met forcast is not very good, and a Shackleton reports there's ice ahead. Be prepared for evasive action. I will con you past any obstructions. That is all."

"And quite enough, too," said Phil. "If it's all the same to you, sir, reckon we might keep that bit about ice to ourselves, like.''

''Yes, I agree.'' Watching *Guardian*'s lights, he guessed why the Old Man had been so damned keen to slip the tow.

Any faint doubts he might have harbored about his captain's judgment would soon go: in five hours, forty minutes, to be precise.

XXIII

Carter relieved Phil at midnight. He had slept for nearly two hours after supper, and while not at the top of his form, faced four long hours' steering with fair equanimity.

The arrangement would work—had to—for one night, but more hands were necessary. So far the task had been to save the ship from immediate disaster. If they got through the next twenty-four hours in one piece, the next problem would be to get the tanker to Cape Town. Labor-saving was one thing; to run a ship with one man on watch, with the entire engine-room staff snoring his head off in a saloon armchair, something else.

Carter hoped the weather would not be bad enough to stop the transfer of two or three seamen. As the night wore on and the wind gathered strength, it became a very faint hope.

The inmates of the company HQ, although still desperate for details of the hijack, were, according to their different temperaments, very excited. In a moment of mad excess, the chief accountant shook hands with the shipping super-intendent, to the latter's surprised embarrassment. The chairman gave a select champagne party, the managing director gave his secretary a long weekend and a lot of attention in Paris. The insurers smiled again, thin sunshine after storm, for it was evident most of the oil had gone, and in Scotland Yard three senior detectives tossed for the plum job, a trip to South Africa to meet the tanker.

About the only people who did not regard the safe return of

AT1 as a foregone conclusion were two or three officers in MOD, and the shipping super, who was also preparing to fly south. This group reserved judgment, and they were the seamen.

And worldwide, press and TV clamored for hard news, all dependent upon the short, factual handouts from the Navy. Editors dreamed of an exclusive interview with Jane Harris, the "Lone Heroine" who had "Gunned Killer," for to a man they billed her as the star of the biggest sea spectacular since the *Titanic*. In their intense search for human-interest background, reporters dug up details of her accident, disfigurement. Tabloids on both sides of the Atlantic presented this "stricken beauty who hid from the world, only to be dogged by tragedy," as a cross between Joan of Arc and the heroine in a Greek play.

The pirates sweated, their only comfort that with every passing day the scent grew colder. The first tanker had discharged its cargo and was en route at its very best speed for the scrapyard; the second was ahead of its schedule. Another week, that was all they asked. Their boss in Switzerland had been far from idle; crews were to be cut to a minimum, the rest paid off and sent to their prearranged dispersal points to await their share of the robbery.

That much was known to all, but he sent other, very secret orders to his lieutenants: the men who had worked in AT1 might be identified, and though they knew little, they endangered the rest. Nothing was to be done until they had dispersed, for the tanker disposal must go through without a hitch, but once these few men were scattered, they were to be got rid of, quietly and permanently.

Only Karl, the German, had the sense to realize just how perilous his position was. He had had no part in the killings, and if he was caught, it was his private intention to turn state's witness. He realized that the boss—whoever he was—would guess that far, and Karl acted accordingly. He collected his considerable pay and left for his dispersal point, Singapore. There he checked in at his dingy hotel, and spent one tension-filled night, knowing the local "import-export agent" would check and report his arrival.

Early next morning he slipped out the back way through the kitchen, got to Paya Lebar airport without trouble, and was in Bangkok by midday. There he changed his name, passport, and plane and flew—via Manila and a twelve-hour wait—to Sydney, Australia. Now an Australian citizen—at least, according to his emergency passport—he took a cheap room in the seedy Kings Cross area. When his moustache had grown, he took a job as a bouncer in a local nightclub and settled down to wait—watchful awake, a gun under his pillow when asleep.

Every hour, *Guardian* called, confirming the course steered. By 3:20 A.M. Carter felt he had spent his entire life at the wheel. Wind and sea had got up, but not enough to stop him yawning frequently. He stopped in mid-yawn, fully awake.

"Carter . . . captain speaking. How does she handle?"

Something had to be up for the Old Man to ask such questions at that ungodly hour.

"She's pretty sluggish, sir."

"I see. . . . Bring her up to eight knots; that should improve matters. There's a rather large piece of ice ahead, making slightly better speed than we are. I'll route you well clear of it. Keep the chief closed up in the engine room. We may want to whack on a bit more."

"Aye-aye, sir." Clutching the wheel with one hand, he could just reach the phone. "Chop-chop, chief! Revs for eight knots, and stay down there. We're in for a few evolutions."

Four minutes later he reported to *Guardian* that revolutions for eight knots were on.

"Very good. Port twenty. Steer two-two-zero by your compass."

Praying for his repairs, Carter altered course; with elephantine slowness AT1 responded. Ten minutes passed before Carter could report he was steady on the new course.

"I've news for you, Carter: slugs are acrobats compared with that damned thing! Come up to ten knots and go to port to two-one-zero."

Before AT1 had steadied on the new course, Phil arrived in the wheelhouse, shivering.

"Who shook you?" said Carter.

"Those flaming engines! What's going on, sir?"

Carter explained briefly.

"Glad old Bill doesn't know. He must be out like a light. He's as tough as they come, but icebergs give him the twitch. Funny." He yawned. "I'll nip off and grab some coffee and bring you some."

He returned with food and drink, a bulky figure now, dressed against the biting cold. Carter glanced at his watch and said ungratefully, "It's all yours in five minutes."

"Thank *you*, sir!" Phil proffered a loaded dish. "Like a cheese sarney? Got pickles in it."

"That's quick work!"

"Not really," confessed Phil, his mouth half-full. "Good old Jane built a stack of 'em before she got her head down."

"Carter—port fifteen—steer two-zero-zero!"

The lieutenant caught the urgency in his skipper's voice and spun the wheel, praying again the telemotor wiring would hold up, his gaze fixed on the compass. "Move, for God's sake!"

Phil stopped chewing. He stared into the darkness, suddenly split by *Guardian's* searchlights. They wavered, then settled. Five or six miles away he saw a long white line, an iceberg even larger than they had previously encountered; he could see why the captain got snappy. One beam panned along the line. At the western end, after a patch of blackness, another, smaller glittering ice island.

"Hard aport! Full speed!"

"Take the wheel!" As Phil jumped for the wheel, Carter grabbed the phone.

The engines took on a new, deep-throated roar, the wheelhouse shook.

"Steer one-nine-five!" In the stress of the moment, someone in *Guardian* was slow to switch off the microphone. "My God! Things like that shouldn't be allowed."

Phil grinned. "I don't think your Old Man likes us very much."

"He's not the only one!"

"AT1, you're crowding me. Am dropping astern. Will come up on your port side. Report when you are steady on one-nine-five."

Carter guessed the vessel running into danger was not AT1 but *Guardian*. Stationed where she was, she had stood a healthy chance of being forced onto the ice by her charge's ponderous movements. At full speed AT1 did prove more manageable, but five minutes still passed before they could report being steady on the new course. Another half-hour slipped away in hectic activity before they had cleared the icebergs and dropped back to a more sedate ten knots and a northerly course.

Guardian's captain had learned something more: the power-tonnage ratio of AT1 was far less than in any ship he had ever heard of, and unmentioned in the brief signaled from London. Ships with human crews would very seldom alter course to clear another ship—or berg—at more than fifteen miles. That was the average maximum visual distance, and radar made little difference. Under normal conditions, AT1's radar would be tracking, and its computer plotting, everything within thirty miles, and once the computer recognized a possible navigational hazard, began making minute alterations of course and speed. With this built-in facility, the designers had less need for a large reserve of power, saving some five percent, which cut capital costs on engines and steering, running costs on maintainence and fuel, and increased cargo space.

After that nerve-racking experience, *Guardian* took station a mile ahead of the tanker, floodlit her quarterdeck, and signaled, "Revert to cruising stations and follow me."

Carter flopped out on his bunk in Jacens' old cabin and instantly slept. In the saloon, Chief Powers decided he'd earned a drink before settling down in his armchair again.

Much brighter and more cheerful after a good night's sleep, Langley went up to the wheelhouse at seven-thirty. The endless, gray tumbling sea and AT1's motion failed to damp his spirits; every minute, they were getting farther away from the south, enough tonic for him.

" 'Morning, Phil. Had a quiet night?''

Several answers occurred to the sailor, but he let them go. "You ever driven a ship, Sarge?''

"Me? No.''

"Now's your chance to learn! Easy as steering a car,'' he said encouragingly and untruthfully. "See *Guardian*? Just keep our bows pointing at her.''

"Here—''

"Just take the bloody wheel, Sarge!'' exclaimed Phil desperately. "I've been breaking my neck for the last hour. Hold the wheel where it is—I'll be in the head.''

Carter found Langley clinging grimly to the wheel a few minutes later, grinned, and turned his attention to the weather. Bang went any idea of a helo transfer that day. He looked again at Langley. Why not? The chap had both hands in use now.

Phil returned and took over the last ten minutes of his watch. Langley joined Carter, looking at *Guardian*, certainly quite a sight. AT1 was rolling, but the Navy ship reeled and plunged in a way that, Langley said, made him sick to watch.

Carter seized his chance. Yes, just watching could indeed make him seasick. Best thing was a job—like steering.

Carter hustled Langley to the steering position; fifteen minutes' tuition, and the apprehensive Langley had the con, under Carter's watchful eye. An hour later, he pronounced the soldier fit—by AT1 standards—to keep a short watch in daylight. Neither Carter nor Phil could go on splitting the twenty-four hours between them on the wheel, work that required constant concentration.

Langley very soon saw the point, and at least he was doing something useful, and even found a wry pleasure in learning the art in a giant tanker in a full gale. *Guardian* preserved a diplomatic silence, watching AT1's serpentine course, taking good care to give the monster plenty of sea room. Carter got an armchair up to the citadel, told Langley to sing out if *Guardian* called, and promptly fell asleep.

Within minutes Langley's barrack-square voice woke him. *Guardian* wanted him.

As he had expected, there would be no flying that day, but

there were urgent demands from Scotland Yard, the FBI, and Interpol: he must interrogate the AT1 team forthwith.

Carter sighed. "Forthwith" in naval parlance meant "this very second—and you'll still be late." Wearily he called the chief up to take the wheel.

Since he'd joined AT1, he'd been helo control officer, technician, deckhand, steersman, naval officer, bomb-disposal officer, and signalman. Now he'd got to be a bloody detective as well.

He got the team together in the saloon, explaining the "object of the exercise," as he put it. He fished out a notebook and looked at Langley, pencil poised. "So, what do you know?"

Bill said shortly, his manner showing how bad he felt, that he knew damn-all. He'd been knocked out in the very first minute of the hijack, and thereafter had seen and heard nothing.

How about before? No, replied Langley, nothing. He'd never liked Colmar, but who had? Langley sank into gloomy silence.

Carter warmed to his work, remembering innumerable crime novels. He nodded sagely. Langley should stay; maybe he'd remember something from what Phil said, recall some vital clue.

Phil tried hard, but did little better. He remembered that Colmar told him he'd been recruited in his last Army camp—Carter made a note of that—and then there'd been this Jerry seaman, "a big bloke, name of Karl. He came from Travemünde."

"Great!" said Carter gloomily. "A seaman from Travemünde called Karl—that's about as useful as a seaman called Evans from Cardiff."

"I'm trying," replied Phil irritably. He frowned at Jane, who was quietly clearing the table of dishes. "Jane, must you do that when a bloke's trying to think?" He got back to the question. "I'm sure I never heard the rest of his name." He shook his head. "No, sorry."

"Let's try something else," said Carter. "How about the ships? You must have some idea."

Phil displayed every sign of mental effort, shutting his eyes, frowning. He shrugged helplessly. "Such a hell of a lot's happened since then."

"Try."

"Well, the first tanker did slide up on our beam for a bit, 'bout a mile off, and maybe steering just that little bit away from us, so as not to give our computer an attack of the nadgers, I expect. Before we realized what was going on, the helo took off, then it all happened so fast. By the time I saw her again, the tanker had dropped astern, and I only got a bow view. All I can say is I reckon she was about thirty thousand tons, one funnel, and bloody ancient. As for the second ship, I only saw her bows-on. She was bigger—and old."

"Of course they'd be old," exclaimed Carter tactlessly. "It's as plain as day the pirates picked up a couple of tankers ready for the scrapyard—probably sold 'em at a knockout price along with the oil. The world's stuffed with overage tankers, too small and too dear to run! Can't you remember any details? Color of the hull, upperworks, positions of derricks—anything like that?"

Phil tried hard, but with no success. "No. It's no good. It's all so muddled." He had a sudden memory, and blurted out eagerly. "Hey, one of the Arab seamen was called Abdul."

He did not go on.

Carter looked at him thoughtfully. "Well," he said at last, "I can't see the cops going raving mad over that lot." He closed his notebook, smiling sympathetically at the sailor's troubled face. "Never mind, Phil. Can't do everything, and you did a damned fine job with the bombs. I'll pass this bit about Colmar and Karl—it may help." He did not sound convinced.

"May a mere woman say something?"

They looked at her with varying degrees of surprise. Carter said politely, "Of course, Miss Harris, please go ahead."

"I don't suppose it's of the slightest value"—she spoke diffidently, and Carter never did make up his mind if her manner was genuine or cloaked deep sarcasm—"but a woman's eye is not the same as a man's. We're interested in people, not things." She hesitated.

213

"Do go on, Miss Harris." Carter's smile was a little tight around the edges.

"I did happen to notice"—she averted her head, smiling apologetically—"that the German, Karl, had brown hair, blue eyes, was the same height as Phil, aged about forty, had two hearts tattooed on his left forearm with 'Gerda' underneath—"

"Hold on! That's bloody marvelous!" Carter exclaimed, scribbling furiously. He paused, looking at her hopefully. "Anything else!"

"Not a lot. He wore a plain gold wedding ring, an expensive-looking gold watch with an expanding bracelet. Oh, yes—he bit his fingernails, and from the appearance of his eyes, I'd say he was an incipient coronary case."

"Well, I'll be buggered!" said Phil. "I must've been blind!"

"No, Phil, just male."

Langley grinned and nodded approvingly at her. Struck by a sudden thought, he looked at his fingernails.

"I . . . I suppose," ventured Carter, now well in retreat, "you didn't happen to notice anything about the ships?"

Jane shook her head. "As I said, women are not very good at that sort of observation"—she threw her lines away with careless, deadly effect—"but I was in my cabin when the first tanker came alongside. I was looking at it, wondering if, as Mr. Langley had said, they needed a doctor; I thought it made a good picture, so I took a couple of snaps—in color. Would they help?"

From there on it was, literally, plain sailing. By the next morning the weather had abated sufficiently for three seamen to be flown in, and Lieutenant Carter lifted out, taking the vital roll of film. Processed in *Guardian*, Carter told Jane on the R/T that one picture was of excellent quality. Showing another of his many sides, he added that while the photos would be required for official use, he would see to it that Navy Public Relations got her a good price for them from the press.

Next day, the first of many charter planes buzzed the

tanker, TV cameras rolling, and two days after that, when the ship was some three hundred miles from the cape, the shipping superintendent and the Scotland Yard man flew aboard by helo, the former bringing nothing but good news for the slightly bewildered team.

Langley would get a two-thousand-pound gratuity, and if he wanted, promotion to sea-guard instructor ashore. Dazed though he was, he jumped at the offer. As he confided to Phil, in a considerable alcoholic haze, he never wanted to see another blurry ship as long as he lived.

In recognition of his heroic work on the bombs, Roscorla would receive five thousand pounds from the company and the same amount from the insurers.

Jane got a two-thousand-pound gratuity from the company and a further thousand pounds from the insurers, but, said the superintendent, the world's press was frantic to pay her a lot more for her story. He added that if her evidence led to the arrest of the pirates, and the recovery of any part of the filched cargo, she would get a large part of the ten-percent reward the insurers offered.

Months later, the officers and men of HMS *Guardian* got thanked, and a two-hundred-pound donation to the ship's amenity fund. The captain was presented with a silver salver and a framed photograph, in full color, of AT1. Salvage money was ruled out on a legal technicality: Langley, as the company's representative on the spot, had never asked for assistance. In the following week, the company got a considerable bill for HMS *Guardian*'s services.

Jane could not hope to escape the newsmen, and for a space endured a torture almost as bad as anything she had experienced in AT1. At the first possible moment, remembering Mark Jacens' words, she slipped quietly away to the States and a long course of cosmetic surgery, and after that, a new life. Well-off, if not wealthy, she could afford the best. For a time she kept in touch by letter with Bill and Phil, but Langley was no letter writer, and Phil but little better, and in a year they were down to the annual Christmas-card level.

Phil returned for a time to his native Cornwall, toyed briefly with the idea of taking a pub, but found that his

215

runaway wife was prepared to run right back, for he too had done well from the press. Further, a ghost writer was producing his story of AT1, which, the publishers said, was an assured success, and putting their money where their mouth was, paid him a realistic advance on the book. Unnerved by it all, Phil fled back to sea. The company offered him the post of senior guard on AT4, which he refused, shipping as one of her team—for one voyage—free of responsibility, and happy to be that way, an unobtrusive oceangoing dropout.

Three months after AT1's triumphant arrival at Cape Town, Karl Friedmann, alias Charles Freeman, was picked up in a waterfront bar brawl in Woolloomooloo, Sydney. A detective with a retentive memory spotted the tattoo, and Karl promptly turned state's witness. His evidence, added to the positive identification of the first tanker, led to imprisonment for many, the recovery of part of the proceeds of the piracy, and more money for Jane.

Needless to say, the boss man got clean away.

Months later, a small orphanage in a Texas township received a very large donation, with only one string attached. For that sort of money, the governors were prepared to go even further than the anonymous donor asked: thereafter it was named the Mark Jacens Memorial Home.